CW01020660

ABOUT THE AUTHOR

Following a career in education, Elizabeth Ellis is now a director of a community Arts and Heritage Centre in North Hertfordshire. She runs writing workshops and a drama group, has co-written several scripts and edited two anthologies. *The Boatman's Journey* is her third novel.

www.elizabethellis.co.uk

Living with Strangers

The Place Where Love Should Be

THE
BOATMAN'S
JOURNEY

Elizabeth Ellis

Matador
Unit E2 Airfield Business Park,
Harrison Road, Market Harborough,
Leicestershire. LE16 7UL
Tel: 0116 2792299
Email: books@troubador.co.uk
Web: www.troubador.co.uk/matador
Twitter: @matadorbooks

ISBN 978 1803135 694

British Library Cataloguing in Publication Data.
A catalogue record for this book is available from the British Library.

Printed and bound by CPI Group (UK) Ltd, Croydon, CR0 4YY
Typeset in 11pt Aldine401 BT by Troubador Publishing Ltd, Leicester, UK

Matador is an imprint of Troubador Publishing Ltd

For the Family of Fred Jay Girling

PROLOGUE

The Poplars Nursing Home

August 1980

Kate is due again today and this time I'm prepared. Even with the sadness I know will come, it's like a ritual cleansing, clearing moss off the lock walls, bathing in a crystal river after the stagnant waters of the Cut. This will be the last chapter, then it's all laid to rest. Moving on, Kate would call it, though I'm not sure where to.

When she arrives, we sit outside again in the safe space on the bench beneath the Albertine rose. I've not brought the sketch pad, or the canvas roll. This time I can tell her all there is to say.

Kate takes out her notebook, sets up the tape recorder and asks where I'd like to begin. I look up at the deep pink roses on the arch above us. Stirred by the wind a petal falls, its edges curled and tinged with brown, a hint of summer's ending. I'm near the end now too, my story almost told. All that's left is this last piece, in the place I've kept hidden for fifty years.

ONE

February 1980

'Thank you for coming William.' Rhona closed the front door and led the way down the hall to the living room. 'It shouldn't take too long but I just can't manage the loft ladder now – especially after your father's fun and games. Tea first, I think?'

She hurried off to the kitchen and clattered around with cups and saucers.

'How's Dad doing?' William called through the doorway. 'Have you been to see him this week?'

'Not yet. I'll go later. Thought I'd wait until we've had a go at the loft.' Rhona searched for a tray and poured the tea, much of which dripped out through the leaky spout. Never at home in the kitchen, she'd have loved a 'daily' but it went against her husband Leonard's principles. Rhona argued that housekeeping went against hers, so more often than not, he took on all the domestic chores himself.

'Here,' Rhona said, handing William a rather thin looking brew, 'let's have a sit down and then make a start upstairs.'

'I'm sorry I haven't managed to see much of Dad recently,' William said, wiping the bottom of his cup with a handkerchief. 'There's a lot going on at work and…' he paused, took a mouthful of tea, '…Evie's had a cold and isn't sleeping well.'

Rhona looked up sharply. 'Well, if Helena did a bit more to help, it wouldn't all be up to you, would it?'

William put down his cup and sighed. 'She does plenty, Mother, as you well know. Let's not get into this again.'

'I just think…'

'Please leave it, Mother. I'll go and see Dad next week.' He finished his tea and stood up. 'Perhaps we can get on with the loft now?'

Rhona dumped the cups in the sink and followed him. On the landing, the loft hatch hung open, the ladder balanced precariously against it. Beneath their feet, a dark stain blended with the floral design on the carpet. William had done his best to clean it but without much success. It was a mystery to Rhona that her husband, such a practical man, had never installed a decent loft ladder or even had a staircase fitted since there was ample space for it. But then, he was full of anomalies.

While William disappeared up the ladder, Rhona cleared a space on the bed in the spare room. The room was already well stacked with boxes for charity but after Leonard's fall, the whole project had been abandoned.

'I'll just bring the stuff down, shall I?' William called. 'Most of it's already boxed up by the look of things.'

On the landing, Rhona peered up through the hatch into the gloomy space. She'd not been in the loft for years – most of the stuff cluttering up the place belonged to Leonard anyway. Before his accident, they'd talked of moving somewhere smaller, hence the clear out, and though a move now seemed unlikely, Rhona had enlisted William's help and carried on regardless. Countless boxes and bags were heaped on the spare bed, covering the whole surface with the damp odour of decades, and Rhona began to wonder if this was a good idea after all.

She picked her way around the room, tempted to shut the door on it all, but the date on one of the boxes caught her eye. Cambridge 1929. Curious, she flipped open the lid to find an old stock of books and maps, neatly packed inside. She pulled one out, checked the spine and then remembered. These were not Leonard's books but her own, from the early days of her career: *The English Downland, Pioneers in Scientific Agriculture, Sustainable Land Use in Urban Environments.* How long had it been since she'd seen them? Even longer since she'd used them. There were ordnance survey sheets too, of East Anglia and the Chilterns, hardbacked exercise books filled with lecture notes from her time as a student. She pulled out the top one and sat on the bed, leafing through the pages of a half-forgotten life, transported in an instant to those blissful days sequestered in the lab or out in the park checking field experiments. So long ago, like meeting someone you once knew well and then lost touch with. Familiar yet utterly changed.

Rhona shoved the books back in the box, old resentments beginning to flair. All part of a life she'd given up, a life she'd had to forgo. It's so different nowadays, she thought bitterly, young women can have it all. They have no idea what we went through. She closed the box and went off to wash her hands in the bathroom.

For most of the afternoon, William stayed in the loft, bumping and dragging the contents around until she hoped some kind of order was established. When he emerged, dropping two plastic sacks onto the landing and brushing his trousers, he clearly hadn't finished.

'I've straightened things out a bit and sorted some rubbish but there's a large chest up there. Do you know what's in it?'

Rhona had settled herself with a book in the armchair by the landing window and didn't feel inclined to move. 'Can you bring it down? I can't very well get up there, can I?'

'It's a chest, Mum. A wooden one – not very easy to move.'

Rhona put her book down on the floor. 'Well, have a look inside and see what's there first – it's certainly not mine. We can probably just throw it all away.'

'It's locked. Do you know where the key is?'

'There might be one in your father's chest of drawers in the box room. Failing that, force it open?'

Unconvinced, William disappeared along the landing into the box room, the glory hole that housed his father's 'projects'. Here were all the intricate models he'd created over the years, fashioned from wood, metal and wires, from old cans and boxes, that tilted and rolled, rotated and hammered and rocked. Some had little motors attached to the back or the underside, minute clockwork engineering put together from scratch. Toys, Rhona called them.

Ridiculous things for a grown man to make. She didn't allow them in the rest of the house, and like so much else, they sat on shelves in the box room gathering dust.

After a while, when William had not returned, Rhona went to find him, eyeing the room with a sinking heart.

'What on earth shall we do with all this?'

'Maybe nothing at the moment. Dad's coming home at some point, isn't he? He'll need these things to come back to.'

Rhona shook her head. 'There are no guarantees, we'll have to see. I can't have him back here the way he is at the moment. Certainly not if he won't speak.'

'That's likely to change, Mother,' William said mildly. 'The doctors think he'll overcome that in time.'

'Well in the meantime he's better off where he is.'

Muttering, Rhona started to open drawers and rummage through the contents. William checked various boxes and tins lying around and looked through the old cupboard on the wall. They were about to give up when Rhona exclaimed, and pulled out a small bunch of keys from the bottom drawer.

'This looks hopeful,' she said, sifting through them.

'Ok. I'll give it a try. But if not, I think we should leave it for the time being. I'll check with him next time I go.'

Rhona raised her eyebrows. 'He's hardly going to tell you, is he?'

'Let's just do one thing at a time, Mother.' William said, always placatory. So like his father. Like his father used to be.

William took the keys and climbed back into the loft. Rhona waited a while at the foot of the ladder then called up.

'Any luck yet?'

There was a long silence.

'William,' she called again.

William's voice drifted back from the murky depths. 'Mother, there's something up here you should probably take a look at.'

TWO

The contents of the chest William had found were now laid out in the back bedroom, some on the bed, some on the floor. Rhona shuddered. Far from a bracing clear out, every surface in the house now seemed to be coated in faded memorabilia, acres of the past in need of attention. First, they had sorted all Leonard's paintings and drawings, the artwork he dabbled at in those early years, most of it dreary images of waterways, warehouses and boats. William said something about taking it to Leonard's nursing home for a new project they were planning to start up there. It all sounded a rather unnecessary fuss, but if it was going to help, she'd best go along with it. At least it got the stuff out of the house.

That just left the rest of it. Folders filled with lesson plans and teaching notes, history textbooks, art materials and sketch books galore. Rhona knelt down on the floor and began to move things into an orderly pile, separating art from teaching, what to keep, what to discard. None of it would be used again, what was the point of any of it?

She shook open a black sack and threw in the pots and palettes of dried-up paint, an assortment of unsavoury grey rags, torn scraps of paper, the exercise books and all the lesson notes. She dragged the sack to a spare inch of carpet by the window and pulled up the next pile for inspection. On top of this stood a large cardboard box, much like the one she had found earlier containing her own belongings, only this one had no date, just a label with *St Mark's* written on the lid. Inside she unearthed more of the same ancient clutter – unfinished sketches, tubes of paint, teaching handbooks and yet more notes. Leonard's thirst for learning was never sated, no matter how much detail he absorbed.

There was an old photograph album, a scrapbook packed with souvenirs all dating back more than fifty years, and half way down the box she discovered a roll of stiff khaki canvas, smudged with paint and tightly laced. Leonard's treasured tool bag, given over to his art materials in the early days, long before they met. Rhona didn't open it, it held no meaning for her, but mindful of William's belief that his father might recover, she placed it with the scrapbook and album in a separate pile, to deal with another time.

Rhona put the lid back on the box, stood up and stretched her back. Enough for one day. But the prospect of another long evening alone with a book or the meagre offerings of the television, did little to tempt her downstairs. For another hour she ploughed through more piles, discarding a satisfying amount of general rubbish but still leaving much of Leonard's belongings intact. Then she dragged down as many black sacks as she could reasonably leave out for the bin men and closed the door on it.

For days Rhona avoided any further visits to the musty piles in the spare room. Not only was the task of checking each box, each piece of paper, tin and book exhausting but her knees ached constantly from kneeling on the floor. Getting down to it was literal for Rhona.

It was not until a week later that she discovered the manuscript. It lay tucked away at the bottom of Leonard's art box in a manilla folder tied with green tape, hidden beneath several blank sheets of cartridge paper. If this belonged to Leonard it didn't seem to fit with the rest of his paraphernalia. Rhona untied the tape, and pulled out a thick wad of typewritten papers but as she read the heading, an uneasy rhythm started up in her chest. Sifting through the pages, the handwriting in the margins rose up to greet her, every loop and sweeping curve spoke volumes. Of course, this was her stepsister Issy's work, the writing she must have done all those years ago. But why had she not found it before with the rest of Issy's things? She had unearthed notebooks and diaries, half-finished attempts at poetry, but this was new. And why was it here, in Leonard's box?

Rhona put the folder back in the spare room, together with the scrapbook, the album and the canvas roll. Perhaps they should all be kept, perhaps Leonard might have use for them one day, but what good would dragging up the past be to him now? Certainly not that long ago past anyway. I'll ask William next time he's here, she thought. He might know what to do with them.

THREE

I'm not sure how long I've been here. Weeks? Months maybe? The young nurse comes into my room wearing her shiny clothes – they make a swiping sound as she moves about, straightening the bed, plumping pillows. She smells of cigarettes. We're not allowed to smoke in our rooms but sometimes she lets me, hands me one from the packet and we lean together out of the window like errant kids. Lucky my room is at the back, overlooking the bins and the greenhouse so no one sees except Tom the gardener and he doesn't mind. She talks about the weather, the green moss gathering on the dark side of the shed. I've forgotten her name – if I ever knew it.

The staff here are pleasant enough, most of them at least. Very caring, though I'm still treated like a child. Questions have stopped beyond the banal: Cup of tea Mr Gardner? It's two sugars isn't it? All this in a loud voice in case I'm not paying attention. They seem to think we're all deaf in here but there's nothing wrong with my hearing. Maybe it's a bid for equality – shouting for one means shouting for all. It could be worse though. I hear stories, when they think I'm asleep. There's a place up the road where the inmates are locked up all the time. A step or two beyond where I am now, a dumping ground for the inconvenient when we can't pull our weight any longer. I think of those years growing up on the Cut. I pulled my weight then, legging it through the tunnels, keeping the boat off the lock walls when a sidewind took it. I suppose the whole lot has gone now: the locks dried up, the towpaths overgrown.

Today the young nurse doesn't offer me a cigarette, or a cup of tea. She's in a hurry, she says. This is her last day as she has to go and look after her mother. Another ageing burden, no doubt, one of the millions like me, jamming up the health service, catching our death. What is it we're called now? Bed blockers. The nurse sweeps from the room pausing only to wedge the door open. When she's gone, I get up and close it.

It's another damp day. Spring is a long time coming this year – constant weeping skies and stiff winds that rock the poplars by the far wall. From the window in my room, I watch Tom dig a long bean trench. The veg will suffer – he won't be pleased if it doesn't brighten up soon but there's no point planting out yet, the soil's too cold. Wait a bit, my wife says, never mind what the books tell you. She knows a thing or two about the soil.

Tom looks up and sees me. He grins and I raise my hand in a half salute. He'd have been too young for the second war, as I was for the first. I can name all the veg he's planting out there, the soft fruit bushes in the kitchen garden, the herbs, even the weeds. Once I knew every tree and plant that grew beside the water, which ones were food and which were not. But the words are stuck now, trapped in a jar and I can't take off the lid.

I leave him to his labours and shuffle downstairs to the day room. I'm never keen to go in there but if I don't, they come and fetch me, tutting in that voice that tells me I'm not playing the game. They've opened the French windows today so it's fresher than usual. Outside a blackbird sings its heart out, there's another I hear each morning from my room, perched on the greenhouse roof. I sit down in one of the chairs, all lined up in front of the windows. Rather a dull lot we are, not much to humour or amuse us. One or two nod off over a newspaper, some of the women take out their knitting. We all have a blanket on our knees, a simple weave in shades of blue. There's a lot of blue around: in the carpet, on the walls. I wonder who chose it and why.

In the next chair there's a fellow asleep, his mouth lolling open, a roll of spit on his chin. There's a shaving nick too and they've put a dab of cotton wool on it. At least they let me shave myself – and all the rest of it. They know I'm not helpless, I just need a hand sometimes, to get from A to B. Just until the ribs heal. Then there's the speaking, of course. Or rather, the not-speaking. They say everything still works as it should, I just can't find the words. In my head it all makes sense, what comes out of my mouth clearly does not. I'm locked in a foreign place, beyond their understanding.

I used to speak when I first came here. I'd ask for coffee and was met with a frown, a quizzical smile and a cup of tea appeared. I asked for custard not cream, but every time my pudding came back with cream. I asked about the grounds

12

around this place, about who built the house and when. I waved my hands a bit for emphasis, to indicate the lawns, the trees that border them. They told me not to get excited, to settle down, it will be alright. So I stopped waving, kept my hands still, and said no more. That's better they said, and gave me another cup of tea. We score points for doing as we're told. I've seen it: extra toast at breakfast, a second helping of meat. Compliance, that's the word. It's what they want. It's what my wife wants too, it's why I'm here.

FOUR

I'm told I have a visitor today – thankfully not my wife but my son William. He's not been here very often. I know how busy he is with family and work, so I'm touched that he's taking the time. I don't want to be sitting in a blue chair when he arrives, so after lunch I fetch my coat and wait for him by the main door. Matron is at the reception desk, starchy and fierce. When she gives me the *look* she reminds me of my wife.

'You're not thinking of going outside are you, Mr Gardner? It's very wet.'

She knows I won't argue, but silence can be powerful too. I carry on standing by the door with my coat on until William appears outside in the porch, shaking an umbrella and dripping onto the tiles.

'Ah,' Matron says. 'It's your son, I think? Good of him to visit.'

I detect something in her voice. Perhaps she should mind her own business. William waves as he comes over to me but Matron intercepts him.

'How nice to see you, Mr Gardner,' she says, all sweetness. 'Dreadful weather, isn't it?'

William wears his surprised look, surprised that anyone would speak to him. 'It's easing now,' he says, taking off his mac. 'The forecast is better for tomorrow. Hello Dad. How are you?'

'Your father's all ready for you, aren't you Mr Gardner?' Matron speaks in the same sickly voice but loudly now. 'I've suggested it's not such a good day for a walk but we know how Mr Gardner likes the outdoors, don't we? Very much an all-weather man, your father.'

William stands awkwardly, holding his wet coat. I give him a hug and head for the door.

'Well, I'll leave you to it,' Matron says. 'Don't stay outside too long. We can't have our patients getting wet and cold, you know.'

As usual, William begins with an apology. 'Sorry I'm late – I had to wait for Helena to get back from work with the car and the traffic was bad.'

I take his arm and we walk to the end of the garden by the wall. We find the seat where I sit when I can escape outside and William spreads his coat out to cover the damp. Never much of a talker, this is hard for him, a one-sided conversation.

He brings out a thermos and two cups from his haversack. I smell the coffee before he pours it: pungent, delicious, the real thing. We don't have it here, they must think it's too much for old hearts to cope with. He hands me a cup and I wrap my tired fingers thankfully around the warmth. We sit quietly for a while – we could be anywhere, he and I side by side. I used to take him down to the Cut, all the scenic bits. William loved the water, took an interest in where I'd grown up. He was the calm one, sitting with me to watch the boats, or spot a heron. At the juncture, beyond the weir, where the Cut meets the river, we had swans nesting, and geese in the winter. There were geese in that other place too, but that was long ago.

'I've been offered another job,' William says at length, shaking the coffee dregs from his cup and screwing it back on the flask. 'Head of archives at the school. It's a step up, I suppose. More money too, which always comes in useful.'

I nod, thankful he's steady and settled. Helena's good for him and he loves his little daughter. It's just as well, William wouldn't cope with upheaval. I drain my cup, savouring the taste and hand it back to him.

'Has Mum been in this week?' He watches as I shake my head, then turns away. 'I didn't agree to this, you know. I didn't want you in here.'

I pat his arm gently, let him know I understand.

'I tried, but you know what she's like, Dad, she doesn't listen. And the power of attorney? Why has she done that?'

I shrug, as bewildered as he is. There's not a lot I can do about it at the moment. Not unless I can suddenly talk sense again and that's not too likely, so they tell me.

William packs away the cups and thermos, leaves his haversack on the ground. I expect him to go now, duty done, but he doesn't.

'I've been thinking, Dad – actually rather more than thinking. Mum and I were tidying up the loft last week – just trying to get things in order for you.'

Alarm bells begin to ring.

'Don't look so worried,' William says. 'Mum's letting me deal with it. But we found your paintings in the wooden chest – all your artwork from way back. Do you remember? It's quite remarkable, Dad. Exceptionally so.'

I'm not sure what to make of this, trying to remember what's up there. The paintings of course, but there are other things too, old things I'm not sure I want anyone to meddle with. Especially my wife.

William's voice drifts in from far away, my heart sets up its thumping. It's what happens when I want to speak but know it won't make sense.

'Book?' I try.

'No, Dad. Paintings.'

I shake my head, make writing movements with my hand. 'Writing.'

'Do you want to write something down? Is that it?'

I breathe out, a long slow breath just as the therapist at the hospital explained before I came here. Relax, she said, give yourself time. That's all very well but not when it's urgent, when there's something important you're trying to say.

I try again, hold my hands as if I'm reading a book. That doesn't work either and I give up. William wants to know about the paintings. He's asking whether it might help to bring them here, I can't think why. I haven't painted for years. I must look at him blankly because he begins to explain.

'The other day I was chatting to the staff nurse. He mentioned that he wants to try new ways of working with patients – ways of using past experiences to keep the mind active. It's just a thought but I did wonder,' William pauses, takes a deep breath, 'whether this might be something that would help you. Help you make connections again, find a link with the past. It makes sense to me.'

I'm not sure what to think. It sounds a bit… eccentric. But whatever helps the days lie less heavy has to be a good thing. I smile and nod, my standard form of assent.

'Thanks Dad. This could be good for you.' He pauses. 'There's just one snag. Because of the power of attorney, it should really go through Mum and given her views, she might not agree. I'll give that some thought. It's been so long since you painted, Dad. I know it wasn't something Mum liked, though I could never understand why.'

William's quite animated now, unusual for him. My being here has triggered something. His mother's meddling a step too far? He's right about the art though, it was another loss, another door that had to close if only to keep the peace, to move forward after what happened.

William reaches into his haversack, brings out a couple of Kit-Kats and in the stillness of the garden, we sit quietly together and munch.

FIVE

Kate Davies liked to think finding Leonard Gardner's work was part of a determined effort to make something of herself, something to hold on to when not much else was making sense. In truth it was the staff nurse Walter Robinson who called her into his office one morning and handed it to her on a plate.

Not for the first time, Kate had slept badly the night before and woken with a sore head. Concern about the new job had prompted an excess of red wine, and Walter's cheery invitation, though kindly meant, did not put her in the mood for a chat. He looked at her sideways and sighed.

'Sit down, Kate. You look awful.'

Kate sat. 'Sorry Walter. Not at my best, as you can probably tell.'

'I can see that.' Walter hitched himself onto the desk and folded his arms. 'What's going on, Kate? You've been here six weeks but you don't seem very settled, very... committed. The way things are, I'm afraid I won't be able to sign off your induction period.

Kate's eyes prickled. 'I know things have been a bit off recently but...'

'But?'

'I've been... finding my feet.'

'Really? I'm not sure turning up on shift with a hangover is quite the way to find your feet, Kate.' He leaned forward, his dark eyes troubled. There was no judgement here, just a wish to help, but even patience could be trying at times.

'I'd really like this to work for you Kate. Apart from anything else, it doesn't do much for my credibility if you leave. I realise that working here can be tough at first but structure can often give you a sense of purpose.'

Kate chewed her lip, wishing the meeting would end. Much as she valued Walter's opinion, this morning was not one for a heart to heart. Care work had been low on her list of career choices and it took some effort to turn up each day. Walter clearly hadn't missed this.

'People come into care work for many reasons,' he said. 'It's not right for everyone, of course, but my guess is you have a lot to offer.'

Kate looked up sharply. Was he joking? She was still getting her head around soiled nightwear and bed pans.

'That's why I asked you to come in this morning. I've had an idea.'

'I see.' Kate wasn't sure she was ready for an idea. She just wanted to do the job, keep her head down and get paid.

'You mentioned at your interview that you enjoy art.'

Kate had thought up a lot of stuff for the interview, stitching a few colourful patches onto the unimpressive years since leaving school.

'I did 'A' level and a pre-diploma – but that was some time ago.'

'And do you remember the new programme of care I'm hoping to start up for some of the patients?'

Kate vaguely recalled talk of a therapy using pictures and artefacts. 'How does this affect me?' she said.

'Well, I think you should take a look at these.' Walter indicated a large portfolio lying on his desk. He untied the tapes and opened it up. 'They were done by Leonard Gardner, one of our patients. He's on D wing so you won't have met him yet.'

D wing was where the special cases were kept, ones with complex needs, not just the usual geriatrics.

'Leonard's son William found them in his parents' loft and thought they might be useful as a resource for the programme. There's a fair bit of history here, especially to do with the canals. Not only is the artwork exceptional, as you'll see, but it tells quite a story – a whole way of life that's gone. A lot of folk around here have a background on the water.'

Kate stood up to take a quick look, the sooner this was over the sooner she could finish her shift and go home. She opened the portfolio, moved a large sheet of tissue paper to one side, but then caught her breath. Laying out a few of the samples, she leaned in to study them closely. The work was stunning – piece after piece of astonishing beauty. Sketches in charcoal and pencil, muted inks and watercolours, the brushwork precise and delicate. There must have been forty pieces altogether – mounted but unframed, all depicting some aspect of the canals, a whole way of life documented with all its intricacies, its beauty and its hardship.

Walter watched her closely. 'Told you, didn't I?' he said.

Kate swallowed, a sudden lump lodged in her throat. 'Where did you say they came from?'

'From William Gardner. This is his father Leonard's work. All done many years ago apparently, back in the late twenties. No doubt his son could fill you in a bit. Leonard is first on my list for the programme, I thought that showing you these would help you understand who he is – where he comes from. Always supposing you decide to take part. There's no pressure.'

Leonard Gardner. The name rang a bell somewhere but Kate's sore head was beginning to spin and this was not the time to make decisions. Replacing the tissue paper, she closed the portfolio and picked up her bag.

'I'll think it over, Walter. Can I let you know by the end of the week? Sorry but I have to go now.'

Walter opened the door for her. 'This is a gift, Kate. Think about what you could do with it.'

Kate left Walter's office and hurried across the garden to the main door, it was quicker than traipsing through the building. One or two of the staff lurked by the greenhouse smoking, hands shoved into pockets, pretending it was fun. Kate didn't smoke now, not on care sector wages, though she still managed to find a budget for wine.

The day crawled past, filled with tasks that would have been unthinkable a few weeks ago. As yet, Kate had little contact with patients, her time spent dealing with the left overs of their personal care. On occasion she'd deliver teas to the day room, where they all sat in a row, facing the window, most of them asleep or staring into space. She'd heard they were heavily medicated, whether they needed it or not. No wonder Walter wants to shake things up a bit, she thought. No one deserves to be abandoned like that, no matter how old or infirm they are. She thought of her grandmother back at home, and shuddered.

Throughout the day her mind returned to the collection of artwork she'd seen that morning, its style and beauty, the story it told. Rarely had she been in the presence of such quality outside a major gallery, work that quietly beckoned, rescuing another sluggish day. And there was a connection with something she'd studied in the past, though for the moment it lay just out of reach.

SIX

At home there were two envelopes on the doormat, one clearly a bill, the other Kate's weekly letter from her grandmother. The handwriting never failed to lift her mood, though much of the content she'd read before. Kate took painkillers and lay on the couch for a while, turning over the meeting with Walter. Had she been ungracious? He'd guessed art had always played a major part in her life, and was simply helping her out, after all.

She heaved herself off the couch and began to search through the stack of books that lay where she'd unpacked them in the corner of the living room. Her tiny rented flat didn't include a bookcase, nor did her DIY skills run to putting up a shelf. Text books from her year at college lay in random piles alongside paperback fiction, ring binders and her collection of publications from all the exhibitions she'd ever visited. Lost afternoons drifting in a gallery, inspired and daunted in turn.

Kate sifted through the piles and picked out her catalogue of 20th Century artists, a well-worn handbook of favourite works she'd compiled over the years, some notable and well known, many simply pleasing, or memorable in some way. There was no entry under the section marked G, and nothing from any of the major movements she'd studied, yet the name Leonard Gardner was definitely familiar. She went to bed but was again restless, the images she'd seen that morning staying with her between bouts of fitful sleep.

The following day, with a clear head, Kate took the long route to work, across the fields to the canal towpath, an overgrown straggling track only recently unearthed. A group of volunteers had started to clear it, hacking back rotting vegetation, fallen trees and hauling heaps of debris from the canal itself. Kate had seen a photo of the spoils in the local paper – four bicycles, a kitchen table, a pram and a mountain of shoes and plastic bags from one session alone. Yet in spite of the dereliction, the place had a certain charm, a past full of energy and purpose, a forgotten heyday once supporting a complete way of life – Leonard Gardner's life, in fact. Rather like life in the Valleys, Kate thought, picking her way around the brambles. It will never be the same again and one day will all lie forgotten.

Kate caught up with Walter in the car park.

'Ah, Kate,' he said turning off the engine. 'Feeling better this morning?'

Kate scuffed the gravel with her foot. 'Sorry about yesterday,' she said. 'It won't happen again.'

Walter raised an eyebrow and smiled. 'We'll see about that.' He got out of the car and leaned on the driver's door. 'So?'

'I've been thinking about the artwork.'

'I knew you would,' he said.

'It's quite something, isn't it?'

'Isn't it just. It's certainly unusual, canal life doesn't spark much interest these days. But I guess there are hundreds of brilliant artists whose work never sees the light of day.'

'And Leonard Gardner is a patient here?'

Walter nodded. 'He grew up on the water, did them all as a young man.'

'And there's been nothing since?'

'Apparently not. His son didn't know much about this side of his father's life. He said it wasn't talked about at home.'

'Are they valuable, do you think?'

'Impossible to say without a proper valuation. They could be, but they could also be very useful for you, Kate.'

'Maybe,' she said, still doubtful.

'Trust me on this, Kate. I knew that stack of work would interest you. But there's more to it than pictures. Remember the boats, the children, the warehouses? There's a whole social history right there. I'm sure William would help if you talked to him – it could shed some light on things, be a living history – and not only for Leonard.'

Walter got back in the car. 'Think about it Kate. Come and see me in a day or two. If you decide to do this, I'll take over some of Leonard's care – help keep an eye on things.'

Kate wasn't too sure she wanted her boss breathing down her neck, helpful though he seemed to be.

'Think of it as support,' Walter said, as if reading her mind. 'It's what we try to do here.'

Kate nodded. 'Thanks, Walter. I'll give it some thought.'

Later, after her shift, Kate set off for the library. In the art history section she scanned the shelves for any information that would shed light on Leonard Gardner, or more importantly, what connection she might have had with his work in the past. After two hours trawling through dull volumes, she gave up and walked home but she still wanted to know more. Besides, if she messed around any longer, Walter might offer the work to someone else.

The following day, she went to see Walter again and found him in the lounge area chatting with a patient by the French windows.

'Have you got a minute?' she said.

'I can make time,' he said. 'Come to the office. I could do with a coffee anyway.'

'So,' he said, handing her a mug. 'You've thought things over?'

'I think I'd like to go ahead with the project,' she said. 'It's a challenge – I think I should probably take it.'

'Excellent! I hoped you would, but...' Walter hesitated. 'I need to fill you in on one or two things.'

'Oh?'

'I've wanted to start something along these lines for a while now. When you joined us, I realised you'd be a good fit to trial things.'

'You mean it's not been done before?'

'Not here, no, but a few more enlightened places have begun to use pictures and artifacts to help restore memories for some of their patients. There's also a move to use drawing and painting as a means of self-expression, especially when there is speech loss, as in Leonard's case. The problem is, Matron hasn't exactly approved the project.'

This didn't sound good. 'So how can we go ahead?' Matron could be fierce, Kate had no wish to cross her.

'Don't worry about that, I'll deal with Matron. My argument is that patient well-being is our prime responsibility and we need to take care of the mind as well as the body. These people have lived long and interesting lives – they need more than food and a quick chat.'

Again, Kate thought of her grandmother, still bright and active in her eighties, how fortune favours some and not others. 'I suppose if it works, and Matron sees the benefit to patients, she might relent?'

'We can hope so. Meanwhile, if you're on board we can make a start with Leonard. I have his son's blessing at least. His wife can be a bit waspish so we need to tread carefully there too.'

Oh God, another one, Kate thought. Did she really want this? But the sight of Walter, so fired up, so concerned for those in his care, was enough to convince her.

After her shift they drew up a timetable for the sessions and planned out how the process might work. The initial sessions would take place over six weeks and to avoid drawing attention, feedback meetings with Walter would take place in the weekly briefing he held for each of his staff.

'And if I'm questioned about the visits?'

'Just say I've allowed you extra time to get to know the patients. It's unlikely Matron will notice anything, she spends most of her time in the office, anyway.'

'And the other staff?'

'They all know what she's like. No one's going to snitch.'

Kate finished her coffee and put the mug down on the desk. 'So, when do I start?'

'As soon as you like. It might be best to meet Leonard's wife first. Unfortunately there's a power of attorney in place, so we do need to go through her. But don't worry, I can sit in with you.'

'Thanks, that might be helpful, but we'll see. If I'm going to do this, perhaps I just need to toughen up.'

Kate was about to leave then stopped at the door. 'You know, I have a feeling I've come across Leonard's work before but I can't remember where.'

Walter looked up and smiled.

'Really? So this could be useful for you in more ways than one.'

SEVEN

'He's very stubborn, you know, and doesn't speak at all now. Certainly not to me.'

In Walter's office, Kate sat opposite Leonard Gardner's wife, wishing she'd not insisted on holding this meeting on her own. Things had not begun well.

'You see,' Mrs Gardner went on, 'that's what started all this – why he's in here. That and the broken ribs, of course. But I can't be expected to look after him if he won't talk to me, can I?'

Walter was also right about 'waspish'. She tried for an opening, something to break the ice now rapidly chilling the room.

'Your husband has been here a couple of months, is that right?'

'Before that he had to be in hospital for six weeks. Kept getting up and wandering about – that didn't help, of course. But his medical state needn't concern you, the doctors deal with all that. I was given to understand you just want to find out about his early life on the waterways – something to keep him occupied.'

Kate took a deep breath. 'It would help to know a little about your husband,' she said. 'To build a picture, so we have something to start off with. The aim is to find links with early memories. It can be helpful for patients who've experienced a brain injury.'

The woman sat back in her chair frowning. 'I see. Well, my husband eventually became a teacher. He even did the training. Surprising really – when you think of where he started out.'

'Did he teach art?'

'Oh no.' Mrs Gardner flapped her hand dismissively. 'My husband left all that art nonsense behind ages ago, when he…' she paused a moment, frowning. 'When he left the canals. He taught woodwork and history, of all things. Of course, he wasn't a proper teacher. Couldn't teach in a grammar school, or anywhere prestigious. Not with his upbringing. It followed him around, you see, holding him back.'

Maybe he didn't want to work in a *prestigious* institution, Kate thought. Maybe he'd wanted to work with kids who didn't have much of a start in life. It would have been more productive to interview Leonard's son rather than his wife. Waspish was an understatement.

The woman sat very still for some time. 'It was all a long time ago,' she said at length. It doesn't account for much now. He's gone somewhere I can't reach him, obstinate old fool that he is. I'm not quite sure why your staff nurse recommended this kind of project in the first place. I don't know what you hope to gain by using his pictures, or whatever. I'd have thought extra speech therapy would be more useful. But what can you do?' She shrugged. 'I suppose you know what you're doing.'

Interpreting it loosely, this felt like permission and Kate took it as her cue to wind up the meeting. There was little point going any further at this stage but the woman hadn't finished.

'You might be interested in this, I suppose,' she said, rummaging in her bag and producing a soft backed book about the size of a small magazine. 'I suppose if you're rooting around in the past, it might help.'

'I see,' Kate said. 'May I have a look?' She sat down again, baffled by this generous new offering. The woman did not exude generosity.

'Help yourself. You'll see it tells quite a story.'

Kate hesitated, then picked it up, laid it on her knee and opened it. It was a scrapbook, inside was a mass of papers, some attached to the curling pages, many loose and flimsy. There were sketches, diagrams, tickets, pressed flowers and maps. There were cuttings, pages of notes – places, dates, times. Forgetting her audience for a brief moment, Kate picked up a small sheet of paper, held it to her nose and breathed in the potent age of it, journeying back to her grandmother's house years ago. Camphor and lavender, mildew and dust. Then she replaced it and closed the scrapbook.

'Thank you, Mrs Gardner. This is most useful. And I'm sure your husband will benefit from seeing all this again too.'

'I should hope so, otherwise there's not much point troubling everybody, is there? I expect reports, you know.'

The woman was an enigma. What she gave with one hand was snatched away with the other. 'I have to feedback to my manager every week,' Kate said, more crisply that she intended. 'I'll let you know how things are going.'

'You'll have your work cut out, that's for sure. I mean, he doesn't speak a word so I really don't know what you hope to find out.'

'It's surprising what can happen over time and in a safe space,' Kate said, placing a respectful hand on the scrapbook. 'Would I be able to borrow this – just for a short time until we get going? All your husband's work will be stored here, it's quite secure.'

'I suppose it couldn't hurt,' the woman said. 'It's just festering in the loft. In fact,' she added with a note of relief, 'as far as I'm concerned you can keep it, though goodness knows what Leonard will make of it all now.'

The woman got up to leave. 'I'd wish you luck,' she said, 'but I know what he's like. Don't expect a miracle.'

When Leonard's wife had gone, Kate took the scrapbook across to the main office, logged it in with Leonard's other personal effects, then signed it out again and headed home. The meeting had at least been fruitful, if not pleasant. All part of the job, perhaps – not everyone was a joy to be with. Kate could only hope the husband proved a little less hostile than his wife. Leonard Gardner may not be vocal, but anyone who could conjure the images Kate had seen, clearly had little need for words. There were other ways to convey meaning, opening up buried memories might be a way to help with that too.

On the kitchen table, Kate sifted through the contents of the scrapbook. Inside the front cover were the dates 1926 –1930. The first three years were well ordered and neat – all the mementos labelled in minute script. But for the final year, 1930, nothing had been secured on the pages, there were no annotations, no labels, no clue to any of the places, simply an untethered pile of scraps.

Kate began to sort the loose items, separating them into categories, noting any relevant dates from the cuttings and arranging them as chronologically as possible, checking the notes she'd already begun against any new information uncovered from the scraps. There was an article that mentioned a place called St Mark's and a faded photo of a waterside building, clearly some kind of institution, that must have been kept for a reason.

Bent over the cuttings, fired at last with inspiration, Kate worked steadily, pausing only to switch on a lamp. By the evening, way past her usual hour for wine, she had gathered together some of his smaller drawings from the scrapbook, pictures she hoped might prompt a memory and entice him into the process. For the first time she began to see the whole project rolling out before her, clearly defined and brimming with promise.

EIGHT

With the power of attorney in place, Rhona no longer needed Leonard's permission to keep or discard anything, yet much as she wanted the space cleared, she began to wonder whether shifting the lot without any consultation was a step too far. The paintings were now deposited at the nursing home along with the scrapbook, the photograph album she would deal with in time. Maybe the nursing home would find that useful for Leonard too, more useful than gathering dust in the loft. But the manuscript was different. Whilst Leonard had tacitly agreed for his artwork to be used, he may not agree to handing over more personal items, and certainly not this. It was over two weeks since she had unearthed it and for the time being, she would keep its discovery to herself. Rhona had so far avoided the temptation to find out what it contained, reading it just an unnecessary voyage into the past. But since the meeting with the young care nurse and handing over the scrapbook, she was beginning to have a change of heart.

One evening Rhona fetched it from the spare room and brought it downstairs. She sat a moment, fingering the green tape then flicked it open. On the first page she read the heading again: *London 1929*. So during Rhona's final year at Cambridge. Issy still lived in London then, though she too had recently flown the nest and now worked for a small publishing house in Bloomsbury. Not the most promising of careers, Rhona had warned. She could have done better for herself, trained as a solicitor like her father, or taken a degree. Anything else could have led her away from the path she took, away from its cruel outcome.

Rhona picked up the folder and held it to her nose, as she had seen the young care nurse do with the scrapbook cuttings. At the time she'd thought it rather vulgar, yet here she was, smelling something slightly familiar and transported by this surprising gift. But she feared an unbearable upsurge of the past. Shameful memories of their early years together, Rhona's resentment at having to share her home with two strangers when her mother married Issy's father. How she'd sought out and relished every opportunity to pitch Issy into trouble. For a while it seemed her sole purpose in life had been to heap unhappiness upon her, laying the blame for every mishap, ignoring Issy's pleas for company and even her cries for help.

With hindsight, and the dampening of the years Rhona did begin to acknowledge how much Issy too had been forced to give up. Her father, Edward Hamilton-Brown, was a kindly man, given to spending what little spare time he had with both girls, hours that had previously been Issy's alone. He took them to parts of the city Rhona's mother Edith preferred to believe did not exist. He encouraged them to read newspapers, talked with them about politics, filled their minds with dreams of a world beyond the confines of their sex. Without this Rhona would never have aspired to study for her degree, Issy would surely have ventured little further than a husband and the Heath.

From an early age, Issy sought comfort in literary escape, reading avidly anything that caught her fancy amongst the well-stocked shelves of her father's library. Rhona, on the other hand, took refuge in the natural world, wandering beyond the gardens to the Heath and the lakes, returning with copious samples of flora and fauna in containers filched from the pantry.

But as the years passed, the two girls did settle to an ordered and disciplined froideur – their temperaments disparate, their looks strikingly dissimilar, there was little of common interest to create a bond. Rhona grew tall, her hair fair and plentiful which she kept long well into womanhood regardless of new trends. Whilst she allowed her hems to rise a little and abandoned the cinched waists of her mother's era, Issy took it all a step further. She did not grow much in height beyond the age of fourteen, yet in spite of this, she grew a great deal in character and looks, shortening her skirts and discarding restrictive underwear. She learned to dance, though unlike many of her generation was not tempted to lose herself in gaiety and drink. Her dark hair lent itself to the chop, Rhona recalled how she would tuck stray curls behind her ear. By the time Rhona left for Cambridge, inspired by Edward and his radical views, they did finally find common ground. The post war years had shaken up the order of things, women were vying for the vote and value in the workplace. Swept up in this, and much to Edith's dismay, both Issy and Rhona had turned down half a dozen offers of marriage. Rhona had no ambition beyond her desire to become an academic, to remain cloistered in a small research laboratory where the demands of fashion and style were no more exacting than blue stockings and a white coat. Issy's bid for freedom however, took a very different turn.

Rhona flicked open the folder, turned to the first page and began to read.

I

PART ONE

London 1929

It was not much of a place, an attic room in a late Georgian terrace overlooking the small green on Percy Square. With its gentle sweeping curve, the building itself still aspired to grandeur but without much real success. This part of London was familiar to me, the canal nearby bringing memories of walks with Father. It was a far cry from Hampstead but all I could afford at the time.

Inside I cleaned and polished, scraped mud off the linoleum and brought in a rug from home. Before leaving, Cook gave me a new dustpan and brush, some dusters and a packet of lye. Don't tell your mother, she said. I bought them from a pedlar – one of those knights of the road, poor chap. The war has been over more than ten years but its deep shadow still stalks.

Against the wall in one corner was a narrow bed covered with a patchwork counterpane in faded blue and purple. Beside it, a small stand chair held my torch and alarm clock, electricity being as erratic as my ability to wake up on time.

On the chest of drawers, marble bookends housed my small collection of books, curated with loving care from Father's library at home. I'd brought only my favourites: the Brontës, Dickens and Hardy, Virginia Woolf, D H Lawrence and James Joyce. There was poetry too, classical volumes learned by heart from an early age, and the recent harrowing voices that speak of war with fresh invective – Owen, Sassoon and Graves.

Since the house was blessed with indoor plumbing, the tiled washstand under the window doubled as a desk and here I'd placed my new stock of foolscap paper, pages that would contain all the elements of my new life, a story waiting to be told.

I brought very few clothes, two pairs of shoes were all I would need: a stout pair for walking, and a lighter pair for the office. I had very little evening wear, nothing to suggest I might have a social life at all. My stepmother Edith could not imagine how I would manage without the array of outfits I kept at home, but I'd no intention of enlightening her. This space, though cramped, was my own, not open for scrutiny.

For one hour each evening I was permitted use of the kitchen, strictly timetabled between six and seven. 'Surely your landlady could prepare a meal for you?' Edith argued before the move. 'Even if it costs a little more?' I told her Mrs Fletcher made it clear she's not a housekeeper. Besides, I didn't want to be looked after. I would teach myself to cook – it would all be fun.

Edith was not convinced, though more concerned for appearances than my welfare. 'It's not right,' she said. 'Young women alone in the city. You'll have no life at all.'

'Oh, but I will, Mother. Women are changing, leading their own lives. Look at Rhona, you were more than happy for her when she went to Cambridge.'

'That's different,' Edith sniffed. 'Newnham is a college, it's... sheltered.'

'You mean there aren't any men?' I teased. 'You know there are plenty of other colleges at Cambridge, don't you? Teeming with men – they outnumber women ten to one. Rhona will have her pick!'

Edith flapped a hand. 'Don't be facetious, Isabel. You don't seem to realise how serious this is. I'm only thinking of your reputation, your... *chances*.'

'It will be fine, Mother, and if it makes you feel better, my job is in a very respectable publishing house in a highly regarded area. It's a literary heartland. I'm hardly likely to come to any harm.'

'Huh!' Edith scoffed. 'I'm well aware what these arty types get up to.'

'Really Mother? Based on what – reliable information from your afternoon tea circle?'

'Now you're being rude, Isabel. I worry about you, that's all. How will you get about after dark? You won't be safe.'

But on the morning I left, Edith waved me off with a fine display of affection, and I have seen nothing of her since.

Edith was not the only one against my move to Percy Square, or the job I've taken. Rhona's opinion as usual was unrestrained. 'It's such a waste!' she said, soon after the interview. 'You have a brain, Issy – can't you think of a better way to use it?'

My stepsister's lack of support disappointed me. I somehow imagined she would endorse the decision, admire the strength I'd found to take such a step unaided. 'I will be using my brain Rhona, really I will. This is what I want to do.'

'But you'll just be an office girl, a skivvy at everyone's beck and call. You've had a good education, Issy you're destined for better things.'

I wondered how Rhona could possibly know what I was destined for. So often we seemed to share so little. 'It may not seem much to you,' I argued, 'but this job is a chance to be close to a world I love – to writers and books and new contacts. And I'll be able to focus on my own writing too, I'll have time.'

'Write? Issy, don't tell me you're still scribbling! What on earth do you have to write about?'

I had not the strength to explain. I pictured all the pages upstairs in my wardrobe: exercise books full of 'scribblings', treasured and stored for years, holding the fruits of endless head-bent hours. The stubs of pencil, the penknife shavings in the bin, all bearing witness to my efforts. Rhona knew nothing of this, how could she when we'd spent so much time in sullen ignorance of each other?

'Well, I'm going Rhona, and mother has agreed – reluctantly I admit but she's hardly going to stop me, is she? I don't think I've ever been high on her list of concerns.'

Rhona shrugged. 'Mother's done her best, you know, especially since your father died.' She stood up to leave but paused at the door. 'Don't sell yourself short, Issy. Life is different now for women. In some ways it has to be – after all, half the men our age were left behind in the Flanders mud.'

We didn't discuss it again, Rhona went back to Cambridge and I moved to Percy Square, gradually finding solace in the cramped space of my attic room, despite the fingers of damp that spread in trails across the ceiling when it rained, or the drops of moisture landing on my pillow that sometimes woke me in the night. And though at times the rain beat into the bucket I'd placed on the desk when writing, a steady rhythm to keep me going, I found joy in the novelty of it all.

II

The office manager Miss Jenkins was clearly a force of nature, having worked for Messrs Arthur Fowler and Son for over fifteen years. A diminutive figure in brown tweed and sensible shoes, I suspected she was not as old as she looked. In the office she was known as the Gatekeeper, amongst other less favourable titles when out of earshot, but in general staff referred to her simply as Miss J.

By the end of the first week, I had gathered a long list of directives and a fearsome hierarchy of penalties should they not be adhered to. Top of the list was Timekeeping: 'Work begins at *Nine Sharp*, Miss Hamilton Brown. Mr Fowler Senior does *not tolerate tardiness,* lunch is *a strict half hour*. Comfort breaks are *not allowed* unless,' as Miss J delicately alluded, 'it is a *certain time of the month.* 'And mark you, I will know,' she added on my first morning. I could well imagine Miss J keeping a diary for all six female employees.

Second on the list was Tidiness, both in the office and in personal appearance. 'Your desk will be kept clear at all times apart from essential equipment: typewriter, pen, ink, blotter, one HB pencil (*just because your initials are HB does not entitle you to more than one*) and a pot of paper clips.

All papers not actually being worked on must be stowed safely in the bottom drawer of the desk. Prying eyes, you understand. Occasionally there are manuscripts to file. These are the product of months, sometimes years of work. They can contain an author's very soul and we don't want to leave that lying around, now do we?'

Miss J did stop short of dictating rules on cleanliness and hygiene but was unambivalent on matters of appearance. 'Hair should be off the face, Miss Hamilton Brown. I see you've adopted this new *short* look. Just make sure you don't adopt the same principle for your skirt lengths. Ten inches below the knee at all times.'

It was worse than school. I spent the first evening after work letting down all my skirt hems.

★

Confined on the first floor with four other women and Miss J, there was little opportunity to discover how the place worked – who came and went apart from employees. I had hoped to catch the occasional glimpse of a visiting luminary, someone to remind me of the core business, of why I was here. But those early days passed calmly enough, I kept my head down, stuck to the rules and learned fast. The main duties consisted of filing invoices and typing correspondence to printers, editors and potential or existing authors. Rhona would be pleased to know that the nearest I got to skivvying was for James Fowler the Son, who clearly followed his own rule book and rarely arrived at the office before mid-morning. At this point, he would ring the downstairs bell and being the newest recruit, I was obliged to stop work, go down to the ground floor, take his hat and coat and hang them on the stand in the entrance hall. Exactly why he couldn't do this for himself made little sense since he passed the coat stand on his way in, but I was beginning to discover it was all part of an elaborate game, and if the job was to remain mine for long, I would rapidly need to learn the rules.

I had a sharp reminder of this one morning about a month later. Apart from the hat and coat routine, I didn't expect to have any contact with senior management, this being strictly the domain of the *personal* secretary, so when James Fowler came into the office whilst Miss J and the other typists were at lunch, I wasn't sure what to do.

Fowler approached my desk and held out his hand. 'Miss Hamilton Brown, isn't it? Guardian of my outer vestments? I don't think we've been formally introduced. James Fowler – deputy to the Upstairs.'

I shook his hand briefly. 'I'm very grateful for this opportunity sir.'

'Please. Forget the *sir*. James is fine – or Mr Fowler at a push if jolly Miss J is around. Don't want to get into her bad books – she's the one who actually runs this place, you know. The old man is terrified of her – so am I, truth be told. Anyway,' he glanced around at the empty desks, 'mustn't keep you.'

He was about to leave when I realised I'd no idea what he'd come for. 'Was there something you needed Mr Fowler, something I could help you with?'

At the door he paused, then turned to look at me. Still smiling he said, 'Well, now Miss HB, that rather remains to be seen.'

Miss Jenkins returned some minutes later, sat down, picked up her pen and began to write. 'What exactly did Mr Fowler want?' she asked without lifting her head. Clearly the woman's hawkish eye missed nothing.

'Actually, he was just catching up with new staff, I think.'

Miss J laid her pen carefully on the desk and folded her hands in front of her. 'Anyone Mr James Fowler catches up with would do well not to mistake conviviality for kindness.'

I sensed there was more, but the straight, pale mouth clamped shut and we both returned to our respective stack of papers.

*

Following Fowler's visit, Miss J kept me heavily occupied and weeks passed without further encounters with senior staff. She issued as many menial tasks as she could muster, clearly nothing beyond the closely defined boundaries of my humble position was going to land on my desk anytime soon. Then, after days of tedium, I ventured to comment on a rejection letter I'd just finished typing.

'It must be heart breaking,' I said simply, a moment of empathy with a hopeful new writer.

Miss J looked up sharply. 'I beg your pardon?'

'I said...'

'I heard what you said. You will do well to mind your place, Miss Brown.' Miss J had long since dropped the first barrel of my surname, presumably it signified a status far higher than I deserved. She then regaled me with a long list of faults and weaknesses including dress, (still too short), timekeeping, (sloppy), and attitude, (disrespectful), none of which I considered to be justified. The reprimand, in front of the entire office staff lasted a full five minutes and I could think of no response polite enough to ensure I would keep my job.

On the journey home, Miss J's shrill voice accompanied me all the way to Percy Square: *Utmost discretion... Who do you think you are?... Typing means typing... Not your place to question or comment on content...*

So I wrote it all down, every word. I had come to realise the artful way to diffuse anger or rationalise injustice, was to let it bleed onto the page, to be stowed away and reproduced in some future fictional narrative. In this way I gathered a host of scenarios, of characters, each one complete with family tree. Dialogues and storylines emerged in which I succeeded in rewriting my own life in a long sequence of witty or moving exchanges. In them, not only did I become the senior typist at Messrs Fowler and Son, but also an indispensable member of the editorial team. Miss J, meanwhile, was relegated to the lowly tasks befitting her great age and incompetence. With any luck, retirement was on the horizon, the same horizon that hailed me as a celebrated authoress. Such dreams kept me from despair when tedium and frustration encroached. More than once I recalled Rhona's warnings and looked into the blunt reality of my life. Perhaps I was wasted there. As yet I had written nothing towards the memoir, the empty sheets stark and challenging. Nothing that inspired a true account had prompted me to start.

III

As spring advanced, I began to spend the evenings outside, sometimes reading on a bench overlooking the green in front of the terrace. More often I would go down to the back yard and dig out my bicycle from the shed. Apart from the books, this was the only other treasured item I'd brought from home, a shared gift to Rhona and me from Father before he died. He viewed it as a rite of passage, a passport to the furthest, deepest unexplored regions of our native city. To complete the gift, he'd given us a map. Just because we were female, he argued, were we not worthy of adventure? Egalitarian in practice as well as principle, Father had espoused the views of the Labour Party since its inception, campaigning for them tirelessly in three general elections. When Ramsey Macdonald's national triumph proved so brief in 1924 and Father died early in 1925, I couldn't help but feel a connection between the two events. Now, with growing insight and a pang of sadness, I saw that father was way ahead of his time, his belief system more in tune with current thinking than that of many men half his age.

One evening, from a quick study of the map, I found a route from Percy Square north through Pentonville that brought me to the canal basin and the towpath – the long narrow highway running east to Hackney Marshes and west to Regent's Park and beyond. I crossed the Maiden Lane bridge and headed east towards Islington. On one side, a wall of sleepers held back the cliff where the canal had cut through and on the other stood a long row of warehouses, many now empty and crumbling. Victims of the railways that were stealing trade from the boatmen, threatening a whole way of life.

Barges and narrow boats still travelled through here, though very few were horse drawn now. There was an aesthetic quality to it that raised my spirits, a determination to triumph against the odds of fortune or environment. Like the flower sellers in the East End or the women who scrubbed their doorsteps each morning knowing it would blacken again by nightfall. History lessons at school had taught me about royal dynasties and the spread of Empire, but it was from Father that I learned the human cost of progress, the social history of the overlooked and the dispossessed. Early explorations with him left me in no doubt about the privilege of my existence. His work as a solicitor took him to visit clients in the East End, pro bono cases I later learned, defending a docker or a drayman wrongfully accused by the authorities. Many times as a small child he would take me with him and while Father sat in the living room of a damp tenement, in earnest conversation with his client, I would play on the floor with any number of children who happened to be there, clapping rhyming games or tossing jacks. In the streets, I'd feel the tug on my skirts of a hand no larger than mine. Women and children in doorways, faces smudged and sore, market traders bawling in a language all their own, rangy dogs that paused at every rotting heap. And everywhere the acrid smell of sulphur and woodsmoke, of sweat and cess and rotting vegetation.

But Father would buy food, pay generously for a fresh loaf or for fruit straight off the docks. He was known here as the Guvnor, much as he disliked the term, and the reverence with which he was regarded included me too. After his death, when I visited the families again, they organised a tribute, a small gathering in Father's honour when those he had helped brought flowers and food and drink.

His work extended to canal workers too, defending those accused of cheating the Weights and Measures Board, or facing heavy fines for a late delivery. My informal education included hours of hopscotch on the towpath of the Grand Junction while Father sat smoking on deck with his client. Or I would huddle in the warmth of the narrow boat's tiny caboose reading stories to the family. I discovered a little of life on the Cut, and harboured no romantic notions about how tough it could be.

*

On the towpath I watched as a vessel slid by, a slow chug at walking pace, the vibrant colours of the livery, the artwork blooming on the sides, floral offerings cascading from the cabin roof: geranium, cornflower and oxeye gathered from the banks. I knew families still lived on board sometimes but on this day I saw only a young man, his face deep grained and weathered, shirt sleeves rolled above the elbow, stout boots. He smiled, raised his cap as he passed and I waved back, touched by this connection. It was only the locks I avoided, fearing the roar and gush of water through the sluice gates. It filled my ears as the river did years ago when

I'd toppled from the bank and fallen in. Though not deep, I'd struggled to stand, the force of its current pulling me under time and again until my cries brought Rhona to haul me out. But here, where the water turned slowly in the wake of the passing barge, I found calm in the quiet murky depths, a gentle throbbing pulse to settle my thoughts and strengthen my resolve to stick with the choices I'd made.

IV

I had been to Cambridge once or twice with Edith during Rhona's early days there, but had never made the journey on my own. It was simple enough to catch a train from Kings Cross and Father's small legacy meant these extras could be indulged even on my wages. I telephoned Rhona in advance but as the train left the grey North London suburbs, I began to doubt the wisdom of my visit. Would Rhona spend our time together listing objections to my career choice as she had done so often before? Was I secure enough to plead my case again now I had to admit that some of Rhona's comments were valid?

This time, however, I fully realised how stark the difference in our bid for independence. As we toured the College and the library, the refectory and the lecture halls, I saw how Rhona seemed to thrive in her glittering world, seizing knowledge with a hungry mind, spending time with others of a similar disposition. All this in such contrast to the limitations of my own tedious routine, grappling with disaffection, maintaining a stubborn pretence that I was somehow in the 'real' world where Rhona hovered aloof. When she asked how work was going, I could find little of interest to say and mentioned only the mundane tasks, the pettiness of office protocol.

After the tour, we took tea in Rhona's spacious rooms overlooking the courtyard. Sunlight streamed in through the leaded windows, casting diamond tiles upon the floor.

'Give it up, Issy,' Rhona advised, ladling strawberry jam onto a scone. 'You owe them nothing. Go to college, learn something.'

'But I only want to write,' I said. 'It's my chance to be at the heart of the business. Not everyone has that opportunity.'

'Not everyone of your upbringing runs errands for upstart office managers. You might as well work in a book shop if that's your real reason! Or better still, become a librarian – at least you'd be using your brain.'

'It's easy for you. You have a subject, a strength. I only have... an idea, a longing if you like.' My defence sounded weaker with every word.

Rhona took a bite of scone and wiped jam from her mouth with a napkin. 'Take care Issy, longing will do you no good. The world is full of girls with longing. Clever, monied young women who long for what they can't have – a man mostly, and we all know there are precious few of those in spite of what you might think from looking around this place. Most of them are all tied up at home anyway – straight back into daddy's business and a sweet girl patiently waiting.'

I stared at my sister. Such radicalism! It was a comfort to think that some of Father's influence had rubbed off on Rhona too.

'No Issy, keep your mind open but keep it concrete. Don't drift or you'll wash up on some undesirable beach somewhere, nearing thirty and quite alone. We may have won the right to vote, but equality is a long way off.'

I wondered which elements of Rhona's mindset came from experience and which through recent debate. Though not yet nearing thirty, had Rhona learned the hard way in her dealings with the world and with men? Now in her second year, was she expected to subjugate all she had experienced here to some inferior role when she left? It was hard to imagine Rhona settling for that.

*

The pages of Issy's manuscript now lay in an untidy pile on Rhona's lap. Some had even fallen on the floor, scattered around her feet, their sequence muddled. Absorbed in the narrative, she'd failed to notice it was growing dark, she had even forgotten to make a cup of tea. Collecting the papers together, she laid them carefully on the side table and went in search of something for supper. The fridge had little to offer apart from some slices of grey-looking ham and a few tomatoes. Without Leonard to cook the thoughtful balanced meals she'd always enjoyed, she was at a loss. Over the weeks of his absence, Rhona's choice of menu lacked much in the way of variety or imagination relying on simple pickings and too much cake. Now as she made her way through two large scones, she recalled the visit Issy had made to Cambridge, how hopeful they had both been then, alive to a new world, a succession of opening doors. Their father's faith and optimism guiding them both towards self-reliance. True, Issy had questioned her role at the publishing house but Rhona could now see how perceptive she'd been, how she had matured and flourished since leaving home.

Rhona cleared the table, turned on the reading lamp and gathered another handful of papers from the folder.

V

Convinced anew that Messrs Fowler and Son held the key to my literary future, I battled on in my lowly capacity, banging out memos and correspondence with increasing efficiency, loading up my desk with as much as Miss Jenkins could procure, often finishing the lot by lunchtime.

One evening as I prepared to leave, locking my desk drawer and stretching the cover over my now familiar Imperial, James Fowler again called unexpectedly at the office. This time Miss Jenkins was also present.

'Ladies,' he said, strolling to the window and standing with his back to the light. 'I was hoping to find you still here, knowing how conscientious you are. Actually, it's Miss HB I'm looking for. Doing a spot of poaching, you might say.'

Miss Jenkins dropped the pile of papers she was holding and scrabbled noisily on the floor to pick them up. 'I see,' she said, when flushed and upright again. 'What exactly had you in mind Mr Fowler?'

She positioned herself behind her desk, the typewriter like body armour before her. 'Miss *Brown* was on the point of leaving.'

Fowler strode back across the room to my desk. 'Shan't

keep you a tick,' he said, 'but I've just heard a most exciting piece of news. Well, it's more hearsay really.'

'So, it's gossip then.'

Miss J's snapped response took me by surprise. I watched closely for Fowler's reaction.

'*Informed* gossip,' he said, unabashed. 'Sarah Paget is working on a new draft, early stuff but she wants a reader.'

Sarah Paget was one of the company's leading names. Novelist and playwright, her output prolific, I had read and admired several of her earlier works, literary sagas penned in tranquil days before the war. There were later works too, a shift away from the norm that chimed well with the current trend for realism and the changing role of women.

'We're still working on her last offering,' Fowler went on. 'That's almost typeset and ready to go, so this new stuff's rather taken us by surprise. Anyhow, long story short – excuse the pun – she's asked for fresh eyes on this one.'

Miss Jenkins listened, her head tipped to one side looking fixedly at the far corner of her desk. I stood motionless and tried not to breathe.

'According to Miss Paget, this is a different angle on things. She's trying to catch a new market – and by that I assume she means a youthful one. Some of her fan base are dying off and that's not good news, even when you're as successful as she is.'

Miss Jenkins stepped out from behind her desk. I noted suddenly how small she seemed. 'So, what exactly do you need from us, Mr Fowler?'

'Actually, I need Miss HB and her youthful brown eyes,' he said.

I heard his words from a distance, as if I were standing in the street viewing the scene through a window, my mind tipping somersaults. Should I speak – express some interest, a word of delight? But the resolute figure of Miss J controlling the scene, kept me silent. I hoped only that Fowler would somehow grasp the enthusiasm now issuing from every cell in my body.

Miss Jenkins studied her feet for a moment, then clasped her hands and looked up. 'I see,' she said. 'This is very irregular, Mr Fowler. Miss *Brown* does not yet have the experience to become a reader. I admit she is *finally* proving to be an asset, but her skills do not lie along the lines that you are suggesting. Besides which, I cannot spare her at the moment. We are working to capacity as it is.'

I leaned forward on the desk, and for a moment caught Fowler's quizzical gaze, willing him to understand this was not my decision.

'Well, that's a great pity,' he said, turning to go. But at the door he hesitated. 'Perhaps I could speak to Miss HB alone? Tomorrow morning – I'll be in early. Come to my office first thing. I'm sure something suitable can be arranged.'

He left, both of us silent, me with excitement, the other, I assumed, with rage. Undermining Miss Js' authority will have justifiably angered her, but there was more. That she had issues with her employer was becoming increasingly evident, but it would be some time before I discovered quite what they were.

VI

I slept little that night: a long, drawn-out restless night, waking fully before dawn. The meeting with Fowler had flooded my mind since the wondrous moment at the office yesterday when he had firmly overridden Miss J's objections. I could almost feel sympathy for a woman so unused to the questioning of her word. Living with Rhona had taught me to accept a pecking order, no matter how petty or unjust. As a child I had learned the consequences, often violent, if this was challenged. Wails of *Issy did it!* echoing from the nursery whenever drinks were spilled or toys broken. I did not expect violence from Miss J, but her disapproval could punish with equal force.

In the morning I made use of the bathroom ahead of the queue, in time to catch some hot water, and chose my outfit with care: a simple grey skirt and pale green blouse, no frills but nothing too severe, something to show me in a good light: intelligent, determined, conscientious.

Mercifully the morning was dry, the sun on Bedford Square cut through the long terraces at intervals and struck gold across the road. When I reached the office, the building was already lit up. I'd hoped the hour would mean Miss J was yet to arrive, but it was clear the woman would not be beaten to the post by a mere member of her staff. She greeted me with a stiff nod, wound a sheet of paper into her typewriter and began attacking the keys. I hung my coat on the peg, ran up the stairs to Fowler's office on the third floor and paused outside the door, willing my heart to settle.

Fowler was seated behind a large desk strewn with papers – clearly no office protocol here. He rose to greet me and ushered me not to his desk but to a club chair, one of two set at angles by the deep window. Instead of the face to face confrontation I was prepared for, I found myself looking at a street view three floors below, the pedestrians diminished, a passing motor vehicle like a child's toy. It did not, however, put me at ease. I smoothed down my skirt and folded my sticky hands together.

Fowler hitched his trouser knees and sat down next to me. 'Miss HB,' he began, 'or may I call you Isabel? Delighted you could make it – ungodly hour this, don't you think?'

I was given no time to reply, other than to smile and look attentive.

'Much better than under Miss You-Know-Who's draconian eye, eh?'

Miss J had her faults but I could not afford disloyalty. I began to wonder whether this was all a plan to test my allegiance.

'It's very good of you to see me this morning, sir. To consider me for this work.'

'Please, Isabel, less of the 'Sir'. James is fine with me.'

It was not fine with me. Egalitarian it may be, but a man so senior in the organisation and at least thirty years old? To use his Christian name would be no more acceptable than calling Miss J, *Freda*.

'Miss Jenkins is right, in that I don't have much – any – experience in this field, only...' I paused not wishing to underplay my hand. 'Only one of the reasons I wanted to join your firm was to extend my experience. I've always had a passion for books, for reading. I was fortunate enough to have access to my father's library.'

Fowler sat watching me, his fingers steepled. 'And what kind of reading matter might ignite that... *passion* I wonder?'

A pink sweat crept up my neck. Bad choice of words – this was not a good start. 'I mean, I greatly enjoy reading – all kinds of material. My father's library contained many law books, some of which – the case histories, were quite fascinating. But it was mainly fiction: Jane Austen, George Eliot, Mrs Gaskell, Mary Shelley. And the Brontës. More recently I've been reading Virginia Woolf, Katherine Mansfield – and Sarah Paget, of course.'

Fowler nodded slowly, appearing to listen intently. 'And did any *male* writers spark your interest, by any chance, or is your list exclusively female?'

In my preoccupation, I'd failed to mention the catalogue of male writers devoured over the years. It struck me now that faced with the question of which significant writers I'd most enjoyed, it was the women I'd subconsciously singled out. 'Of course,' I added hastily, fearing this might not be what Fowler wanted to hear, 'I enjoyed many other works too. Dickens, Hardy's novels of character and the environment.'

Fowler raised an eyebrow. 'Indeed. Coming from a respectable home, I'm surprised you were allowed access to some of his later works. Tess, for instance – not a fine model of young womanhood. Or Jude, content to live with a woman out of wedlock? His ultimate crime against the family?'

If Fowler was testing my moral fibre, I would not disappoint him. 'I believe both protagonists were greatly wronged. Perhaps in ways a little of their own making, but ultimately Hardy's message is that we are all helpless at the hand of fate. The gods ending their sport with us, so to speak.'

'And you, Isabel – are you a fatalist?'

I took a moment to reply. In both novels I'd identified strongly with the main characters, the lure of ambition, vicariously imposed in Tess, self-inflicted in Jude. Edith's wish for me to make a suitable marriage, my own desire for self-improvement.

'I believe we must take responsibility for our actions – have the clarity and vision to carve a path for ourselves and not fall prey to the wishes of others. Remain true to one's own integrity even if...' I paused, again wondering if I'd overstepped the mark.

'Even if?'

'Even if it's not what others may wish for us.'

'I see.' Fowler smiled, adjusting his shirt cuffs. 'I sense you may be speaking from experience, Isabel.'

'Perhaps. My stepmother holds strong views on women in the workplace.'

'She didn't approve of your appointment here?'

'No. And neither did my sister, for the opposite reason. She's up at Cambridge and thinks I should be using my brain, not learning to file memos and type letters.'

I stopped. Fowler was silent. Carried along by debate, I knew at once I'd gone too far. But instead of rising from his chair to bid me a rapid good day, Fowler nodded again.

'As it happens, I wholeheartedly agree with your sister. Hence this offer. My dear old father never could resist a pretty face, but at your interview he managed to see something else in you. A spark. Potential. We are currently beginning to sign more women to our list, many of them accomplished writers but overwhelmed by the predominance of men – both writers and publishers. It's my belief that women like to read other women. Not merely magazines or the Penny Dreadfuls but the meaty stuff, as you've just illustrated. Hence the success of Sarah Paget.'

For the first time since entering the room, I began to feel comfortable, anticipation growing with every word that came out of Fowler's mouth. I had never heard my own views echoed so succinctly by anyone, let alone a man. Even Father, for all his broadening agenda, had rarely sought my opinion, still believing perhaps that at fifteen I was too young to hold one. In spite of this I remained cautious, Fowler may yet have been sounding me out.

'Am I to understand that you need a woman to read, to determine whether the new work coming in is likely to catch on – whether it will sell?'

'Exactly.'

'I see. This would be quite an honour, but as I've said, I have no experience in this area.'

'But you do have a young brain, and it's my guess there are many more educated women now earning their keep, who want reading matter that will challenge – even excite. Women who no longer have to justify what they spend their money on. We need to fulfil that market before someone else does. So,' Fowler stood up and faced me, 'what do you say – give it a go? Can I peel you away from Miss J and up to the second floor?'

How I accepted, or what effusive and garbled thanks I uttered, I cannot remember. But for the rest of the day and for some time into the future, I floated high above even the third floor of Messrs Fowler and Son, up and over Russell Square, coming slowly to rest somewhere in the reading room of the British Museum.

VII

My first meeting with Sarah Paget did not take place in the office. Away from a certain pair of eyes was Fowler's suggestion, better for both of us. On a warm afternoon the following week, I was seated at a table in the window of a small tea shop in Holborn. I'd brought a notebook and pencil, to pass the time with inspired musings, since Fowler had warned me that Miss Paget's timekeeping could be somewhat erratic. To create a semblance of artistic style, I had abandoned my formal office clothes for a pale cotton shift and straw cloche. To complete the image, I'd draped a long chiffon scarf around my neck. But as I sat, restless and waiting, I found myself fiddling with the ends and took it off.

The previous night, my eyes gritty from straining in poor light, I'd finished reading Sarah's last novel, the words transporting me yet again into a world I was beginning to recognise: the struggle for equality, women's rights. I'd prepared an appraisal in case it was required, something knowledgeable but brief I could drop into the conversation. Though I'd memorised what I wanted to say, the longer I sat waiting, the less of it I could clearly recall. The inspired musings I'd planned for my notebook became a list of prompts and queries, the risk of appearing ignorant being far greater than the risk of appearing unprofessional, or worse, inexperienced.

Sarah Paget announced her arrival with a loud clang of the teashop doorbell. She paused in the doorway, squinted briefly around the room and headed straight for my table. 'Miss Hamilton Brown?' she said, offering her hand. 'Sarah Paget. Pleased to meet you.'

I rose to greet her as Sarah signalled to the waitress.

'Have you ordered?' she asked.

'Not yet. I was waiting for you. What would you like?'

'Tea. Lap Sang. No sugar. And cakes.'

No small talk, I noted. No gush. Not quite what I had expected. I ordered while Sarah dumped her large shoulder bag on the floor and sat down.

'So, Isabel,' she said, facing me across the table. 'I gather you're Fowler's new protégée.' Her voice, softer now, had a familiar edge. It was not hard to tell which side of the city she'd grown up in. She opened a small tapestry case and put on an imposing pair of tortoiseshell spectacles, bringing her pale blue eyes into sharp relief. She wore no hat, and with her straight hair cropped short, her dark grey skirt and jacket, she seemed to have stepped straight from a novel herself.

'It's very good of you to come,' I ventured. 'I believe Mr Fowler explained that he's asked me to act as reader for your new book?'

'Ah, yes. How is the delightful James? Not giving you a hard time, is he?'

'It's an honour to have this opportunity,' I said. 'I haven't been with the firm very long.'

Sarah, tipped her head to one side and peered at me. 'You're quite young, aren't you? What – nineteen? Twenty?'

I sat up straight in my chair, wishing for a brief moment I'd not abandoned my stays. 'I shall be twenty-two next month.'

'You're not going to know a lot about life at twenty-two, are you? I know I didn't.'

Whatever confidence I came in with was fast draining away. I'd hoped for a meeting, if not of equals then at least a platform to demonstrate my commitment to the task. This felt like a job interview with no chance of success.

'I realise a great deal of trust has been placed in me,' I said primly. 'I will do my best to live up to expectations. I have always enjoyed your work.'

Sarah leaned forward on the table. 'What, all of it? Even the recent stuff? You know the critics had a field day with the last one. Far too miserable apparently. Readers want light and life these days, not doom and gloom. James took a great risk with it, only got it past the Board because I'm something of a name. Sales have been abysmal.'

I glanced at my notebook and took a breath. 'I saw it as a fitting tribute to those women who sacrificed so much for their beliefs, who fought for their right to equality at least at the ballot box if not in society at large. The details might be harrowing, but the public have been shielded from the truth of what they went through. A convenient cover-up to protect the authorities. And,' I added, 'it's not hard to work out the role model for your first female MP!'

Sarah watched me as I spoke, then nodded slowly. 'Well that's a good start,' she said. 'Very astute. Perhaps James does know what he's doing – professionally anyway. Seems to think you've got the necessary. I can see what he was thinking.' For the first time a smile surfaced. 'Right, then,' she said. 'Let's get to work.'

Shifting the crockery and cutlery to one side, Sarah pulled a large bundle of papers from her bag and laid them on the table. 'This is the new one,' she said, slapping her hand on top of the pile. 'Most of it anyway. It's a bit raw in places but you'll get the idea.'

When the waitress arrived with the tea I straightened the cups and picked up the pot. There didn't seem to be any milk, only a small bowl with some thin slices of lemon and a pair of tongs. The tea, emerging from the pot, resembled lightly coloured dishwater. 'Oh,' I said, dismayed. 'I forgot to stir.'

'Not to worry, it's Chinese – quite normal. I'll take a slice of lemon with mine. I can ask for milk, if you prefer?'

'No, no. Lemon is fine.' In spite of Edith's attempt at sophistication, I had no experience of anything beyond regular Darjeeling. I had an idea that Sarah knew this too. Her eyes, above the tortoiseshell specs softened, and were no longer peeling me alive. 'We're a crazy lot, you know – writers. You'll get used to it.'

The tea was a delight – fresh and aromatic. For the next hour, we pored over the manuscript and polished off half a dozen cakes. Only when Sarah looked at her watch and announced she had to leave, was I aware of how much time had passed.

'Let me know when you're ready to meet,' Sarah told me as we packed up to leave. 'Sooner rather than later would be good – I'm always in limbo at this point.'

Too late to return to the office, I took a long route home, lingering for a while at the stalls on Leather Lane, again retracing steps I'd taken with Father years before. But now with every step, I moved a little further onto new ground.

VIII

The meeting with Sarah Paget stirred up new fires. Not only was it the trust placed in me by James Fowler, but getting to know the inspired mindset of this woman whose achievements outshone those of many fictional heroines. Women in fiction were so often a construct, the product of a male imagination – either wilful, unpleasant characters or at the mercy of their tremulous unchecked emotions. Even in the books I adored, I had always questioned why fiction did not reflect the way many women really were. Our lives had changed greatly since the war and with the vote, and in Sarah's recent writings I'd seen this change, had recognised its power and drew inspiration from it. If I ever manage to produce anything worthy, I thought, let this be my vision too.

Next morning I carried the manuscript to the office with great care, clutching it to my chest, conscious of its unique value and the task entrusted to me. But on the stairs I met Miss J whose sharp eyes did not fail to take in the bundle in my arms.

'Miss Paget's work, I presume?' she said, nodding briefly at the hefty folder.

I tightened my hold on it. 'Yes I'm just...'

'Miss Brown, you've worked here long enough to know that manuscripts should not leave the premises.'

I opened my mouth in defence but Miss J rattled on. 'You realise this is grossly negligent and I should report it? Just because you've moved upstairs doesn't entitle you to flout the rules.' She turned and carried on down the stairs but I was determined to be heard.

'I collected the work from Sarah – Miss Paget – late yesterday afternoon,' I called over the banister. 'There was no time to bring it to the office and I took it home for safe keeping. What else should I have done?'

Miss J stepped up again and faced me. 'Nevertheless, this is most irregular, Miss Brown and you would do well to remember your position here.'

There was no need to say more.

★

My office on the second floor was small but warm and light. I shared it with Joan, a pale spindly woman whose quiet company I valued after the clatter and chat of the typing pool. Here I could work undisturbed and usually at a safe distance from Miss J's unnerving surveillance. Joan too was a reader and fortunately more than generous with her years of experience. I made good use of this, referring her to various passages of Sarah's manuscript that might be considered too controversial, or cause offence. Whilst I understood Fowler's wish to capture a new market, there was still the need to honour Sarah's existing readership.

I worked daily on the manuscript and sometimes into the evenings too, risking the wrath of Miss J by leaving my gloomy garret to sit with it in Percy Square. In a week, I'd completed a second reading, fascinated, absorbed in the special quality Fowler had expected me to find. With any luck, I'd passed the test, convinced that Sarah's work would open minds to a new age. Moreover, it would sell. Impatient and curious for the remainder of the story, I phoned Sarah to ask for the missing chapters.

★

At the table in the window, her demeanour changed from our previous meeting, Sarah sat frowning, rearranging the cutlery, raking impatient fingers through her hair. She'd ordered sandwiches to compliment the China tea but the neat triangles of egg, cucumber and salmon, lay untouched.

'Ok, Let's have it,' she said, before I had a chance to sit down. 'I can't get on with anything until I've some idea of where, if anywhere, this is going.'

I set the manuscript on the table in front of me and took a deep breath. Nothing I could say would do justice to the work, the pure joy of reading it had held me spellbound, breathless with admiration. How had I found myself in this position, how was I qualified to comment on such work, an imposter way out of my depth?

'Sarah, it's...wonderful, simply wonderful. I've read it twice, and each time something new emerges: an element of Joe's character, another piece of his life I'd missed before. I even passed some pages to Joan, the woman I work with, to test her reaction. She's been doing this far longer than I have and I needed her judgement – I couldn't risk getting it wrong. But I needn't have worried – it turns out she's in total agreement.'

'Thank God for that,' Sarah said, losing the frown and dropping her elbows onto the table. 'You know, it's the same every time. No matter how long I do this job, no matter how many books I write, this is always the bit that cracks me. Will it make sense? Does the plot hang together? Does it carry you away?'

'It does all that, and more. It's different, certainly, and there may be some of your faithful readers who will find it... challenging. The war's been over for years yet there are thousands of men like Joe. Finish it, Sarah, I'm longing to know how it ends.'

Sarah started on the sandwiches. 'Truth be told, I'm not sure myself yet. It could go either way.'

'You mean, he could survive or perish?'

Sarah nodded. 'That's the joy of fiction. You're a puppet master, holding the strings. Only sometimes, your characters don't dance to the right tune, they have a mind of their own.'

'And Joe – what does he want? What does he deserve?'

'Perhaps this time I'm trying to say there can be no happy endings, not after so much misery. The world has changed and fiction should reflect that.'

'So he dies?'

Sarah shook her head. 'As I say, this is fiction, I'm not sure yet. Anyway, don't let's bother with it now,' Sarah said. 'Too gloomy. I'd rather just natter. It's good to have company – I don't get much when I'm working on a book and right now I'm in need of gossip. What's going on in the office? Who has the dreadful Miss J found to needle now that you're safely out of the way? Anyone had their heart broken recently?'

I wiped my fingers on a napkin and sipped my tea. I'd never dealt in gossip. At home, for all their faults, Edith and Rhona did at least confine harsh criticism to their own four walls.

'Oh, dear,' Sarah grinned. 'You're shocked! I should have known you'd have more integrity.'

'Not shocked, just...,' I searched for a suitable word, 'uninformed, I suppose. What people do in their spare time is their own affair.'

'But aren't you curious? I'm always looking to gather as many tasty morsels as I can. It's what writers do.'

This was true, but I saw a distinction. After a pause I said, 'There is a difference between storing up observations and relaying information that may or may not be true.'

Amused, Sarah leaned towards me on the table. 'As a colleague, I admire your principles,' she said. 'But as a friend, I'd just love to know what's going on within the hallowed walls of Messrs Fowler and Son.'

I finished the last of the sandwiches and brought the conversation back to business. 'Well, I'm sure the book will be a success. It's different, yes, but powerful and moving. What's more, I think Fowler will be impressed.'

Sarah leaned back in her chair and turned away to the window. 'Let's hope so. He can be unpredictable, you know.'

'So you've said. But I find him quite amenable. I suspect he even has a sense of humour.'

Sarah eyed me carefully. 'Don't let that fool you Issy. We need his blessing on this but...' she paused, about to say more, then thought better of it. 'Let's just wait and see. I've another hundred pages to go and I know he's anxious to get his hands on it.'

'I think we might need to go,' I said, conscious of the waitress hovering by the table. 'I'll get the bill this time.'

'I trust Fowler and Son will be paying?' Sarah called. 'Make sure they do – James can be a stingy rat at times.'

Walking back to Percy Square, it began to rain and as I had no umbrella and wore only a light jacket, I was soaked by the time I reached home. I hung my wet clothes on the back of the bedroom door, pulled on a dressing gown and lay on the bed with a book. But the afternoon had left me confused, joy and gratitude giving way to something more complex and confusing. That Sarah counted me as a friend was an honour, close colleague was perhaps the most I had hoped for. But Sarah's shift from brooding to cavalier, her conversation from erudition to gossip unnerved me. Over the years, I'd grown used to the flick of Rhona's switch from rationale to anger, I'd learned to temper my words and actions to limit such outbursts. But a similar shift in Sarah left me at a loss. Then there was Fowler. Clearly Sarah harboured some grievance against him – what had she called him – a stingy rat? And there was the warning too: *He can be unpredictable.*

I abandoned my book, sat down at the wash stand and began to write. For a while I could escape the complexity of working life and lose myself in fiction of my own making, over which I had full control.

IX

On yet another rainy evening, Fowler stopped me on the front step of the office. I held an umbrella in one hand and in spite of Miss J's warning, had Sarah's manuscript in the other, carefully shrouded in a skirt I'd collected from the laundry at lunchtime.

'You look loaded, Miss HB,' Fowler said. 'Can I help at all?' Sheltering under the front porch, he was standing very close.

'I can manage, thank you,' I replied, stepping away from him onto the pavement.

'But you have a long walk back to... Islington, isn't it?'

'I may take the tram. It's not so far.'

'Then have tea with me first. There's a Lyons on Southampton Row – excellent service I gather.'

Though grateful for the trust Fowler placed in me, I had no wish to extend my working day with him. Sarah had also arranged to send over her remaining chapters by courier that evening and I needed to be home.

'You're very kind, but my mother is visiting and I need to prepare a meal for her.'

'I see,' Fowler said. 'Another time then. Goodnight, Miss HB.'

He raised his hat briefly and left me on the pavement, wondering why I felt guilty when all I'd done was make my wishes known. Edith was definitely not visiting but a social lie did not count as deceit. Yet something about Fowler's manner as he left suggested he was displeased, the look of a man unaccustomed to being turned down. The very attitude Sarah was trying to challenge, I thought, setting off into the rain across Russell Square. Entitlement, as if women are simply here to be moulded, waiting for just such an invitation since there's not much more to life than the company of an eligible man. But by the time I reached Percy Square, I'd convinced myself this was nonsense, he was probably just trying to be kind. Another time, if there was another time, I might accept.

★

Sarah's pages arrived late that evening and I sat up long into the night reading the final chapters. I woke with a pain behind the eyes and a sore head. Papers now lay strewn in disrespectful array across the floor – Miss J would have a fit.

Outside the rain had ceased and through the gap where the curtains did not quite meet, a bright strip of sunlight caught tumbling dust motes. I gathered up the papers, returned them to their envelope and hurried out to the office without breakfast, carrying Sarah's work carefully swaddled as before. In Russell Square, I bought chestnuts from a vendor and sat a moment, soothed by their sweet warmth and the thought of tea in the office at ten. Even lowly employees such as myself were entitled to that.

★

In the teashop, Sarah leaned forward in her chair and viewed me expectantly. 'So, you think it works? The ending?'

I pulled the manuscript from my bag and placed it on the table. 'I think it does. There's balance, you give equal weight to each section of Joe's life and although it's not the conclusion we want, it's the only one that fits, that remains true to the heart of the narrative. I have to admit I cried, but that's no bad thing. I loved it.'

'Well, that's a relief. Treading new ground can be tricky. I'm still not sure what Fowler will think.'

Neither was I, but I didn't want Sarah doubting herself. 'I'm sure he'll see this as we do. After all, he is aware it's a shift from your other work.'

Abstracted, Sarah sat staring through the window, then turned her attention back to the table. 'Now, tea I think.' She selected a large éclair from the cake stand and bit into it, blissfully rolling her eyes.

I poured the tea and helped myself to a scone. Afternoon teas courtesy of Fowler and Son were fast becoming an enjoyable bonus – I would need to watch my waistline.

★

That evening I sat up late, my mind full of Sarah's story. The book and the man who inspired it, the stranger who'd knocked at her mother's door, the account of his terrors and turmoil, the field hospital in France, the women who'd kept him alive with their kindness and care.

Again I thought of my generation, of how indulged we are. An accident of birth that put me in this place at this time. Men who missed the war, women who missed the struggle for suffrage – we simply reap the benefits: a free and peaceful country and the right to vote. There was much to be thankful for, despite a fastidious office manager and an enigmatic employer.

But Sarah's writing troubled me on another level too – its depth of insight, the skill with which she revealed Joe's painful plight, exposed only too clearly the banal inadequacy of my own scribblings, the distance I had yet to travel as a writer. Comparison may well be the thief of joy, but sometimes it was inevitable. Pulling all my notebooks and folders from the wardrobe, I threw them in a heap on the floor. In the morning, I might well be tempted to burn the whole lot.

X

Following the last meeting with Sarah, I spent time on my appraisal, the recommendations I would make to Fowler in support of the book. Although convinced he would be willing and eager to publish, I strove to highlight the importance of the work, to endorse the messages it carried. This was not about the glorious sacrifice of those who died, but rather a celebration of forbearance, the strength and resilience of those left alive and for many, the tragedy of their plight. So much public effort had gone into eulogising over the dead when so many survivors found no homes to return to, no solace and no work. But when I presented the report later that week, Fowler's response was not at all what I'd hoped for.

'Well,' Fowler said, dropping the hefty stack of paper onto his desk, 'this will certainly stir the critics – and she's plenty of those as it is. Meddling, they'll call it. Stirring things up where she has no right to interfere.'

We were seated in Fowler's office, either side of his desk, unlike the convivial arrangement of our previous meeting. It was not a good sign.

'But the account is true,' I said, struggling to remain calm. 'Almost all of it. Sarah has testimony from the old soldier who came to her house, and the others she met as a result. She pieced it all together from real events!'

Fowler eyed me across the desk. 'I doubt the critics will see it like that. Some – those with liberal leanings might just accept what she's saying, but she'll be scorned – the book will be scorned. And that, by implication, means us.'

'But if it's controversial,' I broke in, 'wouldn't that be a good thing? People might buy it out of curiosity, to see what the fuss is about?'

'That's possible, but it's not just the horrors, the graphic description of the battlefield, it's some of the other 'exploits' going on behind the scenes – assignations behind the mess tent and so on. Plenty of chaps wouldn't want their womenfolk reading that stuff – if they weren't deeply offended, it might give them ideas.'

I grew impatient. 'And my report? I've tried to emphasise the novelty of Sarah's story, the aftermath for these men who now have no place in society, the injustice of it! This hasn't been spoken of before.'

'And there's a reason for that, Miss Brown. It's uncomfortable, some might say shameful – the public don't want a reminder of such a failure. True there is the Haig Fund, but we all know that's not enough.'

I had imagined Fowler to be built of sterner stuff, had seen him as forward thinking, supportive of Sarah's radicalism, willing to embrace some of the liberal philosophy creeping across the Channel from France. Something had clearly caused a change of heart.

Tempted to push further, I bit my tongue. Fowler was now holding my report, tapping the sheets together on his desk and I had to let it go.

'It will be seen as the fabrications of a female fantasist, Miss Brown, a popular writer who has lost her calling. I'm not sure we can take that risk.'

I stood up. 'What should I say to Sarah – Miss Paget?'

'Tell her whatever you like, but we can't publish this as it is. We need romance and soft landings from our women writers, not harsh *realities* even if they are true. We took a big risk with her last book – this is a step too far.'

He handed me my report. 'I'll leave the manuscript downstairs, you can arrange a meeting with Miss Paget and return it to her.'

I made my way down to the second floor and sat brooding at my desk, stunned by Fowler's complete volte face. Now I faced telling Sarah that her work would not be accepted unless major changes were made and as I feared, this did not go down well when we met later in the teashop.

'Well?' Sarah's eyes, initially bright and hopeful, clouded the moment I sat down.

'I'm so sorry,' I said, laying the large envelope on the table. 'I tried. My appraisal is there for you to read, you know I loved the book but Fowler wasn't buying, I'm afraid.'

'So,' Sarah frowned, rubbed her forehead, 'things haven't moved on as much as we hoped, more's the pity. I suppose he wants changes – beyond the usual amendments, I mean?'

I nodded. I was finding it hard to speak. This book, I realised, meant more than just a failed contract, it was my first serious responsibility. I had wanted to succeed as much for myself as for Sarah.

'That will be hard,' Sarah said. 'It would change the whole tenor of the book. Knowing what I do, I can't write about the war without honesty, without telling the truth. I might just as well write something else altogether – more slush about the upper echelons of society and their desire to make a good marriage. Jane Austen for the 20th Century without the wit!'

'I can try and speak to Fowler again, if it would help?' This was the last thing I wanted to do, but it might appease some of the clawing guilt I bore for letting Sarah down.

'Thank you but I know how this works. I've done well for them, but I have a box – a *niche*. Readers have certain expectations, that's what the publisher counts on, especially now. Things are tough for small companies and Fowler won't want to take risks. I knew it was a long shot, but hell, Issy, I wanted to do it! The story needed telling.' Sarah tapped the table with her finger. 'You've read *All Quiet*, I presume?'

I shook my head, more inadequacies piling up fast.

'Well, that book has created a sea change in the way war is viewed, at least among the enlightened. There are others too – Robert Graves, Margaret Bonfield. The establishment of course, don't want to know. Our victory has to remain unequivocal,' Sarah waved her arms around, her voice rising. '*We held off the Hun, by gad, sir!* It would spread panic otherwise.'

Heads turned anxiously to our table. This was not the usual sedate discourse for an afternoon tea room. The waitress eyed us nervously, as if the manager might need to be called. But Sarah raised no further eyebrows that afternoon. We drank our Lapsang and tucked into scones with cream. As I rose to leave, I apologised once again. 'I still feel this is all my fault, I should have done better.'

Sarah put a hand on my arm and spoke kindly. 'Think nothing of it,' she said. 'You've done your best, now I have to decide where to go from here.'

At the door, I looked back to see Sarah light up a cigarette and sift slowly through her pages. The rejection, at least outwardly, had caused less distress than I feared. The distress, I realised, was all my own.

XI

The following weeks hung heavily. Above all I wished to avoid probing questions concerning progress on Sarah's manuscript. I kept myself occupied in the office as far as possible, extending my working hours beyond those of the other employees, all except Joan, who stayed with me until the janitor stood in the doorway jangling a bunch of keys. In the morning I arrived at the office early, buying fruit and fresh bread outside the Tube station at Russell Square and hiding it in the locked drawer of my desk. I took pains to guard the key – if such a cache were discovered, Miss J's dressing down would be audible in Battersea.

New manuscripts arrived regularly, many trivial and insipid, familiar romantic nonsense I'd read a hundred times already. Some were daring or pretentious, but none had a fraction of Sarah's depth and insight. And nothing at all dealt with the same subject matter.

One morning, my alarm clock failed to wake me on time and arriving late at the office I ran into Fowler on the stairs.

'Ah, Miss HB.' He stopped on the step below me, our heads at the same level. It was somewhat disconcerting.

'Mr Fowler?'

'I was expecting some progress on Sarah Paget's redraft. Have you heard anything?'

I rested my hand on the banister to steady it. 'No, actually. I met her about two weeks ago but I haven't seen her since.' This at least was the truth. 'I believe she is considering her options.'

Fowler looked surprised. 'Her options? Surely, it's quite simple, her only option is to redraft along the lines I recommended, otherwise it's no go I'm afraid. You did make that clear, I suppose?'

At this very moment Sarah was probably hawking her work unmodified to every publisher in London. 'I'll chase it up,' I said, 'find out what's happening.'

I moved to pass him on the stairs but he stepped in front of me. I could smell his shaving soap, the oil in his hair.

'Perhaps we could arrange another meeting after work,' he said. 'Say tomorrow? Your mother's not visiting again is she?'

I fought for another excuse. 'No, but I have to visit my aunt who's in hospital. She's in Charing Cross. With an ulcer.' Under different circumstances I'd have been rather pleased with my inventiveness – a raft of relatives needing my support. But a touch of menace lurked behind Fowler's disappointment each time I turned him down.

'You have a very warm heart, Miss HB, so many good deeds. However, you should understand what your priorities are. Your future doesn't lie with ageing relatives, now does it?'

I stepped aside and continued up the stairs. 'You'll have to excuse me, I'm a little late this morning. I'll contact Miss Paget and find out where things are.' I ran up the second flight to the office and slumped down at my desk.

Joan looked up and stopped typing when I entered. 'Are you alright?' she said. 'You look ghastly.'

'It's Fowler. He's... difficult sometimes.'

'Oh, *Prowler*, you mean. The girls in typing named him years ago. I'm surprised you hadn't heard.'

Whatever he was called, I'd no wish to create problems for myself. Clearly, he expected me to meet him, perhaps I owed it to Sarah to try one last time to plead her case. I unlocked my bottom drawer, carefully broke off two pieces of bread and handed one to Joan. Then I scooped the crumbs into a paper bag to dispose of later.

XII

With careful timekeeping, I saw little of Fowler in the following weeks. When we did meet, he acknowledged me with a curt nod and to my relief, made no further attempt to engage me in meetings after hours. Once or twice I went to see Edith in Hampstead who welcomed me with tepid enthusiasm and stale cake.

One Sunday afternoon in mid-October, I took a train out to Cambridge to visit Rhona again. Her opinion, though often caustic and lacking in sympathy was at least honest and I badly needed a sounding board. But after we met, and took the river path along the Backs and across the meadows towards Grantchester, London seemed a long way off, my dilemma less than urgent. We sat on a bench by the water, watching the punters take a wavering course upstream.

'Do you remember when we were little and you fell in the river?' Rhona asked.

I had not forgotten. Nor had I forgotten how Rhona stood on the bank watching me struggle without coming to help. I even wondered whether my fall had not been accidental.

'I wasn't very kind to you, was I?'

I stared at my sister, 'What makes you think of that?'

Rhona sighed. 'I'm not sure. I feel a bit out of place here, less than welcome at times. It makes me think of those early days we had, as a family.'

'When father and I first came to live with you?'

Rhona nodded, 'I realise now how hard it was for you. Not the sort of thing you think of when you're ten years old. I just hated the intrusion.'

'It was a long time ago, Rhona – and we're still speaking! I shouldn't worry about it.'

'But I do. Mother was so besotted with your father, I didn't seem to fit in any more. Daft really. I should have known better.'

'I'm sorry it's hard for you here. Last time I came you seemed so settled, so at ease.'

'I manage. It's a means to an end, that's all.'

Soul searching was a rare thing with Rhona, a privilege for me to witness, my own problems trivial by comparison. I might not have mentioned it at all, had Rhona not coaxed it from me.

'In your last letter you mentioned an issue with… what's his name – your boss?'

'Fowler. And yes, things aren't that easy.'

I explained the situation with Sarah's manuscript, Fowler's reaction and what Sarah had decided to do.

'Issy, you do realise you're risking your position by going up against Fowler? Annoying though it is, can't you just knuckle down and accept what he says?'

'No, I can't! It's not fair, Rhona. Sarah's book is brilliant.'

'Clearly Fowler doesn't think so.'

'He's thinking about sales, that's all.'

'That is his job, Issy.'

'Yes, but couldn't he take a leap of faith, shake things up a bit?'

Rhona stood up, straightened her skirt and prepared to move on. 'It doesn't sound as though they are the sort of company to do that. And Sarah is looking elsewhere, you say?'

'She's passionate about this book – opus magnum and all that.'

'Well take care Issy, I know I said you were selling yourself short with this job, but you've done well so far and I can see how much it means to you. Don't throw it away.'

'But in principle it's wrong.'

'You're a woman Issy. Principles don't count for much if they deviate from the norm.'

There was truth in Rhona's words but as dusk fell and we wandered back towards the City I was no closer to a resolution. We stood awhile at the point where our paths divided.

'I hope things improve for you here, Rhona. You deserve this, it's what you've always wanted.'

Rhona gazed into the distance. 'It's not the work, you understand, just attitudes. Science is still very much a male domain. I realise now we were spoiled by Father's enlightened views.'

'It grieves me that he won't see us go to the polls. He was way ahead of his time.'

'That's very true. Most men I meet, in spite of their intellect, are Neolithic in social thinking.' Rhona paused a moment, her head bowed. 'Have you ever thought that might be Fowler's problem? That you might be too forward – too opinionated? Maybe he even agrees with you about the book, but won't admit you're right.'

'It's possible, I suppose. Sometimes I have the feeling it's not my opinion he's after.'

'You mean he's after your virtue?'

For all her forward thinking, Rhona had an innocence about her. Enclosed within the sanctuary of the university, it was hard to believe that she had seen more of life than I had. For almost a year, I had at least been out in the real world unchaperoned, amidst the rub and knock of earning my keep and mixing with the likes of Sarah Paget, whose views on certain matters would shock a sailor.

'I can look after myself, Rhona. Don't worry.'

'Well, make sure you do. You need to be careful, Issy. Men can be... uncompromising. Keep your head down and do the job. That would be my advice.'

'Thank you,' I said, pecking her briefly on the cheek. 'Duly noted. I have to go now – the last train is at eight and you'll miss your supper.'

★

Rhona took off her glasses and rubbed her eyes. Deciphering the text on Issy's manuscript was not a simple task, the typeface small and feint. This was clearly a work in progress. Handwritten amendments crowded the margins on every page, red and green ink denoting which sections to keep and which to discard. Yet for all the uncertainty in her output, Rhona once again sensed Issy's strength and resolve. Determined in her bid for independence, any attempt to caution her had met with little success.

Rhona placed the papers on the side table with the others and went to draw the curtains. Wandering round the empty house, peering out into the dark, she thought of those days as children, she and Issy locked in rivalry, each nursing their own displacement. How sad they'd had so little time as grown women, to shore up the cracks. Cleary Issy had me down as an ingénue, Rhona thought. Less than worldly-wise cooped up in my ivory tower. Hardly a flattering portrait, despite its fragment of truth. But whilst Rhona may not have lived in the real world, she still mingled with some of the finest young brains in the country, and they weren't all male. Rhona had no doubt that Sarah Paget belonged to a similar privileged elite, even if she did appear to slum it from time to time.

With a glass of sherry to hand, Rhona took the last section from the folder and settled again to read.

XIII

The next time I encountered Fowler, I did not escape so easily. Did he wait in his office, listening for my tread on the stairs?

'Miss Brown,' he said, a renewed touch of warmth in his voice. 'So glad I've caught you. I've been thinking about our last meeting – Miss Paget's manuscript. I've been reconsidering and perhaps I have been a little hasty.'

I stopped and turned to face him.

'The woman can write,' he went on, 'that's well established, and I was impressed with your defence of this new work. However, my father will need a little more information when I pitch it to him – he has the final word, you understand?'

I allowed myself a moment of hope. 'Of course, I said. 'Anything I can do...'

And then it came.

'These things are so much better discussed away from the office, don't you think? So, I'd like you to be available say, Friday? I'll book a table at Maurice's – it's a rather bijou French place just off the Strand. We should be able to discuss things without interruption. What do you say?' Before I opened my mouth to respond, the matter was settled. 'Good. I'll send my car for you. 7.30.'

Fowler took off up the stairs whilst again I was left entangled in a situation I'd entirely failed to manage.

Throughout the rest of the day I worked piecemeal at various tasks, sorting papers for filing, typing rejection letters. But I struggled to give anything my full attention. The one mitigating thought was the chance I now had to plead Sarah's case again, even though this could simply have been done in the office. By now I was well aware that Fowler expected more than just my opinion.

And intuition did not mislead me. At 7.30, I waited for Fowler's car outside on the front doorstep. After work I'd sifted irritably through my sparse wardrobe in search of an appropriate outfit, opting eventually for a dark blue satin shift, demure but informal. However, when Fowler rose to greet me at the restaurant, I noted he still wore his work suit, even the same tie. Perhaps, after all I had misjudged him.

'Ah, Miss HB – Isabel,' he said, reverting to his former effusiveness. 'I trust your journey was pleasant? So much more agreeable than public transport, don't you think?'

I offered my hand which he held a few moments longer than necessary, then sat down. The room was small, the tables laid with white crockery on red checked tablecloths. Wooden chairs with no upholstery scraped on the bare floor. But the clatter, the voices, the informality pleased me, it was far less intimate than I'd feared.

'Something to drink perhaps? The house red is worth a try.' Fowler indicated the carafe on the table. 'Or maybe you'd prefer something a little more refined?'

He made a lot of assumptions – was he mocking me? At home with Edith and Rhona, I drank sherry.

'The house red is fine, thank you.'

Fowler poured me a glass and refilled his own, signalling to the waiter for another by waving the carafe in the air.

'Since we last spoke,' he said, 'I've had time to consider Sarah's work in more detail. I don't see why the controversial elements of her story can't quite simply be altered to reflect a more positive, more hopeful outcome. Surely this can be done with a mere change of emphasis here and there?'

I took a sip of wine, then pulled out the folder containing my appraisal of Sarah's manuscript and put it on the table, to firmly establish the purpose of the meeting.

'So, what are the specific changes you would like Miss Paget to make?' I said. 'If we water down this man's testimony too much it will lose impact. If we twist his words, the story will be no different from dozens of others – brave young men, heroic deeds, glory for the country in their sacrifice. This isn't what Joe experienced, nor is it how Sarah portrayed it.'

Fowler was watching me closely, 'But that's just the point, Isabel. The public don't want to read about slaughter. They want joy and restitution and to know that the best side won.'

I took another sip of wine. Mindful of the conversation with Sarah regarding recent contentious publications I said, 'How can there be a *best* side in a war? England doesn't have a monopoly on the dead. Both sides lost millions. Shouldn't that be acknowledged?'

'I can see where your sympathies lie, Isabel. No doubt you align yourself with the likes of Helena Swanwick and Co on the peace crusade, but just because you women now have the vote, don't think you can go around challenging conventional wisdom!'

Fowler picked up the menu and scanned its contents briefly, adding, 'There is a status quo to maintain, society has been rocked enough. People need their fairy tales, not raw facts, even if it is the truth. Let's order shall we? I understand the moules marinières are splendid.'

But my appetite, such as it was, had vanished, along with any influence I may have had over Fowler's decision. There was no evidence that he had reconsidered at all, he had simply presented the same objections as before. The wine, heavy and rather acid, swirled a little in my head and I put the folder away in my bag. This meeting, to which I'd not consented, had already failed in its purpose.

'I'm sorry,' I said, 'but I'm really not hungry. I think I may need to go home. I'm not feeling too well and I have an early commitment tomorrow.'

As I gathered my things Fowler stood up. 'I see,' he said. 'I'm sorry to hear that.'

I shook his hand, but his face did not register concern – it was something else altogether. Scurrying back through the evening crowds, the disappointment of failing Sarah yet again was more than tempered by the fear that my job was now in jeopardy.

XIV

For several days, I put off contacting Sarah. What could I say, how would I explain the devious nature of Fowler's tactics and above all, my failure? As it turned out, Sarah saved me the trouble, phoning me at the office a week later.

'Can you talk?' she asked, a note of excitement in her voice. It was a poor connection and I suspected the operator would be listening in.

'It might be better to meet. Is there any progress?'

'Surprisingly, yes. I think I might have a nibble.'

After work the following day, I met Sarah outside the British Museum. We wandered down Monmouth Street towards Trafalgar Square and found a seat in the churchyard of St Martin in the Fields.

'You've had some luck then? Some interest?'

'Just a bit – tentative but definitely not a refusal. It's a new place, mainly poetry at the moment and the occasional play. But they seemed to approve, and what's more, they liked the honesty, the strength of it. They seemed to think this is the way forward, so that's good.'

In spite of my doubts, I grasped Sarah's optimism and

hung on. Any repercussions from Fowler and Son I would deal with when, and if, they came.

On the way back to Bloomsbury, Sarah mentioned she was meeting up later with a few friends. 'Going for a quiet champagne dip. You should come.'

I suspected a champagne dip involved getting into water that wasn't a hot bath.

'We're trying the pools at Hampstead this time,' Sarah said. 'It's great fun.'

'Thank you, but I don't actually own a costume.'

'Oh, that's no problem – I have spares. Besides,' Sarah leaned in, 'we don't always bother to wear them.'

I was not easily shocked. My former circle of friends were prone to acts of frivolous daring, some of which I too had engaged in, but nothing would persuade me to swim anywhere, not after the river incident with Rhona. From the security of dry land, I loved the water, but had never quite conquered my fear of it.

'I'm seeing my mother this evening,' I said. 'She's not been well.'

Sarah studied me a moment. 'You do need to let rip now and again, Issy. We all do.'

It seemed the more time I spent with Sarah, the less I made sense of my life.

★

'Mr Fowler would like to see you immediately in his office.' Miss Jenkins appeared at my door early one morning towards the end of November.

'I see, thank you.' I removed my coat and hat and collected the latest manuscript from the pile on my desk.

'You won't be needing that,' Miss Jenkins rapped, hands clasped in front of her. 'You must go now, it's urgent.'

I set off up the stairs, conscious of a pair of hawk eyes following me, and waited outside Fowler's office to catch my breath.

Fowler, seated at his desk, did not stand to greet me, or even raise his head. I made a move to sit down but he held up a hand.

'Don't sit, this won't take long.' On his desk lay the usual piles of paper, some typed, one handwritten, the scrawl unmistakeably Sarah's.

The room had none of its former warmth, the winter cold and deep chill reached me across Fowler's desk. Finally he looked up.

'It was not your place to question our decision, Miss Brown,' he said, reverting to formal address. 'I'm disappointed, you have overstepped your position by a long way – and now I find we've lost a writer. A popular and profitable one at that.'

I took a moment to reply. 'But you didn't want her work! You made that quite clear.'

'Miss Paget was obliged to change certain aspects of it, but with modifications it would have been perfectly acceptable. A simple tale of heroism and triumph – that's what the readers want.'

This time I flared up, protocol be damned. 'Are the readers children? Can't they be trusted with the truth? You expected Sarah to write a completely different book! This man, this soldier's story would be totally subverted. Men like him are still tramping the streets because of what he went through! Don't we have a duty to make that public knowledge?'

'We are not in the business of polemic, Miss Brown. I trusted you with too much responsibility. It was your job to persuade Miss Paget to do what was required and quite clearly, you have failed.'

Desperate to flee, I fought to keep a shred of dignity.

Fowler stood up, walked slowly round the desk and stared down at me. 'Of course, there is a way we could rescue the situation,' he said. 'A way that might safeguard your position here. You can start by being a little more gracious with my invitations.'

So that was it, what all this was about. Layers of innocence, fell away – Rhona was right after all. This was so much more than losing Sarah, James Fowler did not take no for an answer.

I took a step back, chewing hard on my lip to stop it trembling. 'I see,' I said.

'I will decide what should be done with you when I've spoken to Miss Jenkins,' Fowler went on. 'No doubt she can find some tasks more suited to your level of... competence.'

I turned and fled downstairs to my room, swallowing the taste of blood where my tooth had punctured my lip. Only then, resting my head on the desk, did I allow myself the comfort of tears.

XV

Joan had called in sick, leaving me grateful for a quiet space to myself. If I stayed put, did not take a lunch break, I would see no one and the time would pass. Most of all, I had no wish to meet Miss J. I reached into the drawer for the day's workload and pulled out a comforting stack of papers, enough to fill the long hours until I could escape the office and my bitter humiliation.

For a while, it worked, losing myself in the usual pile of rejection letters, and sorting the copies for filing. But Fowler's words echoed, his veiled threat clawing its way in and I failed to keep my misery in check. I sat sobbing at my desk until a hand touched my shoulder.

'I take it things did not go well.' The voice was quiet, the tone unfamiliar.

Lifting my head, I found Miss J standing beside me. I groped for my handkerchief lying illicitly on the desk, rubbed my nose and sat up straight. 'I'm sorry, Miss Jenkins. I wasn't... feeling too well. I'm just about to carry on now.'

I braced myself for the tirade – sloppiness, laziness, disgrace and all the other misdemeanours I'd been guilty of, but this time, it never came. Gone was the familiar pinch of disapproval, Miss J's face now wore an altogether different look – the harsh features softened, melted into deep furrows of concern. Neither did she stand rigid with clasped hands, she pulled out a chair from beneath Joan's desk and sat down next to me.

'My poor girl,' she said. 'I did try to warn you.'

'It was my own fault,' I said, screwing my handkerchief into a ball. 'I should have persuaded Sarah to rewrite the book, not encouraged her to take it elsewhere. I should have been more loyal, the company has been good to me.'

Miss J shifted in her chair. 'I think you know by now that James Fowler is not a good man.'

I watched carefully as Miss J spoke, expecting the familiar version to re-emerge at any moment. 'But you've always stressed how important loyalty is. I assumed that keeping us in line was all part of that.'

'Indeed it is. However, sometimes loyalty can be misguided. There can be many reasons to question it. In the end, we may have to make a difficult choice, and stick to our principles. Am I right in thinking that's what you have just done?'

'I nodded. 'I suppose so, yes. You see he – Mr Fowler, wanted –'

'I know what he wanted Isabel, you don't have to explain.' Miss J got up to close the door and sat down again.

'A few years ago,' she said, 'there was a young woman who worked here. Her name was Lilian. She and I were friends – *good* friends, you understand. She was bright, full of ideas – a bit like you. Like you, she had hopes of being a writer.'

I stared at her, tucking my handkerchief into my skirt pocket. By now I was utterly confused. 'How did you know I wanted to write?'

Miss J studied her hands. 'As you know, not much escapes my notice, Isabel. But to be honest, I gathered from Sarah Paget some time ago that you aspired to be a writer, that you hoped your time at a publishing house would equip you well for this.'

'That didn't exactly go to plan, did it?'

'Perhaps not, and it was the same for my friend. All went well for a while, then Fowler promoted her, began asking for extra meetings, insisting they take place out of hours. Only my friend did not have your *awareness,* shall we say? She did as she was told.'

'So, what happened?'

Miss J stared into the distance, for a moment pained and vulnerable. 'He found out about our living arrangements. Threatened to sack her for some petty work infringement. Mixed up invoices or something – I can't even remember now.'

'Unless she obliged?'

'Exactly. But by the time I found out what was going on, it was too late, and rather than approach Fowler, I persuaded her to leave. Selfish perhaps, but I couldn't risk my job as well, especially then. Even though she had family money, I wanted to support her, at least until she found another post.'

'And did she?'

'No. She moved away after a few weeks – back home to the Midlands.'

'But why did you stay? Surely it would have been better to leave too, go with her.'

Miss J stood, gathered her composure. 'It's a job, Isabel. Unlike some people, I have no other means of support. And I was never likely to marry, now was I?'

I sat motionless, waiting for the next disclosure.

'And in case you're wondering,' Miss J added, 'it is the reason I run such a tight ship.'

'Beyond reproach?'

'Absolutely. You were something of a challenge, though. A free spirit.' Miss J smiled for the first time. She was, I realised, not much older than Sarah. 'But I stay to keep an eye on him, to make sure he doesn't try it again. Maybe one day when I've less to lose I'll have the courage to confront him.'

'Thank you,' I said, 'for telling me this. It can't have been easy.'

'You're welcome, Isabel. Just another word of advice – resign before he has the chance to send you back down here. That way you retain an element of control. You know you're wasted here, whatever impression I may have given you, I believe you have a bright future ahead. You will find another placement, I'll give you an excellent reference. Go home now and write your letter. I'll make excuses for you.' Again she touched me briefly on the shoulder then left the room.

For a while I sat at my desk, turning over Miss J's extraordinary revelation. Though comforted to know I'd not misjudged Fowler, my failure still gnawed. If I could not find work elsewhere, what then? It would mean a return to Hampstead and Edith. I had no other income, in spite of Miss J's implication, Father's legacy was not a life support. Worn out by the weight of the day, even though it had barely begun, I fetched my hat and coat from the cloakroom, checked my face in the mirror and washed my sore, gritty eyes.

On the way out, I found Miss J installed at her own desk, the familiar inscrutable mask rigidly back in place. Undeterred, I stopped in the doorway.

'Do you ever hear from her, from Lilian?' I asked.

For a second her face softened again, but there was no response this time. 'Go home Isabel,' she said. 'Look after yourself. I have work to do.'

★

I had no wish to invite gossip by returning to Percy Square at this hour. Instead I set off towards Camden and the canal, where the towpath stretched invitingly either way. Being out at this time of day had an air of truancy about it. As I took to the streets, my boots hammering disappointment into the pavements, there came a sense of freedom, a feeling of calm. Perhaps I'd expected this all along, had known my good fortune to be short lived. But there was relief too, that my ambition had not landed me in trouble deeper than the loss of a job. How strange had been the encounter with Miss J, almost enough to ease the indignity of my meeting with Fowler. It explained much about the workings of the place, the rigidity, the constant battle for perfection. Again, my sense of privilege surfaced – I did at least have options, a home to go back to, undesirable though it might be. Miss J had none of that. She could not even choose who to love.

Whatever happened next, I resolved to keep a clearer head, resist the dazzle of hope and expectation, in other words, to grow up. I recalled Sarah's words at our first meeting: *You won't know much about life at twenty-two.* That may have been true, but I was learning fast.

I worked out a week's notice. On my last morning Miss J came up to the second floor to find me, bearing no trace of the triumph I might once have expected. When she offered her hand, I fought a sudden urge to hug her.

'You've done the right thing Isabel, and I wish you luck. You can write your own story now, even if no one ever reads it. But write the truth – that way it's documented and you have borne witness. Take care, and keep your wits about you.'

Then she left, her sensible shoes clacking loudly on the stone staircase.

XVI

A few days after the extraordinary events at the office, I called Sarah and arranged to meet. I explained briefly what had happened but made no mention of Fowler's threat or my resignation. I met her in the teashop after work on my last day, hoping to find an ally, some sympathy to go with the tea and cake. After all, it was defending Sarah's work that had landed me in this position, that and the unreasonable – if not sinister – expectations of my employer. But Sarah had other things on her mind.

'It's lovely to see you,' she said, beaming across the table as I sat down and took off my hat and gloves. 'So much has happened! It's just wonderful how things work out sometimes. I'd say it was a silver lining, if that wasn't such a cliché!'

As far as I was concerned, the outcome was a disaster. I waited hopefully for the right moment to begin, but Sarah rolled on. 'You know it's perfect timing, as if everything's come together at once. All that fuss with Fowler and Son and the book, the effort of sparking interest elsewhere, finding another publisher.'

It's not been a picnic for me either, I thought meekly. Did Sarah even acknowledge that? 'I can't see how any of this applies to my situation,' I began. 'It's actually been quite distressing. And now…'

'And now what?'

'I've left Fowler and Son.'

Sarah stopped beaming. 'Why on earth have you done that?' she said. 'Was that wise?'

Perched uncomfortably on my seat I briefly outlined what had happened in Fowler's office the previous week. 'So, you see it was the best thing to do – the only thing to do, under the circumstances. My sister warned me,' I said, 'and so did Miss J, in a roundabout way.'

Sarah picked out another vanilla slice. 'Well at least you'll be shot of her now. That's one less thing to worry about.'

'I'm not so sure. She was strangely sympathetic – very kind, in fact.'

'Really? That does surprise me!'

'There's more to her than meets the eye,' I said, about to reveal more of our conversation. But then to do so seemed disloyal, breaking the brief and valued bond that had formed between us that miserable morning in the office. I was also aware of Sarah's need for gossip and feared where it might end up. I said no more, but watched as she tucked into her flaky cake.

'Oh well,' Sarah said, emptying her mouth, 'you'll find something else. London's full of opportunities for a young thing like you. Think of how much experience you have now.'

This was not quite the support I had hoped for, no endorsement of my principled stance, not even much interest in what would happen next. Perhaps I had expected too much and I sank into my Lapsang and cake with little enthusiasm for either, while Sarah brought the conversation back to her own affairs.

'Anyway, as I was saying, things have worked out really well for me. I'm going to miss this place. In fact, I'm going to miss London.'

I stared at her. 'Miss London? Are you leaving?'

Sarah nodded, her mouth full of cake again.

'But why? I thought all was well now the book had found a new home?'

'It's quite simple really. I've had enough of the Smoke – I've been here quite a while remember. The lease is up on my rooms – it's time for a change.'

'But where will you go?'

'Ah, now that's the exciting bit! I have a couple of friends who run a small theatre down in Cornwall. They want me to join them, focus on play writing. They're great advocates of new talent, all very encouraging.'

You're hardly new talent, I thought, ungenerously. But Sarah in full flow was not in need of generosity. She spent the rest of the afternoon outlining her plans, how fortunate she was, how much she would benefit from the change of scene. I could not muster the energy to break in, nor find anything to say that did not betray my disappointment. With every word that came out of Sarah's mouth, my temper was wearing thin. I had thrown my support behind this woman, to encourage acceptance of a story that begged to be told. Now Sarah was deserting me, heading off to start a new chapter whilst I tried to pick up the pieces of an old one. Maybe my support for Sarah's work had been overzealous – even misguided, but it cost me dearly – an injustice that Sarah, now lost in new horizons, had not even bothered to acknowledge. Even a few weeks ago, I might have caught Sarah's excitement, felt the same fire. Now all that emerged was a void, a gaping well of sadness. It had been a long week, I had heard more than enough and began to gather my things.

'Sarah, I have to go. My mother has some friends coming for Bridge and she's asked me to make up a four.'

Only now did I have Sarah's attention. 'Bridge? Issy, really?'

I nodded, another social lie I had become so gifted at delivering. I would no more play Bridge with Edith and her crowd than suffer another meeting with Fowler. But I hadn't endured Sarah's diatribe to have my own choices questioned, even if they were an invention.

'Yes, Bridge. And why not?' I snapped. 'It's all very well having friends connected in all the right places – how very convenient for you! I've been listening to your eulogy all afternoon and I'm very pleased for you. But now I have to go – even if it is just to play Bridge!'

Yet again the room had gone quiet. I stood up, shaking a little and picked up my hat and gloves. 'And I also have to start looking for a new job. Goodbye, Sarah. I wish you luck with your new venture.'

If Sarah had the grace to look contrite, I did not witness it. I escaped as swiftly as my battered dignity would allow and hit the cold streets back to Islington.

XVII

Reluctantly, I gave up my room in Percy Square. Though the rent was paid until the end of the month, I had no wish to stay without work to occupy my time. Failure sat heavily with me, in my job and my integrity. Even my writing did not amount to much: diary entries, ramblings and a couple of short stories, none of it of any consequence. I packed my belongings in a few boxes and took a cab back to Hampstead, keeping the details of my banishment as guarded as possible. Edith would delight in a jubilant *What did you expect*? But my welcome came with indifference, Edith's main concern being the disruption to her social calendar.

'You won't know I'm here, Mother,' I assured her. 'I shall look for another post and be off again.'

The reality though proved harder. Each publishing house I tried drew a blank. Since the Crash, companies were cutting back on staff and I still had very little experience to draw on. Weeks became months, the dark winter days dragged on. I'd seen nothing of Sarah since our last meeting and though the friendship existed more in time than substance, the space this left in my life gaped, sore and unresolved. I attempted to focus on my writing, to use my recent experience to add honesty and depth to my work. But ideas would float enticingly beyond reach, refusing to be captured on the page. The poignant irony of this was not lost on me, the life I had wanted so badly at the heart of literary glitz, had turned foul in more ways than one. Events had stolen my writing soul, inspiration that flooded my thoughts a year ago now evaporated like rain on a hot city street.

As winter advanced, I abandoned my writing altogether and took long walks on the Heath or on the muddied towpaths from Camden down to Paddington. I lay for hours in the library reading from Father's case histories, moved and angered again by the injustice served to those with so little security. Boatmen ruined by fraudulent carrying companies, haulage charges unpaid. Amid the ease and comfort of Hampstead, I itched for change, to use my skills for some benefit, to settle on a cause beyond my own needs.

I did not expect to hear from Miss J again, and by early spring, I had finally begun to put the Fowler and Son debacle behind me. But one morning in March, a letter arrived with Miss J's impeccable script across the envelope. I took it with me on my walk to the Heath, found a bench and sat down to read it.

Dear Isabel,

You will no doubt be surprised to have word from me, and I hope you will forgive the intrusion into your privacy. I am well aware how distressing those final weeks at Fowler and Son were for you, and how unjust and insulting your treatment by those in a position of trust. As I mentioned at the time, until such attitudes are challenged, there will be no opportunity to change or modify unacceptable behaviour on the part of those in power. It is to my shame that I have yet to find the courage to speak out, I fear it will be many years before women are able to do so without recrimination.

But I digress, which brings me to the point of this letter. You may remember I mentioned a close friend Lilian, who left London to return home to the Midlands. Her background being somewhat privileged, a large country estate near Leicester, it was yet another reason she and I could have no future together. However, Lilian's sister Annie is a weaver and their mother Geraldine has long been a patron of the arts. A few years ago they set up a small workshop on the edge of the canal at Stanford.

At this point, I had a mental image of carpentry or metalwork but Miss J went on to explain.

It's more like an Atelier, a gathering of craftsmen and women, along the lines of the Suffrage Atelier that operated before the War, you may remember, only less political.

I had been a mere infant before the War, but Father had talked of such places, the attempts to democratise the art world.

It seems they would like to have another member, someone with a commitment to their calling, who needs time to establish themselves. The idea is to work as a cooperative with shared responsibilities. I've met Annie and her husband Michael – they are good people, welcoming, inspirational and very well connected. They have contacts *in every aspect of the arts: galleries, theatre, publishing – Geraldine supports them all quite generously I'm told. Michael is a printmaker, his work is very popular and has found a growing market in publicity. The London Underground has commissioned him to design a couple of posters already, I believe.*

Now, I am not sure what your position is at the moment, or how you have coped since Russell Square. You may already have found a suitable post, but I do know that you would do well there – it is a great opportunity and your writing would thrive.

Again, forgive the intrusion but do let me know if this proposal is of interest.

With all good wishes,
Yours sincerely,
Freda Jenkins

Astonished by its content, I read the letter twice and sat a long while gazing across the Heath. In the distance a family gathered by the lake, a small child crouching, threw bread for the ducks. It touched me in its simplicity, a longing for an innocence that was gone. I read the letter yet again then stuffed it in my pocket and took a long walk back across the Heath, past Kenwood House and out into Hampstead Lane. By the time I reached home, a weight had lifted.

Hiding away in my childhood home was no therapy, it simply stifled all I'd tried to nurture over the past year. That evening I composed a brief and courteous reply to Miss J and arranged to meet her at the teashop in Holborn the following Saturday. Then I pulled out all my notebooks and all the abortive scribblings and laid them on the dining room table. I skimmed through most of the papers and shamed again by their raw, unpolished innocence, took them to the kitchen and burnt them in the range, prodding the ashes until every scrap had gone.

By the end of March, I had a plan. Again I packed a few essentials, as many books as my luggage space would allow and a few clothes I thought suitable for life in the country, among them a white muslin dress I hadn't worn for years. Though Edith thought it cheap, it was always a favourite, full of rustic summery charm and perfect for my new beginning. Then I left London and travelled to the Stanford workshop, hopeful of better things.

NINE

Rhona put down the last sheet of paper and searched for a handkerchief. From the outset she had half hoped to find the pages empty of any narrative that might resurrect those early days. But this was not at all what she found. What she had found was a connection, her half-sister reaching out across the decades, offering at last some clue as to who she really was.

She flicked through the pages again, rereading sections she'd skimmed over before, the full force of Fowler's arrogant menace, Issy's spirited self-defence. Now, so much later it heartened her to acknowledge Issy's strength and determination, even though she bore some guilt for not recognising it sooner. But what puzzled her was why the narrative ended when it did. The last sentence would indicate that Issy had gone off to the workshop to develop her writing, yet her story made no mention of this progress, no indication of what happened there. Perhaps by this time she had found broader, deeper subjects for her skills. There would no doubt be a good reason, just as there would be a reason why the manuscript was in the box with Leonard's things. In any case, it hardly mattered now. Rhona placed all the sheets in the folder again, took it back to the spare room and left it on the bed with the album.

When William arrived the next day, he brought down the remaining items from the loft and swept the floor.

'That's it, Mother, all done. You can forget about it now. When Dad's better, he can look through this stuff and make some decisions.'

Rhona surveyed the contents of the room and sighed. 'I appreciate all you've done William, but it's still a bit overwhelming. Can't we shift anything else?'

William leant the broom against the wardrobe and wiped his hands on a handkerchief. 'It's not ours to deal with Mother, power of attorney or not.'

'I know you don't agree with what I did, William. But I had to make sure I could deal with things if I needed to. If your father didn't…'

'Recover? You might have waited, had more faith in him.'

'Perhaps it was a little hasty – but it's done now. And I won't move anything else, not without consulting him.'

'Promise?'

'Promise.'

William picked up the broom and set off downstairs but Rhona called after him. 'I did want to ask you about this,' she said holding out the folder. 'It might be of interest.'

'What is it?' he asked.

'It belonged to your Aunt Isabel. Something she wrote long ago, a sort of memoir, an account of her time in London.'

William sat down on the step and opened the folder.

Rhona settled beside him, watching as he slowly turned the pages.

'This is quite something, Mother. Had you forgotten about it?'

'That's what's so strange. I've never seen it before.'

'So how come it's here?'

Rhona picked a speck of fluff from the stair carpet. 'It came out of that chest, with your father's things. Goodness knows why.'

'Didn't they know each other though, Dad and Aunt Isabel? Wasn't he the lock keeper at Stanford?'

'Yes, for several years. As you know, it was because of Issy that I met your father.'

William handed back the folder. 'That probably explains it then. Maybe she left it with him to take a look at? Or maybe one of the others she worked with was helping her with it.'

'I've no idea. Not that it really matters now. But I have a feeling there are some pages missing.'

'What makes you think that?'

'It's... unfinished. There's no part two.'

'Well, that's not surprising, is it? Given what happened.'

'I mean before that. There's no mention of her life after she left London.'

'Perhaps she wrote something else that covered that time.'

'I didn't find anything. Nothing relating to her life there – it was all general stuff. Quite lyrical but it didn't describe what she was actually doing. She sent me letters – kind words of encouragement when things were tough after Cambridge, but she kept me at arm's length, and never wanted to come home.' Rhona eased herself off the stairs. 'But then, having read her story, she may not have wanted a reminder of her office days.'

'Could I borrow it?' William asked, putting the broom away. 'It might be fun to catch up on some family history.'

Rhona tied the tape around the folder. 'Not yet, I think. I'd like to mention it to your father first, even though I doubt he'll shed much light on it.'

'That's fair enough. But I'd be interested to know about the missing pages.'

William fetched his coat and fished in the pocket for his keys.

'Not staying for some tea, William?'

'Not this time, Mother,' he said kissing her briefly on the cheek.

'I'll see you soon then. Drive carefully.'

TEN

It's Tuesday today and I'm awake early this morning. The sun filters through the thin curtains and lies in patches across my bed. If I'm quick, I can get to the bathroom before I'm told to, before the routine starts. I can still manage all the personal stuff, though they insist on hovering nearby. It's not easy sorting out your bowels with the door ajar and someone asking if you're alright, even if you were brought up on a boat. That was different, that was family and the same for all of us.

It's a bit chilly in the bathroom, the water takes a while to run hot. I lather up and start to scrape, stroking slowly down my jaw. It feels good, makes me smile. I'm half-way done when there's a loud knock on the door. Damn! My hand shoots in the wrong direction, I've nicked my ear and it starts to bleed, a large red blob on the snow-white foam trickles down my face and onto my dressing gown. Someone won't be pleased. There'll be a fuss about laundry, there's always such a fuss about keeping clean. My wife is the same. But winter and summer, my mother would wash and dry the essentials for all five of us and hang them on

119

the cabin roof if it was fine, inside above the stove if not. I never once heard her complain. She could teach people here a thing or two about fuss.

There's another knock, louder this time and a voice calls, 'Mr Gardner? Are you alright? Can you open the door!'

I take a paper towel from the dispenser on the wall, half a dozen fall out and lie in a wet pile on the floor. I mop my ear and hide the bloodied towel in my pocket. I don't want it seen, they might lock me in my room if they think I can't cope. They do that here too sometimes, *for our own safety*, so they say.

I unlock the door, prepared for disapproval on the other side, but surprisingly there's no grumpy face, just a young man I've seen around the place a few times. I think he's the staff nurse, he was in matron's office when my wife first brought me here.

'Morning Mr Gardner!' he says cheerily. 'Or can I call you Leo?'

It's been a long time since anyone called me Leo. He's taller than I am, dark skinned, his hair twisted into neat rows that end in tiny plaits at the back of his neck. He steps into the bathroom and gently takes the razor from me, rests it on the washbasin and checks my face still half covered in foam.

'Not bad, Leo – good job.'

He doesn't shout or sit me down on the stool and do it all for me, he asks whether I can manage or would I like some help. I pick up the razor and carry on, finish the other side of my face and hope my nicked ear won't give me away. Only when I'm done does he hand me the towel.

'All decent then?' He holds the bathroom door open and we make our way down the corridor to my room. I count the three doors we pass – I've noted them so I can find my way at night if I need to. They expect us to use a bottle, they don't like us wandering about after lights out. Well, bugger that.

'Ok, I'll leave you to get yourself dressed. I'm Walter, by the way,' he says, pointing to his name badge. 'Call if you need anything, I'll just be outside.' He grins and closes the door behind him. I wonder if he'll be in trouble for bending the rules.

When I'm dressed, I let him know I'm decent and haven't cracked my head open in the process. He asks the usual questions: would I like to come down for breakfast, or have it in my room. I usually eat it here, it's good to be away from the bibs and slops of the dining room. I like the quiet too, and the way the sun moves across the bed to the chair where I sit. Early morning is the only time I see the sun in here and I don't like to miss it.

Walter comes back later with a tray, different from usual, neatly laid, a small posy of flowers in one corner. Cowslips and violas. I touch the petals as he puts the tray down on the side table, smile at his thoughtfulness. He stays a while, seems happy to chat.

'I'm fond of English flowers,' he says. 'And gardens with the greenery and the space. Where I grew up, we had none. Just a small yard big enough to kick a ball. In the dry season it turned to dust, and when the rains came it was a mud rink. But on the edge of town, in the big white houses where the rich live, there are walls and walls of scarlet and blue, like a blood red waterfall. And the smell –' his face is alight now, 'you can't imagine!'

I wonder where this place was, who he's left behind.

My breakfast is good, the toast warm and wrapped in a napkin. He hasn't poured milk on the cereal so it ends up a soggy mess. The milk is in a small jug next to the toast and the tea is still hot. I take a sip while Walter straightens my bed and shakes the pillows. I give him a thumbs up and he leaves, says he'll be back later for the tray.

ELEVEN

Leonard was sleeping in his chair by the window when Kate first found him. Walter had suggested an introductory meeting in his office, or visiting him in the day room, but that seemed far too formal. 'I'll just pop up and have a chat with him in his room, if that's ok? It won't take long this time.'

'Do you want me to come too?' Walter asked. 'Moral support?'

'Does he bite?'

'Less than his wife, I know that much.'

'I'll be fine thanks. I'll check back later, let you know how it goes.'

When Kate entered, Leonard woke with a start and pulled himself upright in the chair. His nose began to run and he patted his chest as if he'd lost something. Kate handed him a handkerchief, a real one not a tissue. She'd been told such things could be a talking point, a comforting throwback to the old ways.

'My name's Kate,' she said. 'I'm sorry to wake you. Did you know I was coming?'

Leonard clearly didn't remember. He looked at the

handkerchief then blew his nose and searched again for somewhere to put it.

'You can hang on to it,' Kate told him. 'I've plenty more at home.'

Shaking his head, Leonard stuffed it in his trouser pocket. Kate reached into her bag and found the card she'd made, like a business card only more colourful. She hoped it would draw his attention, be something she could use to introduce herself, to explain the project and what they'd be doing in their sessions together.

'As I say, my name is Kate and I've come to ask for your help, if I may. I've heard about your artwork.'

Leonard frowned and shook his head again.

'I'm sorry,' she said. 'I should explain. I recently started to work here and I've been lucky enough to learn about your paintings.'

Something clicked. He stopped frowning and stared at her.

Encouraged, Kate carried on. 'Last week I had a meeting with your wife and she…'

Mention of his wife didn't go down well. He began to wave his hands, as if in panic, wanting her to leave.

'I'm so sorry,' Kate said. 'I can see I've disturbed you. Shall I come back another time, when it's more convenient? If I leave you this,' she showed him the coloured card, 'next time won't be such a surprise.'

She put the card on the bedside table, picked up her bag and headed for the door.

'Goodbye Mr Gardner, I hope to see you soon.' Then she left and went straight down to find Walter.

Kate scheduled another meeting with Leonard for the following week. Walter advised leaving time between visits, especially if things did not go too well. She realised with some regret that Leonard Gardner wasn't suddenly going to accept her with open arms and start spilling out his life story. If anything, her lack of experience had set the whole process back by scaring him. As his wife had suggested, Leonard Gardner would not be an easy start for her.

There was a fragility about Leonard, stuck in a space that seemed so alien to him with his rights signed away and his wife having full control of his affairs. Not surprising, having met the woman. Yet beyond the frailty Kate saw strength, recognised a body used to movement, to labour. He'd lived a long life, his artwork a testament to a talent that now lay undiscovered and unsung. To work with him was indeed a gift, she must find a way in and eventually hope to get it right.

Walter had already filled in some of the clinical details for her, the accident, the broken ribs that had healed well but left him stiff and breathless at times, the blow to the head, resulting in severe aphasia. There was no actual memory loss mentioned in the medical report but the distress caused by his condition, the inability to access the right words were the reasons he had chosen to stay silent. Much depended on the next meeting, finding the trust, the right path, the beginnings of a bond.

Kate decided it would help to begin with a few sketches, perhaps the simple act of watching her draw would trigger something. It was worth a try and she didn't want to mess it up again.

TWELVE

On the table, there's a small card – bright yellow with an arc of colour, like a rainbow. *Catherine Davies*, it says. *Assistant Care Nurse*. The young lady with the large bag. I'm not sure why she came to see me or why she's left this note. Maybe young people visiting is something they do now, like basket weaving. My wife thinks I'm a basket case anyway, it's why she's left me here.

After breakfast I wait by the window, looking for Tom in case he's around this morning. I'd rather be outside giving him a hand. It never suits me to be shut up for long, even if the weather is bad. But they don't like us getting damp, or too cold or too hot. No extremes, as if the poor old body won't cope. Where I grew up, cold was what we knew, there were no soft options.

Tom's not there today so it looks like the dayroom for me, unless I can escape. As I've discovered, it can be tricky getting out of here. If I make it past reception, Matron is sure to stop me and scowl. She'll tell me I shouldn't be outside on my own and take me back to the dayroom. This time I try the back stairs that lead to the door beneath my window, but on the bottom step is another nurse, taking a cigarette break.

'Not thinking of going out, are we Mr Gardner?' she says, opening the door and throwing out her dog end.

I've no choice but to turn round and go back up to my room. I sit by the window for a while, then head downstairs the right way this time and wait in the dayroom. The interminable wait until lunch. In the chair next to me, my neighbour Angela is stirring. It's rare to see her down here, she has the room next to mine and these days scarcely leaves her bed. I don't recall many visitors either. Angela's inclined to rant, especially at night. I go to her room sometimes when the terrors overtake her and, though she bats me away, I stay with her until help arrives. She's a bit confused when she comes to, doesn't take kindly to strangers.

When the gong sounds, we all stir like Pavlov's dogs and heave and shuffle to the dining room, those that can. Others are wheeled off to the feeding bay. I'm halfway across the room when a nurse stops me.

'Mr Gardner, you have some company today. It's one of our new care assistants – she's going to have lunch with you.'

There's a moment of panic – does she think I need feeding too? I've not reached that stage yet and I hope they shoot me before I do. But then I see the young lady who came to my room. She's here again – how odd. She smiles, takes my arm and says, 'Hello Mr Gardner. I hope you don't mind but I've invited myself to lunch.'

Her voice is pleasant, quiet with a slight lilt, not from these parts, I think. I didn't notice when she came before.

I've never had company for lunch. Will the food taste better, I wonder? Perhaps she's brought her own – I've seen visitors do that. They bring out sandwiches and a flask, not trusting what's on offer here, what it might be laced with. But when we sit down at my usual table in the corner and face one another across the blue checked cloth, there's no sign of a lunchbox, just the large straw bag which she puts on the floor by her feet.

'So, what's on the menu today?' she asks, surveying the room brightly. I hope she's not expecting too much. Food is always predictable – soft and wet, but working here she's probably used to that. Today it's shepherd's pie with cabbage and peas. The young lady takes her helping from the trolley as it comes round, the dining assistant checks her list to make sure I'm not forbidden anything. Anything more solid than mashed potato is out of the question, but it's not easy to complain. I poke at the tasteless mass in front of me, swallow small mouthfuls, try to empty my plate. They tell me I have to keep eating, otherwise the muscles will die and I'll never speak again, apparently. It would help if the food were just a bit more appetising.

Either my companion is very hungry or doesn't want to dwell on what she's eating, but in a few short minutes her plate is clear. Such solid constitutions the young are blessed with. But then she pushes her plate to one side and clasps her hands together on the table as if something is about to begin.

'I expect you're wondering why I'm here,' she says. 'I'm sorry my last visit seemed like an intrusion. Has your wife spoken to you?'

My wife has said nothing of importance for years, except the day she told me I was coming here. I could try to tell her about William, but that will only complicate things. I don't want her wearing that sad, puzzled look, the one they get when I try to speak.

But the young lady doesn't look puzzled at all. She has brown eyes, a small face. A dark curl escapes from behind her ear and falls across her cheek. She hooks it back, and in my head a corner lifts, stirring a dusty layer in the old house by the lock.

'This must all be a bit of a mystery to you, so I'll explain.'

She smiles a lot, shows her lovely teeth. I force down my lunch and try to be encouraging this time. The others are looking in our direction, our corner of the room a welcome distraction. I manage to finish the shepherd's pie and put my knife and fork together neatly on the plate before it's whisked away by the washer-up. Then I turn to face my companion and concentrate.

'I'm an assistant care nurse,' she says. 'I haven't been here long and Walter – Staff Nurse Robinson – wants to start up a new programme of activities for the residents. He's asked me to…'

There's a pinch in my stomach where the shepherd pie sits. Am I an experiment then, a lab rat?

'Don't worry,' she says, picking up on my dismay. 'It's not an experiment, nothing like that. It's more…' she pauses, searching the yellowed panels on the ceiling. 'It's more a kind of *therapy*.'

Now I think of white coats and couches and people with more money than sense.

'I'm not talking about psychoanalysis, of course! This is different, but we're hoping it will help – help you find things you may have lost.'

Like words you mean, and making sense?

'Sometimes it can bring back things from the past, a memory of people or experiences that may have become distant or buried under more recent events. Especially if there's been some trauma. It's simply a way to help you move forward, to move on with your life.'

Will it get me out of here? If it works, can I go home?

'Of course, there are no guarantees but we hope it will help towards your recovery. It's all quite new, very innovative. I suppose you'd call it a... project. We're on a project – together. It involves trust – and by the end, hopefully, you'll have some insight, some understanding.'

Is this what William was talking about? It still sounds like an experiment. The young lady takes a notebook from her straw bag and while we wait for pudding she writes in it, looking up at intervals. She's working something out, there's anxiety there, as if she thinks I might disappear.

I nod slowly, still cautious, but she has an open, earnest look about her that puts me at ease. The trolley comes back, stacked with dessert bowls and an oversized tin of strawberry jam. This means semolina. The dining assistant serves us both and plonks a spoon of jam on without asking. I'm old, so I must like jam, must have a sweet tooth. I don't, as it happens, I only eat Kit-Kats because William brings them. I feed the biscuits they leave me to the birds outside my window – digestives go down very well with the starlings.

I push my dollop of jam to the side and eat round the edge of it. My companion is tucking into hers, swirling the jam into whorls of pink and purple. She looks up and smiles, a flash of glee.

'Can't help it,' she says. 'Has to be done.'

When she's finished, she puts her spoon neatly in the bowl and wipes her mouth on a napkin. 'Thank you,' she says. 'Best meal I've had for weeks.'

I find this hard to believe, though I do know what it's like to be hungry. Hunger years leave a mark that never fades. The dining room is emptying and one by one the residents are wheeled back to the French windows for the post prandial nap. We mobile ones are left to our own devices. My companion asks whether I'd like to go outside. 'It's a beautiful day and… please don't quote me on this but canteens always smell of cabbage, don't they?'

She slings her bag onto her shoulder and stands by my chair while I get to my feet. Not hovering, just waiting as if she has all the time in the world. As I make my way to the door, I hear her tuck in my chair.

THIRTEEN

Kate had taken a risk with lunch in the canteen – it was rather more than 'getting to know the patients'. But Walter had thoughtfully scheduled her sessions with Leonard on Matron's weekly visit to the regional office which meant she'd be away for most of the day.

In spite of the mild weather there were no other residents in the grounds. For Kate, it was good to be away from the lingering cabbage smell – a stark reminder of school dinners. Here the air brought the scent of bluebells, flowering in clumps beside the garden walls. Leonard led Kate to a seat beneath an arch at the bottom of the lawn, a budding rose scrambling over it. They sat facing the house, a gloomy mix of style and structure, built largely of red brick with stonework framing the windows and the main door. Upstairs, on the first floor, casement windows led onto a wide stone balcony, the limestone balustrade now grey with age. They used to leave the beds out there once, she'd heard, when the cure for consumption was rest and the cold night air.

Kate searched in her bag, brought out a large sketchbook and pencil case and laid them on the bench beside her. Not something she'd imagined doing again so soon but given Leonard's situation, she hoped the process might reach him.

'I thought I'd do a sketch of the building,' Kate said. 'It's quite dramatic, isn't it? Rather like a film set.'

There was no response from Leonard, he continued to sit, looking up at the high windows. Kate took out another smaller sketch book and began to sketch the view in front of them – a detail of the windows and the balustrade.

'I've seen some of your work,' she said. 'Paintings of the boats – the waterways? It's beautiful!'

Leonard turned to look at her then dipped his head. Did he remember his young days as a painter, the success he'd known?

Kate finished her sketch and put it on the ground by her feet. Then she produced a small notebook and handed it to him. He looked at it carefully then flicked off the elastic holding it shut. In it, Kate had placed a series of 'memory papers' she'd taken from the scrapbook collection, most of which now fell out into his lap.

Kate waited, then Leonard lifted his head and turned towards her, a slow smile emerging. His hands shook a little and he rested them a moment on his knees, then turned the papers over one by one, studying the images. A kettle, a water can, a profusion of roses and daisies – bright emblems of a distant life.

Kate watched as he opened the sketch book and searched for the right pencil, feeling it settle in his hand. He looked up at the stone balcony again, tilted his head, closed one eye. As he began to make his marks on the page, his body seemed to settle, the posture innate, the angle of his head and shoulders easing into the movement, fluid and natural.

To give him space, Kate left the bench and wandered around the grounds, noting the broken flagstones, neglected flower beds, the crumbling brick wall that surrounded the property. Only the vegetable garden showed signs of attention, well-stocked with row upon row of new growth. To one side was the greenhouse where the smokers congregated; inside a figure moved back and forth tying and tending with deliberate care.

When Kate returned to the bench, Leonard looked up, put the pencil back in its case and passed the sketch book over.

'May I?' she said.

To Kate's surprise, it was not the stone balcony he'd drawn, but a boat, a narrow boat, moored up by a bridge. The lines of his work had not simply pulled out a shape, but a memory. 'Was this where you lived, Leonard – where you grew up?'

He nodded and looked again at the paper, at the object he'd drawn. It bore all the same hallmarks, the lightness of touch Kate had seen in his early work.

'Did your family live here too?'

He nodded again. Kate dived into her bag, brought out a box of pastels and placed it beside him on the bench. Leonard stared at it for a moment then pushed open the drawer. His large fingers hovered across the colours, then he picked one out and started to fill in, yellow and pink for the roses on the water can, red, blue and gold for the livery. As he worked, Kate saw another layer emerge, fresh and vibrant, that brought the whole thing to life.

'Did the boat have a name, Leonard? Are you able to write it down?'

His fingers began to pluck at the corner of the sketchbook. He shook his head, closed the book and handed it back to her. Enough for one day.

'Thank you,' she said. 'I'm sorry if I've tired you, if it's been too much.'

Fearing another blunder, Kate packed everything away in her straw bag and they made their way back to the house.

At home that evening, Kate took out the sketchbook and flicked through the drawings she'd done with Leo. Though hasty and unfinished, they were a sharp reminder of the love she had for her art, the comfort and strength she'd always found in its promise. Art had been her sanctuary, the power she harnessed when things were tough, the company she kept when friendships failed. Now Walter had offered her this new challenge, a different direction, and already things were looking up.

FOURTEEN

Rhona stood in the kitchen eating a sandwich. She'd spent the morning sorting out a large patch of the herbaceous border, her back was playing up and it hurt to sit down. Lying or standing were the only options when this happened, as it now did with irritating frequency. Creeping fingers of age that poked and prodded in all the weakest corners, hampering her progress with the garden or dealing with the remains of Leonard's loft collection.

William hadn't been over for weeks, the new job taking up much of his time. Never sure of a welcome, Rhona hesitated to invite herself down to his home. Since the baby, Helena had struggled – constantly tired according to William – and Rhona's tentative offers of help were not met with much enthusiasm. Helena liked to do things her own way it seemed and that meant leaving far too much to William.

She was still unsure about what to do with Issy's manuscript. Not long ago she might have been tempted to destroy it, along with all the other memorabilia in the loft. If we cannot influence the past, why hang on to it? Too much of Rhona's past had been an exercise in forgetting, of moving on from loss, from events over which she'd had no control. But mindful of William's feelings on the matter, she now hesitated to go against his wishes. Besides, she would dearly like to know why Leonard had kept this particular item from her. Had he simply forgotten about it? Quite possible after so many years. Yet still she could not fathom why Issy made no mention of her time at the workshop, no reference to her work there or the companionship she found. Something was missing, an era of her life that had meant so much, given no space at all. It didn't make sense.

That evening Rhona took courage and phoned William. 'Is this a good time?' she said. 'I don't want to disturb you.'

'It's fine, Mother. Evie's asleep and Helena's out. How are you?'

'Oh, you know. The usual aches and pains.'

'Too much gardening?'

'Probably. I miss your father now he's not here.'

'I'll try and see him again soon – it's not that easy at the moment. But I do write, he knows I'm thinking about him.'

'Actually William, I'm phoning to ask a favour.'

Rhona didn't often ask for favours and William paused before answering, his voice cautious. 'How can I help?'

'I'm not sure what to do with Aunt Isabel's manuscript – I wondered whether you have any ideas. And, there's the mystery of the missing pages too. I remember how significant that time was for her.'

'Maybe she was working on other things while she was there. Didn't she write poetry too?'

'Yes she did. I kept some of it but none of it referred to the workshop.'

'Is it possible Dad would know something about it?' William offered. 'He was living there too, after all.'

'I'm not sure it would do your father any good to see it, even though he is involved in this 'memory' project. He wouldn't be able to tell us much anyway.'

William was silent for a while. 'You may be right,' he said. 'But you could still show it to him, or talk to him about it at least.'

None of this offered a solution. Increasingly Leonard seemed withdrawn and irritable when she visited. Even allowing for his lack of speech, another wall had gone up between them. She had tried to be positive towards the project, had taken in the artefacts to help the young care nurse make a start, now she felt excluded from the whole thing.

'I think not, William,' she said. 'Not yet at any rate. I'll see how the next few weeks go, then decide.'

'Perhaps if I read it, I could help you decide? I could come up to see Dad next week and collect it at the same time?'

Rhona thought a moment, then she said, 'Why don't I pop down with it? I won't stay long but it would be nice to see you all.'

Again a long pause at William's end. 'Ok, Mother. When were you thinking of coming?'

'As it's the weekend, how about tomorrow?'

The visit did not go well however, in spite of Rhona's good intentions. It rained heavily and they were forced to spend the afternoon cloistered in William's small living room.

Rhona had never engaged easily with her daughter-in-law and they struggled to find much to talk about. William did his best, clearing a space on the couch for her to sit and fetching tea and some biscuits that had clearly been in the packet too long. But Evie, going through a timid phase, hung back and refused to leave her mother's side.

It was a relief for Rhona to be back in the familiar spaces of her home, in spite of those now empty of Leonard's presence. She had at least handed over the manuscript and could now wait for William's thoughts on what she should do with it.

FIFTEEN

On her next visit, Kate found Leonard in the day room, one of a nodding row lined up by the French windows. He wasn't asleep this time, surprisingly. It must be 100 degrees in there.

'Hello again Leonard. Hope I haven't disturbed your nap?'

This time, Leonard smiled a welcome, struggled to his feet and indicated the garden beyond the French windows, clearly anxious to be out of the day room torpor. They found the bench beneath the rose arch and Kate took out her sketchbook and a pencil.

'Maybe you'd like to do some drawing again?' she said.

Instead of waiting for her to begin, Leonard took hold of the sketchbook and pencil and began to draw. It was a rough, quick sketch done at speed but not a bad likeness: her features clear and even, the long nose and neat jaw, even the sweep of hair behind her ear.

Kate watched, fascinated. 'Thank you,' she said, offering to take it. But Leonard hung on, trying to write something in the corner. It came out as a G. Had he forgotten her name, or lost the card she'd given him? Or maybe the G was a question mark.

Kate pulled her name tag from her pocket and showed him the photograph. An awful thing, like a mug shot – the drawing was a big improvement and she told him so.

'And see,' she said, pointing to the words beneath the photo. 'My name is Catherine Davies – but everyone calls me Kate. I should wear this round my neck but for our meetings it's too official – and it gets in the way.'

When Leonard smiled, Kate guessed she'd got it right. She found the page from their previous session and showed it to him.

'This is the boat you drew last time,' she said. 'Where you lived with your family. It's all here – even the lace curtains and the water can. See?'

Research so far had taught Kate a little of life on the water. The Cut, they called it. There was a myth, in days gone by, that it was all a quaint romantic idyll like working the land, or digging coal, cooked up by the affluent out of ignorance and guilt, the reality so far removed. Kate knew all about the effects of digging coal.

'It must have been hard for you, on the water in all weathers?' she said.

Leonard looked up at her, nodded slowly and picked up the pencil again, trying to hold it steady, impatient with his stiff fingers. As he started to draw, details seemed to return with the marks on the paper. This way and that, shapes emerged as if they lay just beneath the surface. Perhaps the past had not deserted him, perhaps a memory or two came back with the simple act of drawing. For Kate too, being here in the presence of such skill, such quality, was a joy in itself. How could she ignore a process that was the very substance of her? Walter was right. Kate had much to learn from Leonard Gardner.

SIXTEEN

She's told me her name is Kate. I've logged it in but
goodness knows how long it will stay. I think she gave
me a card with her name on it but I'm not sure what I've
done with it. Taking the sketch book, she finds the picture
I remember from before. I lay a finger on it, trace over
the sections of the boat, feel the warmth of the sun on the
panels, smell smoke in the air. My home from long ago.
The past has not deserted me, even since I drew this, a few
more clouds have lifted. I think of how folk shunned us
on land but stole our designs, copied them onto plates and
coal scuttles, or water cans filled with flowers for a neat
suburban doorstep. I wonder whether Kate is aware of this.
Does she know our only clean water was stored on the roof
in just such a can? Most of the time we washed in canal
water, if we bothered to wash at all. Is this what she wants
perhaps – the rambling memories of an old boatman? Is
this what's behind her *project*?

I want to speak, I want to tell her that five of us lived
there on the boat, that our home was named the *Albert Jack*
after my grandfather. But between the memory and the

voicing lies an ocean of effort. The words I want and the sound that comes will not be a match. Kate's eager face will fall, a cloud of disappointment. She too will think me a fool, or that she has failed. I take up the pencil, try to hold it steady, cursing my stiff fingers.

It's Riley this time, our old tow horse – his name comes back to me as I draw. We named him when he first arrived, a bargain handed on from a family who'd switched to steam. He refused to work before sun up and my mother declared he must have lived a life of luxury, just like the O'Reilly in a song she'd heard. He soon learned to knuckle down, plodding the paths faithfully for fifteen years. I'd plod behind him, switching his backside with a length of willow. What was I then – nine? Ten? Twenty miles a day sometimes. Mother took over when her chores were done and my legs stung with fatigue. I'd climb back on board and fall asleep on the roof if it was warm and Mother didn't notice. She was strict about the water, chastising me when I slept outside. But more than once I rolled off with only the splash to warn them where I was.

When my drawing is done, Kate studies it for a long time. She points to the two figures I've drawn either side of Riley, holding up his midday bucket of oats.

'These are your sisters?'

Again, I want to tell her their names, but I can't risk the words. Then she says, 'Would your wife know their names? Could we ask her? Maybe she could fill in some of these gaps.'

I don't want my wife involved. This is mine, she can leave me this, she's taken everything else.

Kate puts her hand on my arm and speaks softly. 'It's ok,' she says as if she knows. 'Just a thought. What happens here is between us.'

I let out a long breath and close the sketchbook. She collects her belongings and takes me back inside.

SEVENTEEN

It's raining today. Kate and I are sitting either side of the window in my room. Before she came, I remembered to look at the card with her name on it. I'd hidden it in the wardrobe with the sketch book as my wife tends to snoop.

I'm glad she's here and didn't wait for a fine day. I can smell her shampoo, tangy and fresh. A lift to the spirits like Walter's flowers on my breakfast tray. Small gifts, a small joy. It's not the same when my wife comes, when the room is just too small for both of us.

We've looked at the drawing I did last time – Riley with my sisters and his bucket of oats. This time unprompted, I've drawn a portrait which Kate studies carefully. She's thorough, taking her time.

'This is your mother, I think? It must be, there's a strong likeness in the eyes. And here,' she points to the area around the mouth, 'she has the same smile.' She dives into her straw bag and brings out a notebook. 'Can you tell me your mother's name?' she says. 'Can we find it here?'

Kate opens the notebook towards the back. On a double page there's a list of names, a large F above one set, an M above the other. I scan the list and find my mother's name halfway down. Lucy. It never quite seemed to fit her – such a gentle word for a woman so hardened by life. Yet even with that toughened edge, I knew a softness remained at the heart of her. Kate writes *Lucy* at the bottom of my picture, then adds: *My mother.* Then she picks up the drawing of Riley and my sisters and hands the notebook to me.

'Are their names here?' she asks.

Again I scan the list and find Alice and Win. Kate writes their names beneath the figures on the drawing, but Riley's name is not there and though I try, making hopeless marks on the page, I cannot remember how to write it. Not even the first letter. Does it matter, I start to wonder. Do I need to remember every detail? My head begins to ache.

Kate puts the sketch to one side, turns to another page in her notebook and shows me some figures set out in two columns. More reading. Is this a trap, another test to find out how mad I am, like the ones they put me through before I came here?

'These are your dates,' Kate says, seeing my concern. 'Your timeline. We take these details when you first arrive here. I thought it might help to show them to you, to put you in context.'

Next to some dates is a small star. Are these dates important? Did something happen? But then I see the first figure is 1904, and remember it's the year of my birth. I run my finger down the list and note the others: my wife, 1905, my sisters, 1906. William, 1942, his brother Edward two years before. But my finger runs on past the rest, speeding down to the end, to now. My whole life, on a page. It is all too much and I close the book.

Kate puts it away and leans over to wipe condensation from the window. 'I could read to you, if you like? Or we could go for a walk. It's looking brighter over there.'

We take the back stairs to the ground floor. Today the coast is clear and we escape through the side door. I offer my arm and lead her through a gate into the small kitchen garden at the back, a fenced off space about fifty feet square near the greenhouse. I found it on one of my forbidden rambles – there were plenty of those when they first put me in here. This one's a runner they said, each time I left my room. I thought my wife would have mentioned my need to be outdoors, that I can't be cooped up for long. When I started taking myself out, they moved me up to the first floor, in case I tried to climb out of the window, I suppose. I can see the greenhouse though and Tom when he's around.

We wander, along the cracked paving slabs, between the beds of loamy earth, newly turned and ready for planting. Winter's leftovers straggle at the far end: yellowing beets and brassica stalks, beds of parsley, marjoram and rosemary, cat mint, dead nettle and borage. Grown for their healing properties according to Tom, though I doubt any of it ends up in our food. A little mint would do wonders for the mashed potato. Mother used to send us foraging along the towpath searching for nettle and dandelion, wild garlic and chives. Hung up and dried, infused with smoke from the cabin, they served us well in winter months when greenery was scarce. I remember the hedgerows in March crowded with blackthorn and dog rose, the tall shifting grasses in June, peppered with ox-eye, poppies and campion. Or the hips, sloes and brambles we gathered in September and helped Mother to preserve. Stowed in jars beneath the ledge where my sisters slept, this wholesome harvest too kept us in sound health through the long and freezing winters.

It smells good here after the rain. I love the fresh, damp warmth, brimming with earth and new life, away from the antiseptic and the cabbage. A patch of watery sunlight opens up and we sit on the old wooden seat against the far wall in comfortable silence. I look across at my young companion and am thankful for her presence. Quite why she's spending so much time with an old fool, is still something of a mystery, but it's one I'm beginning to enjoy. I have to be careful though. There are many reasons for burying the past and I wonder how much good can come from digging it all up.

Something wakes me in the night, raised voices from the room next door. It's my neighbour Angela. The rumpus carries on, growing louder. I wonder whether I should investigate again. There is screaming now, fit to wake the whole building. I heave myself out of bed, scrabble for my dressing gown. It's cold in the corridor, the screams louder, and through the open door I see Angela lying on the bed, her face screwed in terror. By her side Walter tries to sooth her, a calming hand on her shoulders as she thumps his chest, her fists tight. He sees me, beckons me over to the other side of the bed and I too try to take her hand, to calm her. Then Walter steps back and her face relaxes a little. She stops screaming and tries to speak but we can't make out what she's saying.

'What is it, Angela?' Walter says gently. 'Please, tell us what we can do for you.'

She lies back, opens her eyes and stares at the ceiling chewing her lip. Then she lifts a bony finger and points at Walter. 'Him,' she croaks. 'Get him away from me!' She grows agitated again, writhing on the bed. 'Him!' she yells, 'get him out of here – we're not safe.'

Then I realise, and more memories surface. I've heard these words too, and seen the fear. We were not much liked, us canal folk. I had it all back then, betrayed by my cracked and leathered skin: the pointed fingers, the whispered threats, the spit. No, Angela, I want to say. This is Walter, he's here to care for you. You were frightened and he came to help. But nothing comes, my throat is a void, the muscles seized. I fear the words would be a waste in more ways than one, for Angela will never change, her fears run as deep as the blue of her blood. Walter knows this. He stands by the door, his face set. He too has heard it all before. I nod to let him know it's alright, I'll stay with her.

Angela is calmer now and drifts back to sleep and when I return to my room, Walter is there by the window, looking into the darkness. It's what I do when nothing makes sense. He turns and I see his despair.

'What can I do, Leo? I love this job, I need it. Not just for my family but for me too.'

I nod slowly, put a hand on his arm.

'Even the night shift is not a problem. But this…' he indicates the wall between my room and Angela's, 'this is not good. Not for me, and not for her.'

It's cold in my room. I forgot my slippers and my feet are numb. I drop onto the bed and Walter snaps out of his troubles and back into mine. He finds me a pair of socks and put them on my cold feet tenderly.

'Do you need the bathroom before you sleep, Leo?'

By way of an answer I clamber back under the covers and he tucks them around me, a simple act of caring. To him I'm not just a body in a bed, a carcass to ship from pillar to post. Separated as we are by age and race and provenance, we are linked in some small way.

EIGHTEEN

Kate was finally making progress. In spite of the shaky start, the spiky nature of Leonard's wife and her ambivalent generosity, the work was going well, Leonard's calm and courteous presence an inspiration in itself. The dossier of notes she'd been keeping since the outset was growing – observations, recordings of her 'conversations' with Leonard, his responses to the drawings that came out of each session. So far she'd unearthed his boat, his mother, his sisters and the tow horse, his artwork responding for him, drawn literally from deep within, a skill neglected and forsaken but clearly not forgotten. His early tentative moves now gave way to confident, comfortable pieces, and for Kate, the project fired up more than a professional interest. She began to look into aphasia, what was happening in the brain and whether it could ever be corrected. She did some research on elective mutism and although the subject was vast, the more she discovered, the more it drew her in. In time Kate knew he would give up his story but time was limited and they hadn't even started on details of his schooling. She would have to go and see Walter.

'You're asking for an extension?' Walter tapped his fingers on the desk looking more concerned than annoyed.

'I'm sorry,' Kate said, well aware of how tolerant he had been so far. Not all new staff were given this much support. 'I know it's asking a lot but this is such an opportunity to use original source material and since Leonard doesn't speak, it's not that simple.'

'How much time are we talking about?'

Kate swallowed. Two years ought to do it. 'Another month perhaps?' she said.

Walter looked doubtful. 'Given what you're trying to do, I understand but we've been lucky so far, we don't want to push it.'

'Thanks Walter, I won't let you down.'

'You'd better not – it's probably more than my career's worth. Now go – do some work, empty a bedpan!'

That evening Kate sat down to read her grandmother's letter. It had arrived days ago but preoccupation with Leonard meant she'd promptly forgotten it. Poor Gran, she didn't deserve neglect.

Cariad,

Kate read,

> *Thank you for your lovely letter. As always it cheers me to hear from you and to know you're doing alright. Everything is just fine here, weather brightening up at last – even the slag heaps look better!*

Tuesday I took your Mam to town on the bus. She didn't want to go, mind but I think the trip did her some good. It's not healthy moping around indoors all the while. I bought her a little scarf from that new shop on the corner of the High Street, pretty it was with roses on. Not real silk I don't suppose, not at that price, but still. Your Mam said she wouldn't wear it and best give it to you, but we'll see.

I've been having a little think about this project you're doing – the one where you're trying to help the man who's lost his voice…

Kate put down the letter and thought a moment. Is that what was going on, or was it the other way around? To begin with, certainly. Walter had brought her in to work with Leonard as a favour, to keep her afloat, but perhaps things had shifted a little. Time spent with him more a gentle interlude than a job. Kate carried on reading.

…Well I remember what my school days were like and if I were him, I'd really rather not be dragging them all up again! Perhaps it was different where he grew up, but I know I often went home with a sore backside, or I'd have to keep my hands hidden for days until my palms healed. There were some good times though, we got to draw on our slates first thing in the morning, something we'd seen on the way to school. I loved that. Anyhow, Katie bach, it's a good and kind thing you're doing and I'm so proud.

Keep well and write soon,
Gran x

Kate put the letter back it its envelope and stowed it away with the others, but something she read this time stayed with her. Gran would be about the same age as Leonard and though from mining stock, brought up in the valleys of South Wales, would her schooling have been similar to his?

For their next session, Kate and Leonard were again confined to the dining room amid the stale cabbage and clash of pans from the kitchen. Heavy rain kept them indoors and the plumber had taken over Leonard's room to fix a leak in the washbasin. Together they studied the drawings he'd done last time, the one of his mother and the other of his horse Riley with his sisters. Kate opened her notebook at the list of names.

'I've added a few suggestions, names that might be suitable for an Edwardian workhorse. Is it here, do you think?'

The list was short, and though at first glance Leonard shook his head, he suddenly placed his finger between the names Rex and Romany and gave her a thumbs up. Progress after all. It began with an R – no doubt Kate would find it somewhere among the scraps. Encouraged, she took out another item from the depths of her bag. After numerous phone calls inspired by her grandmother's letter, she'd found an old school slate in a junk shop in the city. She passed it to Leonard together with a stick of white chalk cased in a short metal tube. He didn't take it, instead, a flash of pain crossed his face and a deep frown appeared.

'I'm sorry,' she said, struck again by how delicate this path they were treading and how without speech, she would ever unlock his story. In spite of clues from the scrapbook, all the details of a first-hand account were missing, which was exactly what Leonard's wife had told her in the first place.

Kate took out her sketchbook, hoping Leonard might begin to draw something. If nothing else, she could enjoy the gentle communion of working with him side by side, of watching his skill emerge. Moments later Leonard did pick up the slate and the chalk but after inspecting them closely, turning them over in his hands, his breathing changed and the troubled look returned. Kate feared she'd got it wrong again.

NINETEEN

It's a shock, seeing the slate. There's the pinch again, and now a knock in my chest. I breathe slowly, deeply, bring it under control. What I'm feeling, I think, is excitement. I run my fingers round the wooden frame, in my hand it sits at odds with my white swollen knuckles, my thin skin laced with blue. It must be more than sixty years since I held such things, since we ventured off the Cut and into school. Many times we had tried to avoid it, dodging the law whenever they showed up. At the loading bay, if word passed that 'his lordship' was afoot, the children would all leave the boats, scurrying like rats to hide in the timber yards or amongst the cargo. Much as we knew schooling was now the law, none of us wanted to go, it broke families apart and left our folks to cope without us. Pa did his best by way of learning, he'd acquired the basics from his sister and passed it all on to us children. But my mother was against it, said it filled our heads with fancy notions that life could be different, and we would only end up disappointed. 'Their lot was settled the moment we set foot on the Cut,' she told my father, many times. 'Schooling's not for the likes of us, law or no law, and there's an end to it.'

My mother had a way with words, a persuasive tone that would convince a clergyman to sell his own grandmother if need be. Few men could argue against her and it came in useful in our line of work when faced with an unpleasant option for cargo, tardy wages or a trumped-up toll charge. It served us particularly well when faced with officials from His Majesty's School Inspectorate.

Once when the warning system down the Cut had failed, an inspector turned up unannounced. I'd have been about twelve, tall for my age and sturdy. I could pass for fourteen and so beyond the legal age for schooling but Win and Alice were younger and slightly built, there was no way they would escape notice. We had a cargo of timber on board at the time, sawn logs due for unloading two days travel away. Covering them was an oilskin tarpaulin, lashed down at the corners.

My mother greeted the inspector in her business voice. 'Good morning, sir,' she said, taking a pipe from her apron pocket and packing it carefully. 'Can we help you in some way?'

The inspector stepped aboard, his dark suit, smart shoes and cane so misplaced amid the rough bright colours of our home.

'Good morning, Madam,' he said, lifting his hat briefly. 'You will be aware I think, of the current law regarding schooling for all children under the age of fourteen?'

Ma sucked on her pipe and nodded wisely. 'Indeed I am sir, and a very fine law it is too.'

'You will therefore be aware that the law applies to all children, regardless of… *circumstances*.' He lifted his cane and waved it at the general surroundings. 'According to the Braunston Parish records, you have twin girls, Alice and Winifred Gardner, born 1906 in the county of Leicestershire.'

Ma rested a hand on her hip and took the pipe from her mouth. 'Well now, they must belong to some other Gardner family because as you see sir, we have no girls, just Leo here, my fine strapping lad and he's all of fifteen next year.'

The inspector's eyes took in the entire surface of the boat, the cabin roof, the galley steps, the walkways, he even peered over the edge to see if somehow, we had suspended the girls in the water.

'I think we'd have noticed if there'd been any young girls around, eh Leo?'

I mumbled in agreement and busied myself with the tow rope, steadying Riley as he grew restless on the path. But the inspector persisted and made his way round to the bow end where he stood awhile studying the tarpaulin covering the cargo. Mother followed on the other side, watching him closely, but as he was about to lift the corner of the tarpaulin with his stick, she called to him, 'I wouldn't do that sir, if I were you. On account of the *particular* cargo we're carrying at present.'

Whether it was the firmness of her tone, her fixed stare or the fact that she smoked a pipe, but the inspector withdrew his stick and stood upright again, a look of distaste across his features. 'By that you mean…?'

Mother leant towards him and gestured with her pipe to the mound beneath the tarpaulin. 'Night soil, sir. We don't want to be disturbing that, now do we?'

The inspector grunted, cast another suspicious look over the boat and hastened back to the stern end. 'In that case madam,' he said, stepping smartly onto the bank. 'I'm sorry to have troubled you. Good day.'

It was as well he left when he did, for I could hear eruptions from beneath the tarpaulin, shrieks of muffled hysteria. When he had safely disappeared, we drew back the cover and found the girls in a helpless heap lying amongst the timber.

'Night soil, Ma?' they shrieked. 'Really!'

My mother's skill at spinning a good tale when authority called, became famous down the Cut. Another time, when a warning did reach us, I hid the girls in their sleeping cupboard while Mother hung black fabric from the cabin windows. When the inspector came knocking, she put her head out between the galley doors and said,

'Oh, sir, I wouldn't trouble you to come aboard unless it's to bring a doctor, maybe? My husband is very sick – I fear it's the typhus fever.'

Without a word, the inspector withdrew, clambered off the boat and disappeared at speed down the towpath. We doubted he was on his way to find a doctor. Meanwhile my father, oblivious to the ruse, was safely in the snug of the local hostelry enjoying a pint or two of his favourite porter.

But for all my mother's tactics, at the heart of it lay her wish to keep us together. Aside from our presence needed on board for work, she could not bear to have her children taken from her. She allowed my father to impart what learning he had and by the age of ten I could read, recite great chunks of the Gospel by heart, and understood the mechanics of basic arithmetic. In time I came to manage our accounts, to keep an inventory of each cargo and a log of each loading and delivery. Together with Mother's sharp tongue, we gained a reputation with the Canal Company for integrity and fair dealing. We avoided swindlers and opportunists, and unlike many of our fellow workers, my father kept a firm hand on his love of drink.

My future, it seemed, was assured, I had a steady grounding in a way of life that I loved. Yet something in me yearned for more. Pa's teaching had set down a solid foundation, but I grew restless, knowing the world held horizons far wider than those contained within the banks of the Cut, beyond familiar towpaths that grew ever more tedious through treading. For two years the war had been raging far from our narrow confines, young men little older than me were dying in their thousands and the limits of my life began to pull and to chaff.

I'm still holding the slate and chalk, white traces of it cover my fingers and I rub it off on my trousers. Lost in the past I've forgotten I have company beside me. It's a wonder Kate is still here, among the remnants of lunch, leafing through her notebook in no hurry to leave. I place the slate on the table, steady the chalk in my fingers and with great care, write down two words.

TWENTY

It's way past breakfast time but I've missed mine. I had a bad night, dreamt a lot, got overheated. When Walter arrives, he peers at me for a while, then disappears and comes back with Matron. She tells him to leave though I would like him to stay, a sympathetic face amongst the starchy rigour.

Matron takes my temperature, measures my pulse, then shakes her head. 'So, what have you been up to Mr Gardner. We can't have you getting yourself all hot and bothered, can we?'

She speaks in the loud voice, as if I've done it just to be a nuisance. 'Now we shall have to send for the doctor. He's not due again until Thursday so that will mean a special visit.'

I may be mistaken, but I thought we had a health service now – that the days were long gone when 'inconveniencing' the doctor meant a bill that couldn't be paid. Matron tells me to stay in bed, that nurse will be along shortly to 'see' to me. I know this is code for the dreaded bottle, and I won't stand for that. It's no fun getting old.

When she's gone, I throw off the bedclothes and get to my feet. The floor is cold, I root around beneath the bed for my slippers and when Walter comes back I'm halfway across the room. He puts my arm around his neck to steady me and we limp together down the corridor to the bathroom. I have a feeling he knows a thing or two about dignity, even though breaking the rules might cost him his job. He stays with me when the doctor arrives, hands him the chart Matron left hanging on the end of the bed. If the doctor has indeed made a special visit, he doesn't seem unduly concerned. He pulls out a stethoscope, listens, prods and pokes for a while then puts it back in his case.

'Any dizziness Mr Gardner? Headaches?'

I shake my head.

'Appetite alright? Waterworks?'

This time I nod, grateful for his simple questions. He asks about my ribs, about the pain and stiffness but I don't try to tell him any of that, just give him a thumbs up.

'Looks like it's a slight infection, your chest's a bit lumpy but nothing much to worry about. Best to get plenty of rest, and fluids of course. I'll be back in a couple of days. Meanwhile I'll put you on some antibiotics – that should sort you out.'

Walter leaves with him and I must have slept because when I wake, my wife is sitting in the chair by the window reading the paper, the rustle and tap so familiar I could almost be back at home.

'Matron phoned me,' my wife says, pulling off her spectacles. 'She sounded anxious, so I thought I'd better come and see for myself. The doctor's been, I gather? I told them it would take more than a slight infection to keep you in bed.'

She puts her spectacles on again and picks up the paper.

'I went to see William last week,' she says. 'You know I'm not at all sure about that wife of his. I was rather hoping they might just drift apart, but since the little one arrived, I suppose he's stuck with her.'

Not this again. William's wife is a charming girl and just what our son needs. She certainly put a spring in his step when they met.

My wife carries on talking to the newspaper. 'I really thought he'd do better for himself, at least find someone with a few brains. What was it she did – book keeping for her father wasn't it?'

And that's what I did too, remember?

'Well, you know William, anything for a quiet life. He's always been lazy. Not at all like his brother.'

It's the same old story, the stuck record. You've always been so hard on William. How can we know what kind of man his brother would have been? How he would have turned out or who he would choose as a partner? If my observations were correct, I don't think you could have counted on a daughter-in-law at all. Wired up differently was Edward. Not that you'd believe it, even if the evidence were still here in front of you. But dying at eighteen, leaping on impulse from a rock above the river in spite of our warnings around water, set his memory in stone, forever sacred, his selfish folly indulged, his youth and passion unspent. And William – cautious, loving, living

164

William – never stood a chance. My anger rises but with nowhere to go, it fills up the space, spoiling the air.

My wife folds the paper and pulls herself out of the armchair. 'I'd like a cup of tea,' she says. 'Can I get you one?'

She doesn't wait for my response. Even when I had words, my opinion was rarely sought. We managed, side by side for all those years, part of the deal. But we were never a team, she and I, even with the children, our touch points few and trivial. When she returns with a tray and two cups of tea I'm calm again, but not for long.

'I've been wondering about this project the young care assistant is doing with you. I'm not sure how experienced she is and if you ask me, it's far better to leave the past where it belongs. Anyway, William seems to think it's a good idea, so we'll see, but I might have to speak to Matron about it.'

I climb out of bed, pacing the few short steps between the door and the washbasin.

'Oh, sit down for goodness sake, Leonard. Getting agitated won't help, you know. It'll only send your temperature up again.'

I don't need this. Please, finish your tea and go. I don't want you knowing about Kate and the work we do together, about the past that is opening up, that is starting to speak for me. But there is evidence across the room, lying on a shelf in the wardrobe and if my wife starts to rummage, it will all be gone. I sit back on the bed and start to drink my tea. If I comply, perhaps she'll stop questioning.

But she's on her feet now, muttering. 'I would like to know what you're doing with her, you know how it works now. I was promised a report but I haven't learnt much except you seem to be *responding well*, whatever that means.'

She lifts my washbag off the chest of drawers, as if I might have hidden something incriminating underneath. She opens the top drawer and roots around amongst my socks, then looks at me as if waiting for a clue. Hot? Cold? Warm? I give her nothing, not until she moves to the wardrobe and begins to turn the handle. I'm not sure how it happens, but my cup of tea is suddenly upturned on the floor with a thud.

'Leonard! What on earth have you done?' My wife bangs the wardrobe door shut and comes to inspect the damage. The cup lies shattered and a pool of tea trails slowly away towards the skirting board. She looks around to find something to mop up with and grabs a handful of paper towels from the dispenser.

'Really Leonard, you must be more careful. It makes so much work for people if you're clumsy like this.'

I could argue that I'm not usually clumsy at all, or that clearing up after clumsy people comes with the job, but even if I found the words, they would fall on deaf ears. For now, the crisis is averted, my secret lies safe and that's all that matters.

I ring the bell above my bed while my wife mops and I put soggy paper towels in the bin. Moments later there's a knock on the door and Walter appears.

'Everything alright, Leo?' He sees the broken cup, the spillage, and my wife on her hands and knees by the window.

'Ah, now let me do that for you Mrs Gardner.' He helps my wife upright and she straightens her skirt.

'I'm so sorry,' she says. 'You shouldn't have been bothered. I've cleared most of it up – just the broken bits left.'

'I'll see to it Mrs Gardner, please. Have a seat.' He disappears and returns with a mop, a bucket and a large yellow sign. He clears the fragments and mops the floor, then he puts the *Caution Wet Floor* sign across the damp patch.

'Is that really necessary?' my wife says, looking sceptical. 'Isn't he more likely to trip over the sign?'

'It's our regulations, I'm afraid – Health and Safety. Leonard's room is a public space in the eyes of the law.'

My wife tuts, shakes her head. 'Well, thank you anyway. I'm sorry you've been troubled. I don't know what came over him, he's not usually like this.'

'Is everything ok Leonard? Not feeling dizzy?'

I shake my head. Unlike Matron and my wife, Walter doesn't talk as if I'm not in the room.

'Can I get you some more tea?'

Again my wife responds for me. 'Thank you but he's probably better off with water. Safer, don't you think?'

Walter picks up the mop and bucket. 'Ok then, I'll leave you to your day.' But as he turns to go, he catches my eye and winks.

TWENTY ONE

I'm awake early this morning, my head's a little clearer. I manage to clamber out of bed and get to the bathroom, I even remember to take the medication the trolley nurse left beside the bed before lights out. When Walter arrives, there's nothing to be done apart from wiping a small blob of shaving soap from my chin.

'Looking better today, Leonard,' Walter says, putting my breakfast tray on the table: toast with marmalade and two cups of coffee. 'It's my break,' he says, seeing my question. 'Thought I'd join you, if that's ok?'

We sit together by the open window watching the day unfurl. This is my favourite time, those years of blissful summer dawns and chilling predawn winters have never left me, steeped and stored in my old bones. At the far end of the garden is the bench where I sit with Kate when she comes, and there's a surge of joy, an uplift at the thought of what she might bring next.

'I love the early morning,' Walter says. 'At home as a boy, I always rose before the sun, set off for school before the heat.'

Again, I wonder about his homeland, his family, why they left. Would it hurt, I think, to risk a few words with him? Would it matter if it all came out wrong? He's holding back a life I know little about. It can't have been easy to leave so much behind, coming here to find the cold and the abuse. I've no doubt there was plenty of that.

'I believe Kate is with you today,' Walter says with a small smile. 'Would you like me to check for you? It'll be in the book.'

It's also on my calendar but he disappears before I can show him. When he comes back, he's grinning broadly.

'Two o'clock. Better make sure you've had your lunch – unless you'll be dining together again? Caused quite a stir last time, didn't you?' He nudges my arm, takes a swig of his coffee. I know he's teasing but it makes me uneasy. I don't want to stir anything, it might bring my wife here too often.

Kate collects me from the dining room and takes me into the garden. It's our routine now, each time we build a little more. She takes out the sketchbook together with the slate and chalk and puts them on the bench between us. There are two words on the slate, just as I wrote them last time.

Kate points to the first one. 'This is your tow horse, is it? You called him Riley?'

I nod, pleased she's made the connection. Then I point to the other word – *Daniel,* but have no idea how to explain who he is. I remember the day he turned up on the boat. It was springtime, unusually hot. We were docked in the basin at Brentford after a long trip, carrying pottery down from Stoke. Mother and Pa had gone ashore to stock up on supplies and had taken the girls with them. Freed from chores for an hour or two, my nose in a favourite book, I did not see him until he called me from the mooring.

'Sorry to disturb your studies but I'm looking for a Mr Gardner. Would you know where I might find him?'

In his crumpled brown suit and cap, he did not have the air of stuffy authority we had so often witnessed, but nor was he one of us.

'What is it you want, sir?' I asked. 'My parents will be back shortly.'

He took off his cap and wiped his forehead. 'My name is Spiers,' he said, 'Daniel Spiers. I'm not here to create problems, but I wondered whether I might explain a few things – to you and your family.'

I studied him carefully, then scrambled off the roof. 'As I said, my parents are not here, sir, but you're welcome to come aboard and wait.'

Daniel installed himself against the stern rail and crossed his feet. Unlike the 'official' visitors, he seemed very much at home.

'I'd better explain what I'm here for, then you'll know whether to throw me off before your folks are back.'

Intrigue now had the better of me. Daniel Spiers, it turned out, was not an inspector but a teacher, working at a new school set up for children from the Cut. 'It's called St Mark's Mission School,' he said. 'But don't let that put you off!'

He went on to explain what a formal education could do for me, and for my sisters too. How it was possible, even within our life on the water, to attend school and still contribute to the family livelihood.

'Believe me,' he said, 'I understand how this life works. It was mine too, for many years.'

I began to realise his concerns were genuine. 'And is this a school for all ages?'

'Mainly the younger ones. We're only able to teach the basics with the facilities we have. But there are boarding rooms too – the idea is that you lodge with us for three or four weeks at a time while your parents take a long trip, then go back on the water when they return. When you've had a chance to help out, you come back to the school for another spell.'

I listened intently as he spoke, taking in every word, running over the case I would put to my parents the moment they returned. This was the chance I had begun to long for, but I could not imagine how it would work. Mother would never agree and I was needed here. Pa's health had worsened each winter, we knew his strength was giving out and there was no way I could leave them. There would be costs too – clothes, footwear and books. I began to realise that whilst it may be possible for the girls, this would not be an opportunity for me. I thanked him but explained that my help on board could not be spared.

Daniel Spiers studied his feet a moment then looked across the water to the looming warehouses that surrounded the Basin.

'What if I tell you we could help? That we have a few young lads, a little older that yourself who've been with us a while? I have someone in mind who could work for your father whilst you're away at school.'

Again, I knew this would not be possible. 'We have no funds for paid help, sir. My father would never agree.'

Undeterred, Daniel ploughed on with his next proposal. 'We have ways around that too,' he said. 'Come and visit the school – we can discuss the details then. What do you say?'

As we heard the family approach, he leapt down from the boat and waited for them on the towpath. Pa climbed on board with a cursory nod and disappeared into the galley – when it came to dealing with strangers, he left my mother to it. But for once she stood bemused while Daniel introduced himself, relieved her of an armful of provisions and chatted amiably as if he'd known her all his life.

I watched nervously as she listened, nodding slowly as if taking it all in. I waited for the snort of contempt, the appearance of the pipe and the vitriol to send him packing. But it never came. Whether on this day she was too tired to object, or whether she was impressed by Daniel's gallantry, for the first time in my life I saw her lost for words.

'So you see Mrs Gardner,' Daniel concluded, 'We believe all young people have the right to learn, regardless of their circumstances. Education is no longer simply for the privileged, but the threshold to a future full of possibilities for all children.'

Lying on the cabin roof, Win and Alice too were listening to our visitor, their eyes alight, following every word as he talked of the value an education would bring, not only to us as children, but to our way of working. We knew how Pa's meagre learning had helped me, how that in turn meant I could improve our bookkeeping and prevent us from falling prey to swindlers. Daniel talked of engineering in other lands, of canals in Holland and Italy, in Arabia and South America. Now I longed for books to open such knowledge to me.

For a long time my mother was silent. Then she sighed, a strange, defeated sound and looked over at the three of us. 'I suppose you have thoughts on this, Leo? Something you might like to add?'

Now it was my turn to be speechless. Never did I expect a consultation, I had shut down hope before it dared to fly. My father appeared up the galley steps and leaned against the cabin roof. 'Well, close your mouth, boy,' he said, 'or the gentleman here will think you an imbecile and change his mind.'

'Would tomorrow suit you for a visit?' Daniel said, replacing his cap and stepping back onto the towpath. 'It's half mile from here – a new building, you can't miss it. Not too early mind, as we'll all be in chapel.'

'Tomorrow will suit us just fine,' Pa said, before my mother could raise any objection.

Kate leans forward on the bench to look at me, her expression anxious again. I've been lost in thought too long and the stillness concerns her. Then I remember how I can explain, how drawing acts as my side of the conversation. I open up the sketch book and begin, bringing alive the place that became my home in those years after leaving the water, where my love of learning began and the man who'd made it all possible.

When it's done, I hand the drawing to Kate and wait

while she studies it, though even my unfocussed eye can see I've not done it justice. It's far from perfect, the proportions incorrect, the roof line sloping to the left, the ridge tiles too large. I've drawn a group of children playing on the veranda at the front of the building by the water, but now I think of it, the veranda ran along the back.

Kate looks up and I realise that she isn't here to judge, she simply wants to understand, to work out what I'm trying to tell her. And once again she gets it right.

'Is this where you went to school?'

I nod.

'Did your sisters go too?'

I nod again.

Kate takes the slate from me and points to Daniel's name. 'And I'm guessing he was your teacher?'

He was indeed my teacher and a great deal more besides.

The afternoon warmth has shifted. Kate looks briefly at her watch and starts to collect her belongings. 'Goodness,' she says, stowing them back in her bag, 'I hadn't realised the time! Thank you, Leonard, it's been a good session. I hope it hasn't tired you, you must let me know if I stay too long.'

She slings the bag over her shoulder, helps me to my feet and for a moment leaves her hand resting on my arm. A kindly touch. I add each one to the mounting store.

TWENTY TWO

One afternoon after her shift, Kate bumped into William Gardner at the main entrance. It could only be him, the resemblance to his father was striking.

'Mr Gardner? William?'

William glanced at his watch then turned. 'Can I help you?'

Kate took a step back. 'It's Kate. Kate Davies. I work here as a care nurse. I've been spending time with your father as part of the rehabilitation programme. Sorry to hold you up, but I thought we might have a quick word?'

'Of course – Kate.' William smiled. 'I should have known. Dad showed me the picture he's drawn of you – it's a good likeness.'

'Your father has an incredible talent. You must be very proud.'

William studied the gravel for a moment. 'Oh, I am. You know he had some success in his younger days but he hasn't done anything new for years. I guess life takes over and... well, not everyone thinks as I do.'

Thankfully, William resembled his father in manner as well as looks.

'Before he came here, did your father ever talk about his early life?'

'Not really. Mum didn't…'

William was about to say something, then thought better of it. 'You've met my mother – let's just say she can be…'

'Assertive?'

'I would have said *formidable*, but then I've known her a long time.'

Kate searched for a tactful response. 'I'm sure she wants what's best for your father, even if she doesn't quite agree with the process,'

'You're probably right. This recent business, it's all been rather difficult.'

'I can imagine it has. You know your mother did bring me a scrapbook to work with – there's a lot of material there.'

William smiled. 'I'm glad she let you have it – I didn't know whether she would. And I've just given Dad the old canvas roll that holds all his painting kit. That might help too if you ask him about it.'

'Thank you, I will. Everything you and your mother have lent us has been useful – your father is responding well, becoming more confident. He seems to enjoy drawing again so something must be right.'

'Well, thanks for all you're doing, Kate. Dad hasn't…' he paused. 'Dad hasn't had an easy ride one way and another. But he's tougher than he looks – growing up on the canals does that for you. Thanks again,' he said, searching for his car keys. 'Perhaps we can meet up a bit further down the line – see how things are going.'

'Thank you, yes. We'll keep in touch.'

Kate stood watching William drive away then headed home. She began to take stock of how much progress Leonard was making, how far he'd come in the weeks they'd been working together. He seemed stronger too, less confused, less frail. Not that she could take credit for that, but going back to his roots, picking up old skills, seeing him flourish with every new image he created, had to be part of it.

And Kate too was starting to thrive on these sessions together, back where she'd always found shelter. Perhaps after all it didn't have to be income or art, a binary choice without compromise. Perhaps there was space in her life for both.

TWENTY THREE

Today the tables are turned and this time I have something to show Kate. I've kept it out of sight in my jacket pocket on my way down here, in case beady eyes think it's unsuitable.

Kate and I are outside walking in the herb garden. Tom isn't in the greenhouse today, he's burning parts of an old shed he took down last week. The thick smoke rises, sweet and familiar, stinging my eyes.

Kate's holding my arm, though in truth I should be holding on to her. She's taller than I am and a lot more steady on her feet. We sit down at the old table with a wooden seat where Tom drinks his morning coffee. I hold on to my surprise until I see where this morning takes us. Kate dives into the bag and pulls out a folder full of type written papers and newspaper cuttings neatly clipped together. She flicks through them, selects a small slip of paper and passes it to me.

'I found this,' she says. 'I thought it might help a little after our last session.'

I like the way she calls them *sessions,* as if they're something important. When I study the piece of paper, I realise that they are, that all this is building into something, whatever it may be. I'm holding an article about St Mark's School cut from a recent newspaper. There's an old photo underneath the headline and though the detail is creased and faded, the building is all there. The red brick appears grey, the white stucco grimy and peeling. Parked at the front is a large vehicle, obscuring the door. I hand it back and point to the headline.

'Would you like to know what it says?' Kate asks.

I listen as she reads, her voice calm and clear in the morning air. I hear a lot that is known to me: about its Arts and Crafts style, how it formed the first part of a new development around the West London basin, how it saved many of us from the harshness of a life that was fast becoming obsolete. What I do not know, is that after such schools were forced to close, the place was sold into private ownership and is now worth more than my father would have earned in ten lifetimes.

When she's finished, I hand the photo back and point to the folder, hoping there may be more, something to do with Daniel, but there's nothing much of interest, only dry facts of how the schooling system worked. No depth to the accounts, no warmth or humour, no colour to paint it as it really was.

I open the sketchbook and tear out a single sheet of paper. It's not the right texture for paint but it will have to do. In the greenhouse I find an old jam jar and fill it from the garden tap. By the time I return, Kate has already placed a box of paints and a paintbrush on the table.

Then I reach into my jacket and take out the canvas roll that William left with me and hand it to her. She smiles, as if she might already know what it contains. Inside there are pencils, broken sticks of charcoal, a scalpel, its blade beginning to rust, and all the brushes I've ever owned – fifteen, twenty of them, some from school, and some from that later time, a place I'm not yet ready to go. I begin to draw, sketching the school again, this time getting it right. And when that's done, the colour comes in a slow sweep, washing the page with life.

I remember St Mark's School that first morning, standing close to the water, a short distance from where we were moored at the time. How fresh and impressive it was, its recent structure a glaring challenge to the dismal surroundings. How, amid the familiar colour and bustle of the narrow boats and barges, dereliction gnawed at the heart of the place, warehouses boarded up in spite of the uplift in trade brought on by the war, with the railways shifting troops instead of cargo. I had never noticed it before. It was that morning, standing on the wharf, Daniel on one side, my family on the other, that confirmed my nascent discontent. I knew then what Daniel hinted at when he spoke of a future full of possibilities. I began to realise that mine might lie somewhere other than the Cut.

Rarely had any of us spent time inside a building, and mindful of this, Daniel offered us seats on the veranda. My mother remained standing with Win and Alice close behind whilst Pa and I sat with Daniel as he went through the formalities of enrolment and the equipment needed for our stay. As we were leaving, he handed Pa a written sheet of paper which he promptly passed over to me. On it was a list of a dozen items, few of which I even recognised and certainly did not possess. *Spongebag? Nailbrush? Night clothes?* Night clothes were day clothes with the top layer taken off.

It took a full week after our visit to persuade my mother to let us attend on a regular basis. And there were conditions, negotiated at length with Daniel. We were to stay away no longer than three weeks at a time, and be back on board if needed as soon as the boat returned. But as I suspected, my parents declined Daniel's offer of a lad to travel with them while we were in school. Food was still scarce and my mother, now reconciled to the fracture in our family, justified the change by having fewer mouths to feed.

Win, Alice and I left our home in September 1916, my life an open stretch of water, stepping stones to a different world. My mother's sacrifice was my reward, she had given me the chance to transform my life.

'It must have been a very different life for you,' Kate says, when I put down my brush. 'Staying in one place, being indoors for a large part of the day.'

For me it was a joy, one that I came to appreciate with every hour I spent there. But for my sisters, it was not so, the pull of their old life as ingrained as the grime on our skin. But I'm tired now, even a little hungry and though my thoughts are easing up, the past is still a place I'm not keen to dwell in too long. There are pitfalls and shadows, every backward step brings me closer to the one I have battled fifty years to forget.

TWENTY FOUR

I'm concerned about Walter, his eye is bruised and bloodshot this morning. There was another incident with Angela last night, more terrors with her screaming blue murder. Poor Walter took the brunt again, it's a good job he's a tough one. I heard her first about eleven and went in to see what could be done, but as usual she was having none of my help. She pushed me away, trying to get out of bed but her foot caught in the bedclothes and she fell before I could get to her. When Walter came a few moments later she was lying on her back on the floor, still yelling, her hands in the air batting and fretting at an unseen assailant. For a moment I saw Walter hesitate, mindful of the last time this happened, but then he knelt down and spoke quietly to her. I couldn't make out what he said, in any case it was hard to hear above the noise, but it seemed to calm her and she lay still, staring at the ceiling. Walter looked at me, relieved, but as I took a step or two closer, Angela reared up again and swung a clenched fist hard at his head. I heard the thump, the raw smack of knuckles on flesh and he toppled sideways against the bed while Angela flailed and kicked and struggled to sit herself upright.

Walter got to his feet and pulled the emergency cord. When Matron arrived, they lifted Angela back into bed and smoothed the covers.

'What on earth has happened here Walter?' Matron asked, studying his eye. 'And why is Mr Gardner out of bed?'

Calmer now, Angela again lifted her finger and lay glaring at Walter, chuntering incomprehensibly. One or two other residents had gathered in the corridor, peering through the doorway with drowsy curiosity. Ushering them back to their rooms, Matron left us with a warning. 'Wait here,' she said, 'I need to talk to you.'

When she returned, she was carrying a kidney dish with a large syringe, the contents of which she swiftly emptied into Angela's restless arm.

'Take Mr Gardner to his room, Walter. I'll be along in a minute.'

Walter and I trooped back to my room where he helped me into bed, then paced back and forth chewing his knuckle. A trickle of blood ran down his temple, a bruise already flowering against his skin. When Matron reappeared, she checked me over briefly then beckoned Walter and they left without a word.

It's a relief to see Walter this morning, despite the state of his face. I worried he would not be here, that he would have switched to other tasks, or another floor. Worse even, he will have gone altogether. But he arrives at seven-thirty, as he always does now and sits on the edge of the bath while I finish shaving. On his cheekbone below the bruised and bloodshot eye is a small plaster shaped like a butterfly holding the wound together. These night happenings have become part of life here now, part of our routine. Walter makes no reference to it but I sense an increased bond between us, fellow conspirators, that's both a comfort and a privilege – a duty to have his back as he in turn has mine.

In my room, breakfast is laid out neatly on the table as usual. Walter lingers awhile, straightens the bedding, hangs my dressing gown on the back of the door.

'So what's happening today, Leo,' he asks. 'Are we venturing downstairs?'

I cannot face the thought of the dayroom and shake my head.

'Ok, that's fine. I'll tell them you're sleeping off a bad night.'

I wonder whether Walter slept off his bad night, whether he wants to talk, but he seems distracted now and I don't like to pry, even if I could. He still came this morning and I'm thankful for that.

'Anything I can get you, while I'm here?'

I haven't given much thought to what I can do today. With a sinking heart, I see on the calendar that my wife is due this afternoon, which means that Kate is not. I open the wardrobe and indicate the shelf above my clothes where the blanket lies, the one concealing my work. Walter helps me take it down, together with the papers, and we spread them out on the table. Then he hands me the canvas roll and I know exactly what I want to do. I sift through the pieces one by one, everything I've done since Kate's first visit, some alone but most of them in those treasured hours we've spent together. The great unveiling I feared so much at the start, is now clearing my head like field mist burnt off by the sun.

Kate has left me some of the photos too: of coal scuttles and water cans, the school, the basin at Brentford. It can't have been easy digging them up, to rediscover a way of life that's hardly common knowledge – an era long gone and consigned to history. Defunct, rather like me I suppose, and most of the inmates here. Old Father Time sidling up to snatch us. But my drawings are not bad, now I look again. There's something there still and I grow hopeful, remembering with fondness the school when the drawing began and all the work that followed. For without Daniel, without the school, there would have been nothing further for me than the banks of the canal, nothing deeper than the Cut. Without them I may never have met my wife but more than this, I would never have known her sister.

TWENTY FIVE

Rhona stood by the pond at the bottom of the garden feeding the fish. Leonard had dug it out some years before, when young children no longer roamed in the wild spaces. The goldfish were now the size of small trout, probably an excess of food. He had often warned her to leave them alone.

The house itself, a large Edwardian place, Rhona had bought with proceeds from the Hampstead home after her mother died. Leonard had taken some persuading and was only lured away from London by the promise of cleaner air. But Rhona had wanted a new start, more space for the boys, more land for herself to tend and plant. In addition, the university nearby had a decent science faculty. After the war, with the boys away at school, Rhona had begun to look for work again but her years away counted for little it seemed, things had moved on, her knowledge and skills sadly outdated. Still competing in a male domain, she now had a raft of young women graduates to contend with, they too all jostling for recognition. She was never able to secure a decent post, the most she could achieve was a few hours a week as a lab assistant testing additives for a local food company. Not what she'd trained for at all.

Rhona looked up to see William coming towards her across the lawn.

'I thought I'd find you down here,' he said. 'Still feeding the fish?'

'Don't you start,' she said, rubbing the remains of the fish food on her gardening apron. 'I haven't killed them yet. This is a surprise, William. I wasn't expecting you.'

'Sorry, yes. I should have phoned. I can't stay long but I thought you might like Aunt Isabel's manuscript back.'

'So, what did you think?'

'It's a fascinating read, quite a social history apart from anything else.'

'What do you suggest I do with it?'

William shrugged. 'I still think you need to let Dad know about it. Talk to him, see what his reaction is.'

Rhona sighed, if anything, disappointed. That was the trouble with William – always too bloody sensible, too rational, too much her own alter ego. Not like his brother at all. Edward's wild side may have claimed his life but she had loved it nonetheless.

They walked slowly back up to the house. 'When are you going to see Dad again?' William asked.

'This afternoon. It doesn't give me much time to decide what to do.'

'You'll work it out, Mother. You always do.'

In spite of William's faith in her, Rhona found no easy answer. Uncertainty was not something she dealt with lightly and until now, leaving the past in its place had always been the only way to move on. But Issy's story was no ordinary narrative, no simple log of facts and figures, times, dates and places. This was a memory book, a detailed, heartfelt account of her sister's waking moments, tempting her to cross lines she had always resisted. Rhona had known so little about her, the woman she became after leaving home.

Then there was the intrigue of finding it hidden away among Leonard's belongings. Why had he not mentioned it – or given it to her long before now? Despite knowing that Leonard and Issy were acquainted through the workshop, it still did not explain why it was here in the loft and not with Issy's effects. Rhona could only imagine it had been swept up in the turmoil of that time and then forgotten, like so much else. Fifty years was a long time. But at the back of her mind lay unanswered questions, a growing unease that the writing held some other significance, that the missing pages held a story she had tried not to suspect. I'll ask him about it this afternoon, she thought. There's probably a simple explanation and if so, I'd rather find out what it is before that young care assistant does.

So far she had received only two reports on Leonard's progress with the project, and neither had much substance. It all seemed rather vague, cooked up to satisfy the stakeholders, no doubt. But if it helped a little, kept Leonard from his aimless wandering, perhaps it could do no harm. He was at least being cared for, far better than anything she could do for him at home. Caring was never her strong suit, and caring only led to pain. Perhaps if she'd tried to accept life without her work, bearing the constraints of motherhood, things might have been easier for them both.

Rhona ate a sandwich for lunch, packed her visiting bag and tucked the folder away beneath the knitting, her book and Leonard's clean underwear and pyjamas. When she arrived at the Poplars, she expected him to be hiding away in the grounds or up in his room, but he was still in the dining room waiting for the wheelers and shufflers to move. She could imagine why he liked to stay there a while, watching the staff go about their business, clearing and stacking, spraying and wiping. Normal people doing normal things. No doubt it was helpful when your own world tipped the wrong way.

'There you are,' she said, taking his arm. 'I've been looking all over for you.'

Leonard's expression never changed when he saw her, his smile once warm and open, no longer greeted her. She tried to steer him into the day room without success, he didn't want to go outside either, despite the warm afternoon.

'What's the matter?' she asked. 'Does something hurt? Shall I fetch someone?'

Leonard shook his head and sat down in one of the small chairs by the main door. Rhona eased herself into the other, cursing the weight she'd put on these past months – too much sherry and cake, not enough exercise. She fiddled with her bag awhile, then put it on the floor by her feet. It wouldn't do to show Leonard the folder here in the hallway – far too public, especially as she had no idea what his response would be.

'So, what do you want to do, Leonard? We can't just sit here, it looks bad. Why don't we go for a walk? I could do with some air and you don't look as if you've been outside for a week.'

But Leonard didn't respond. He continued to sit as if no-one minded at all.

Rhona shook her head. 'Have it your own way. You always were a stubborn so and so. Being in here clearly hasn't changed that.'

She took a book out of her bag and started to read, bending back the spine with a noisy crack, thinking of all the years they'd spent together, two cold lives bound by frost and grief. They had walked in separate channels for so long, nothing could alter that now.

TWENTY SIX

It's quiet here in the hallway. Through an open window I hear the rooks' raucous cawing in the poplars, the rumble of Tom on the mower at the far end by the wall. I'd like to be out there with him, or on the bench with my drawings. But if I get up and go, my wife will follow, cursing me under her breath for changing my mind. And the art is still a secret, the drawings still hidden from her. I can't risk discovery – I gave it all up once, I won't do it again.

I'm rescued from my reverie by Matron. 'Ah, Mr Gardner,' she says, stopping to search for something on the reception desk. 'I'm glad I found you. Actually it's Mrs Gardner I'd like to speak to.'

My wife looks up, frowning. 'Is there a problem? Has Leonard done something?'

'No, nothing like that. Well, not exactly. Perhaps we could step into my office and I'll fill you in.'

My wife puts away her book, heaves herself out of the chair and follows Matron down the corridor. Clearly I'm not privy to whatever this is about. I fear it may be to do with Angela and my part in her nocturnal episodes. Walter never told me what Matron said last night.

With my wife gone, I step outside onto the porch. It's fresh out here, the smell of new mown grass strong in the breeze. Tom has finished his rounds, he's putting the mower back in the shed and I cross the lawn to meet him. He looks over and waves.

'Hey, Leonard. How are you? Did I see you with a visitor?'

I look back at the house and nod, hoping my liberation won't be too short-lived. Tom closes the shed door and we walk round to the greenhouse. 'Come and see what's happening in here, there's plenty to keep us busy for a while if you're at a loose end.' He doesn't enquire further about my visitor. Word gets around.

Inside the greenhouse a damp warmth rises from the seed trays lined up in rows along the benches on either side. Courgettes, lettuce, beans, tomatoes, all flourishing. At one end, emerging from a large barrel is an ancient vine, its gnarled and twisted stems wind around the left-hand wall and across the roof. Tom has placed a series of sturdy wooden props at intervals along the bench, and at the far end what looks like a section of railway sleeper supports the main stem. Every twist and turn will have threatened the windows, and each time it's been guided elsewhere. The vine is as old as the house itself, tended by generations of patient devotion. The grapes are sharp, Tom tells me, not liked by many, but in season there are restaurants in town that take them and they always do well on the market.

I like to think I've helped a little with the veg, made myself useful. The garden at home covers over half an acre, much of it orchard and lawn, but the vegetable patch thrived under Rhona's watchful eye. I loved the land, the fields and hedgerows and what they could offer, but the garden was my wife's domain, she knew just what to do and when. Now I come to think of it, perhaps the garden was all we did share in life, including the boys. I'm not sure it's what kept us together, but it helped. Even our offspring couldn't do that.

Tom gives me a job to do, pricking out the lettuce. It's good to be working, using my hands, clumsy though they are these days.

'You're welcome anytime you know,' he says, passing me a rag to wipe my hands when we're done. 'You're better off out here, not stuck indoors like the rest of them.'

He's right. At least now they allow me the freedom to wander, now they know I won't kill myself or get lost. There's a six-foot brick wall around the grounds anyway – I've walked every inch of it many times – three hundred yards up and back and heavy wooden gates kept permanently closed. Where do they think I would go?

My wife is waiting for me in the hall, stressing about my disappearance. 'We need to have words, Leonard, especially after what Matron has just told me. We'd better go to your room, I don't want anyone overhearing.'

Part of me is curious, it would be good to know what's been said, the other part just wants her to be gone. We traipse upstairs and I sit by the window, while my wife perches on the bed.

'I'm really not sure this is working, Leonard,' she says. 'This business with your neighbour and the staff nurse chap. What's his name – Walter is it? I gather there are problems at night and you've been wandering about getting in the way. Leonard, you're here to be looked after, not to do someone's job for them! Matron thinks it would be best to move you to the other side of the building, where it might be… quieter.'

I've heard enough. I won't have a different room, not again. I need my window, the view of the greenhouse and my chats with Tom. I'm not having that choice taken away too. I thump the arms of the chair and stand up, my angry heart racing. *Please, just stop.*

Startled, my wife moves off the bed and backs over to the washbasin. I turn to the window, and signal her to go. She collects her bag, I hear the door open and close and I'm alone again, in the quiet stillness. Below in the greenhouse I see Tom finishing work for the day. He takes off his cap, wipes his forehead, then looks up and salutes.

TWENTY SEVEN

Exhausted by the time she arrived home, Rhona poured herself a large sherry and collapsed into an armchair. Leonard's situation seemed to grow more hopeless with each visit, in spite of all the words of encouragement from the staff. *Cheerful, helpful, as active as he can be given the injuries.* Why did she never see this side of him?

Perhaps she should have kept quiet about her conversation with Matron, avoided the suggestion of changing his room. It was so hard knowing where to begin or what to say – all of it beyond her experience, and she had to admit, beyond the boundaries of her patience. She'd not even been able to show him the folder, now she doubted it was worth mentioning. The longer he was in there, the further away he seemed to drift.

After supper, Rhona made a start on the stack of pots in the sink. Time and again she had tried to persuade Leonard to invest in a dishwasher but he'd never been keen – another vestige of his early life. With clean running water from a tap in the kitchen, he reasoned, why would anyone need a machine? She left the dishes on the rack to drain, poured another sherry and took it into the living room. By the time William phoned, she'd mellowed a little and sat reading in the evening sunlight.

'How's Dad?' William's quiet voice anxious as always. 'How did it go today?'

'It's hard to say. I don't have much luck getting through to him, I'm not sure why. All the reports suggest he's doing well, but that's not what I see.'

'It's hard for him, being so confined. He's not used to it.'

'I understand that, but why won't he speak? Surely he could try and say something? We know there's nothing wrong with his voice.'

'He's a proud man, Mother. Perhaps he doesn't want to appear foolish when the wrong words come out. You remember how it was to begin with?'

'Yes, but this is us, William – his family! If he won't let his guard down with us, he's hardly going to do it for complete strangers, is he?'

William took a moment to reply, his words slow and guarded. 'I think that's just the point though, Mother. Perhaps…' he paused again, 'perhaps he feels under pressure with us. Perhaps we don't have enough patience, or the right experience. We just need to let the staff do their job.'

Rhona emptied her sherry glass and put it down on the coffee table with a thump. 'You may be right. But I still think progress is too slow – he's been there for months already.'

'Let's just give it a little more time,' William said. 'I'm sure it will all be fine. How did he respond to the manuscript? Did you have a chance to discuss it with him?'

'Not this time. As I said, he seems to grow more distant the longer he's in there.'

'There will be other opportunities, Mother. Do what you think best, but let me know if you find out about the missing pages. Is there anything else we found that could help him? What about the photo album? He wouldn't need to talk about that, he could just look at it, take it all in.'

Rhona chewed her lip. 'It's an idea, I suppose.'

'And if you don't want to confront him with it directly, give it to Kate.'

'Thank you, William. Perhaps I will.'

'Sorry Mother, can you hang on a minute while I turn the potatoes off?'

'Can't Helena do that?' she snapped, then hoped William hadn't heard. She really should try to be more tolerant. The line went quiet and in the distance, Rhona heard voices singing an old nursery rhyme. Bedtime for the little one she presumed, something else she'd never been part of. A moment later, William was back.

'Sorry Mother, I'll have to go now. We're about to eat.'

Hearing the edge in his voice, Rhona ended the call and went back to her book, staving off solitude with another glass of sherry.

TWENTY EIGHT

It's three o'clock in the morning and I'm trapped wide awake in the dark. My wife's visit stirred me up. Afraid of her meddling, it sets the panic rising. I didn't want to come here, but now I find it's not a bad place to be. Despite the food, the moaners, the shufflers and the broken nights, I have respite here, a refuge. My thoughts are my own and most of the time my head is clear. In any case, she won't want me home, not yet.

The window is open, Walter knows how I like it and leaves it this way every night now the weather is mild. Another rule broken, another bond between us. Night noises drift in: an owl, the cry of a vixen impatient for a mate, winds that snatch dead leaves from the beech hedge by the greenhouse. There's another tug at the dusty layers and I'm back at home on the Cut, only the gentle rock and slap-slap of the water are missing. I calm myself thinking of Daniel and the school. I see him on the quayside, waiting to welcome us that first morning. I remember Mother's frenzied ablutions before we left, the laundering and head inspections. We were as clean as we'd ever been that day, the smell of lye and coal tar drifting after us down the towpath.

It did not take long for me to settle into this new way of life, an awareness that overtook me each day as I sat at a desk in the warm and spacious school room. I watched and listened in wonder as other worlds, peoples, climates, dynasties were all revealed in words and images upon the page. Not only did I see and understand what was before my eyes, but could now unroll centuries of change or leap thousands of miles to the other side of the world. I came to love the routine and rhythm of learning and would choose to set out the chalk and slates each morning. I'd fetch books for the day's lessons, unfurling a map of distant places. Africa, Asia, the Americas, Australia. On the days we studied science, I'd prepare the classroom early with burners and test tubes, batteries and wire.

But by far the greatest revelation was through art. I began to discover so much more than the colourful simplicity of my canal heritage or my own childish attempts at creativity. Now there were 'Movements' and 'Grand Masters', there were oils and watercolours, pastels, charcoal and gouache. Daniel was quick to notice my interest and under his watchful eye, I began to draw and paint, to gather a growing body of work that even I could see improving with each new attempt.

I spared little thought for home or how Mother and Pa were managing without us. The weeks away passed so rapidly, I came to resent the time we had to spend back on the boat, confined again in such small spaces. I sulked over chores, impatient to return to the school, to my learning and my art. I neglected my sisters too and for months, failed to notice the toll school life was taking upon them.

One afternoon towards the end of our second term, Daniel came to find me as I sat sketching in the classroom.

'Your sisters,' he said, pulling up a chair beside me. 'Are they well, do you think?'

Immersed in a still-life I'd set up on his desk, I continued to draw without responding. Daniel nudged my arm.

'Leo, I think Win and Alice are struggling.'

Emerging from my work was like being woken from a deep sleep. I became aware of his hand and reluctantly put down my pencil. 'Really? They've said nothing to me.'

'I've found Win in tears on more than one occasion. She won't talk to me and I don't want to insist. Perhaps you could shed some light on it?'

That evening after supper, I tried to take the girls into the classroom but they pulled me outside and we sat by the water in the dark. Only then did I realise how much they missed the Cut, how they struggled with the order and confinement of the school.

'I miss Mother and Pa,' Win sobbed into her dress. 'I miss home. It's not fair to make us stay here.'

Cramped as we'd been at home, we did at least have air and movement, a changing landscape, seasons and routines that tied us to each hour of the day. The time I spent here buried in books, in images and artefacts, held little joy for them. The strain of listening for hours at a time, the proximity of strangers, did not entice or excite them in the same way. Any spare moments they had were spent outside at the water's edge, searching up and down for a sign of the life they had left behind. I did my best to reassure them, reminding them of our need for a new future, for options

200

and opportunities, but they remained unconvinced. What for me had become the key to a new way of being, a portal though which I could view a glorious future, was for my sisters a suffocating disillusion. The following day, though in breach of the law, Daniel made a plan for their return.

On the day I took them home, I remember how my mother's face softened at the sight of them, a sudden joy in her life that usually rendered so little. But when I confessed that in exchange for the girls, I was to stay at the school, her mouth clamped to and she turned away.

It was Easter time, Pa had snared a rabbit and, though we feasted on stew with the last of the winter turnips, an air of resignation hung about the boat. My mother packed me a supper of bread and cheese for the long journey back to school and the four of them stood together on the towpath, waving till I was out of sight. This time however, I found it hard to leave, the ties I thought to have severed were stronger than I knew.

Looking back, I sometimes think I adapted too well to school life, seduced by the ease of regular meals, a place to wash, and space between the beds. But for all the joy of this, I still cannot think of my time there without some sense of guilt, that the price my parents paid was too high, that they gave me up to a better life, at the expense of their own.

TWENTY NINE

I don't see Walter at all the following day. It unsettles me to have a different person in the bathroom with me, especially since it's a woman. Walter must have briefed her well because she sits calmly on the edge of the bath and doesn't interfere. In fact, she doesn't take much notice at all and spends a lot of time studying her nails. I want to ask where Walter is, and worry that his shifts have changed. There's no breakfast in my room either, and I'm obliged to sit downstairs with the others eating cold toast. How did I ever get into this state, shuffling from day to day like a sick tortoise?

The hours creep through the morning. I take a look at the newspaper but even the headlines are a struggle. That leaves the television. There's a hostage situation in the Middle East, an interview with the new Prime Minister of Zimbabwe Rhodesia, a woman is jailed for murdering her husband. Not much to lighten the day.

Back in my room I check my calendar and am disappointed to see Kate isn't due today. It will be a long haul till bedtime unless I can get outside. I collect my raincoat, my sketch book and the canvas roll and head downstairs to check if the coast is clear. Matron is busy in the office, speaking loudly into the telephone. I escape through the main door and head round to the back of the building in the hope of finding Tom in the greenhouse. But even he's not around and that's another blow. Still, it's good to be outside. I begin to walk, circling the wall twice, like a prisoner, counting my steps. One thousand and twenty-five, all told, more if I'm tired. The bench I share with Kate is damp from overnight rain so I lay out my raincoat and sit down, spreading the canvas roll beside me.

Kate is winning me over, our time together now lifting the flaps like a tarpaulin in the wind. I need to carry on, even if she's not here. My last drawing was the West London basin, a study in contrast: the bright beauty of the narrow boats, the creeping decay of the place itself. I remember how even without Win and Alice, I slipped back into life at the school as if nothing had changed. By the time I was fifteen, I had taken on pupil teacher duties with the younger children, assisting them in number and written work, encouraging their reading. My world widened daily, I had access to all the books and materials I could ever need, I grew giddy with new perspectives.

Then in the winter of 1918, with the country in the grip of joyful celebrations following the armistice, my father's health finally collapsed. The years of damp, and the fumes that issued from the new engine we'd installed to replace Riley, took first his strength and then his life. My mother managed a year or two alone with the girls, Daniel's young lad did join her on the long trips and I helped out when I could. But she herself did not survive the influenza that took away so many in those post war years. At the age of sixteen, I found myself the sole bread winner with two young sisters in my care.

For a while, we managed well. Since my father owned our boat we did at least have a home, and though I moved back on board, I was able to continue as a pupil teacher for another year. When my schooling was complete, I received a small much needed payment for my work whilst Win and Alice took in mending and laundry for other families on the Cut. They even conceded to help out with laundry for the school, provided they did not have to stay indoors, or go anywhere near a desk.

I still found time for my art. Daniel encouraged and supported my efforts, and sometimes at weekends, he took me to visit places away from the water, in the heart of the City and beyond. I wondered at the size and grandeur of the buildings, the scale of which could not be gathered from a book. Westminster Abbey, St Paul's, the Royal Observatory at Greenwich. I carried my sketch pad like an extra limb, made notes when there was no time to stop and draw. Daniel bought a pocket camera and took photographs which I later used as inspiration. My body of work increased weekly, Daniel even talked of introducing me to a dealer, someone who might be interested in showing or selling my work. But this was never to materialise and the life the girls and I had secured since the loss of our parents, changed yet again.

THIRTY

For once I'm tempted inside by a rumbling stomach. I've no idea of the time, but the smell of cooking reaches me even here at the edge of the garden. I've not done much today, more thought than production. But it's growing, this new portfolio, my secret pride. In my room I stow it away in the wardrobe beneath the spare blanket.

Despite my appetite, lunch is the familiar disappointment, though I still manage a second helping of mash. It sits uncomfortably for several hours, and I regret the delusion that I could fool my body back to its youth. My lunch is still there later, and instead of going down for tea I stay in my room and watch Tom through the window – he's back in the greenhouse tying up the tomatoes.

When it grows dark, I get myself washed and changed for bed, I don't expect Walter will be back today and I don't want anyone else to help. By the time the nurse comes in at nine-thirty, I'm in bed. It's the same one I saw this morning; she bids me goodnight then checks the taps are off and the window is closed. When she's gone, I get up and open it.

I wake soon after two and again at five. This sedentary life doesn't suit me at all, it's little wonder I can't sleep. Until my fall, until I came here, I'd still be up at midnight reading or making things – the little automata I hoped one day to share with William's children. Or maybe it's the stirring of old memories, digging up the past my wife was so against. Maybe she does have a point. It all sits there with the mashed potato, undigested thoughts, churning and unchecked.

I wait a little longer, until my eyes adjust and a dim light spreads through the room, then I go to the wardrobe and take down the drawings. Setting them all out on the bed, I can see there is a pattern, the stages of my half-forgotten lives Kate is helping to uncover. I'm running through time, as if my time is running out. I pick up the latest drawing and take it to the window. My sisters on the boat, moored at the Basin, Win bent over her needlework, Alice with the mangle. I remember when my tenancy at St Mark's ended after the school closed, part of a sweep to bring all schools under local government control. Cut off from my work, I had no choice but to go back and join my sisters on the boat. Daniel too found work elsewhere and took up a post at the other end of the city. Although he left me his address, our paths diverged and did not cross again for several years.

Win and Alice, now beyond the legal age for school, stayed on the *Albert Jack*, scraping a living from the local community. For some time, I stayed with them, recommissioning the boat and transporting loads up to the Midlands. But competition for cargo was fierce, boatmen we had known as friends in Pa's day resenting our intrusion on their patch. The sense of an ending was everywhere on the Cut – the war, the pandemic, bringing change in their wake, a new and different energy amongst the young. There were those like myself who had missed the action, there were those who were damaged, and those who had survived wanting only to forget.

Yet, throughout this time of churn and uncertainty, I still longed for another life away from the water, where I could expand the learning I had acquired and my art could flourish. After a year, despite misgivings about abandoning my sisters, I knew it was time to leave. Win and Alice begged me not to go, but their dreams were small, contained within the habits of their life to date, unchanged by the winds that carried others away.

There was a young man Alice spoke of with fondness, a waterman working on the refuse boats. Not the finest of cargoes, but like the rest of us, he took whatever was on offer. They planned to marry when Alice turned eighteen later that year, and as her guardian I saw no reason to deny her this. They would have another income and it suited my plans, once I was assured that Win would have a home with them too. A week after the wedding, I left the Cut and took to the road heading north, my rucksack packed with few essentials: a little money, a change of clothes and my beloved sketchbook.

THIRTY ONE

Kate was in the middle of breakfast when Walter phoned.

'You want me to come in *this morning*? she said, her mouth full of cornflakes. An unscheduled summons was not a good sign.

'Is it urgent, Walter? It's my day off.'

'I'm sorry Kate but I need you to come in for a meeting. It's to do with Leo.'

Kate stopped chewing. 'He's not ill is he?'

'No, nothing like that. It's just that his wife has been in touch and wants to see you. She's coming in at 11.'

'Do you know what it's about? She hasn't made a complaint, has she?'

'No. But I am concerned she might have uncovered something, found out we're doing this off the radar.'

'Is that likely? Leo won't have told her anything and from what I can gather William is all for it.'

There was a long sigh at Walter's end. 'She wouldn't tell me anything over the phone, I'm afraid.'

Kate cast an eye around the flat, the table loaded with books and scraps of paper from her research, the laundry piled in the corner, dirty pots in the sink. 'Ok,' she said. 'I'll see you later.'

In his office, Walter made coffee, opened a packet of biscuits and sat down at his desk. 'Sorry about this, Kate, but as I said on the phone, Leo's wife wants to see you and I didn't want to put her off. You know how hard it's been to get this thing off the ground, I just don't want to rock the boat.'

Kate was aware she'd have to meet with Leo's wife again but this was sooner than she'd hoped. 'Are my reports ok?'

'There're fine. In fact they're excellent. The more detail we collect, the more likely we are to make this official.'

'And nothing else is wrong?'

'Not as far as I know, but we do need to tread carefully we don't want her chatting to Matron. I can be with you if you like. It might be a good idea.'

Kate had managed before, it wouldn't be any worse than that. 'Thanks for the offer but I'll survive,' she said.

Walter smiled and stood up. 'Don't worry. I'm convinced you're doing all the right things. Leo's definitely improving, spending time with Tom, painting and drawing again.'

Small comfort, Kate thought. She positioned herself behind Walter's desk braced for business.

When Leonard's wife arrived, she took off her scarf and sat opposite Kate, restive fingers tapping the arm of her chair. 'I'm glad I've managed to see you,' she began. 'There are a few things we need to sort out.'

Kate swallowed hard. Every moment spent with this woman shed yet more light on Leonard. 'Of course,' she said. 'As I've outlined in the reports, your husband is making good progress.'

'So you say, but you've given me no details. Whenever I visit, I don't see any improvement at all. I was hoping for a little more evidence, something with a bit of science behind it!'

Kate chose her words with care. 'It's early days. What we're doing is not really a science. As I think we discussed initially, coming here to the home, being confined, can be confusing – even distressing when you've been used to a very active life. We are simply trying to revive an interest for your husband, something that will connect with past skills. He was a very talented artist, that's why we're using this in our sessions together, hoping it will bring some meaning back to his life. It may even help him to speak again.'

'Isn't that rather unlikely now, after so much time?'

Kate picked up a pen that was lying on the desk and began to fiddle with it. Sinking slowly out of her depth, she wished she'd taken Walter up on his offer.

'It is possible,' she said, 'that even with severe aphasia, patients can regain quite fluent speech. Sometimes it's a matter of confidence, or even willingness. Fear of saying the wrong thing can be very debilitating, particularly when…'

Kate stopped herself from finishing the sentence. *Particularly when you have your head bitten off on a regular basis.*

The woman studied her hands then clasped them in her lap. 'I just need to ensure that he's getting the right care, that you have his best interests at heart.'

'I can assure you,' Kate said, as evenly as possible,

'Leonard is treated with the utmost care and respect at all times. Like you, we want the very best for him.'

The woman looked far from convinced. 'Well,' she said, neatly arranging the folds of her skirt, 'that goes without saying. I'm just not sure this is helping.'

'We would like to continue for the time being,' Kate said, not at all certain the woman had Leonard's best interests at heart. 'I understand your concerns of course. Let's review in another two weeks. I think we're very close to a breakthrough.'

The woman looked up sharply. 'Indeed?'

'All the material you've lent us so far has been extremely helpful. Leonard is drawing again, he's even done one or two paintings. I'm sure he's recalling a great deal about his early life and where he was brought up.'

'I see. Well, I suppose we should be thankful for that, if it's helping. I just never imagined he'd want to drag all that up again. He had a hard life early on you know, living and working on the water.'

'So I gather. I'm learning a lot too,' Kate said. 'It's like a giant puzzle and I'm trying to work out how it all fits together. But as I say, in a week or two, with luck things will be a little clearer.'

She put down the pen, pushed back her chair and stood up. 'Thank you for coming, Mrs Gardner. We'll keep you informed.'

The woman also stood but didn't attempt to leave. Instead she fished in her bag and pulled out a small photograph album which she placed on the desk.

'There is this of course,' she said, looking at it with an odd mix of contempt and distress. 'It might be useful.' She paused, her permanent frown growing deeper. 'This above all.'

Kate picked up the album and held it a moment. Scented with storage, it was aged and worn like all the other items she'd been given, the cover a soft suede bound with silk cord. She turned it over carefully, forgetting her irritation.

'Does it belong to your husband?' she said.

'I won't go into it all now,' the woman said. 'You'll find out soon enough when you see what's inside.'

'Well, thank you for lending it to me. That's very thoughtful.'

More than ever, Kate wanted her to go, but the woman seemed reluctant to move. 'Was there something else, Mrs Gardner?'

She flapped a hand, dismissively and set off towards the door. But then she turned and said, 'You know my husband is something of a mystery to me too. There are things that never did quite add up.'

At home, over the remains of yesterday's macaroni cheese, Kate tried to work out what was behind the morning's bizarre conversation. The woman's curious manner, her critical tongue, yet at times she too seemed lost and uncertain. Perhaps the journey Leonard was on, had become a voyage for his wife too.

Kate took out the photo album she'd been given and put it on the table with the rest of her research items. She'd glanced at it briefly in the office but not had time to study any details. It covered the same time frame as the scrapbook but now, despite the quality of the photos a clearer picture began to emerge. There were many images of the landscape surrounding the canal and a group of young people gathered by a row of cottages, a dog at their feet. She looked for Leonard among them but then realised he would be taking the photos. It was not until she came to the end of the album that she found him, posing with the same group outside a large country house. *Stanford Manor,* she read beneath the image, in the same neat copperplate lettering. August 1930. It was then she remembered how she knew Leonard's name. He'd been one of the *Stanford Four*, a member of the art workshop formed as a cooperative in the late twenties to promote equality in the arts.

Kate rummaged through her pile of textbooks and picked out a small well-thumbed volume. Turning to the index, she ran through the headings until she found him: *Gardner, Leonard, page 98.* So, that was it. Tucked away in an essay she'd done years ago on the principal art movements of the interwar period. Flicking through, she found his entry: *1904— Fine artist. A lock keeper by trade, his work largely inspired by his early life on the canals.* Beneath this was an account of the workshop, founded on the ideals of the Suffrage Ateliers that had sprung up before the first World War. The Stanford group had been strong advocates of diversity – an integrated approach to the wider creative process not simply the visual arts. Of the three other members, one was a print maker greatly influenced by the Grosvenor School, whilst his wife, a weaver, favoured the Bauhaus movement. There was little mention of the third member except a brief line describing her as an aspiring writer. The photograph itself, must have been a press shot taken at the opening of their first exhibition. The show had received some critical acclaim but there was no mention of any subsequent public success and the workshop, it seemed, had folded sometime later.

Kate put the book and the album away and though late by now, allowed herself a small glass of wine to celebrate. Her commitment to Leonard as well as the project had grown steadily over the weeks, she found his past life beginning to unfold, drawn out in silent, slender threads. Finding the way in without words had been more of a challenge than she'd imagined, but there was a shift now and with this new piece of the puzzle to tempt him, Kate hoped he might be able to offer more.

THIRTY TWO

Next morning Walter is back. 'You'll be pleased to know Kate is working with you again today,' he says, handing me a towel in the bathroom. 'At eleven, so we'd better get you smartened up.'

In my room I finish the slow methodical task of pulling on my clothes while Walter straightens the room. It's not untidy but I've seen how he likes to adjust things – the small mirror by the washbasin, the jug of daffodils on the windowsill he brought earlier in the week. He picks out a faded flower head and throws it in the bin.

Angela has been quiet recently, I wonder if they give her something to help her sleep. Walter doesn't discuss what happened last time, the soul of discretion.

When I'm decent, we collect my drawings from their cache in the wardrobe and head down the backstairs to the garden. Walter's always keen to avoid the day room when Kate is due and I settle outside on the seat to wait for her. I think about what she might bring this time and what it will reveal. Pieces of a scattered past unfolding, as if we are travelling a long road together.

We've reached a point I well remember, the road I took after leaving the Cut, how soon my dream of a new life disappeared. I had not accounted for the desperate labour situation, not only boatmen were being laid off. Unemployment had risen sharply over the past year or so and the chances of farm work were already slim. Demand for goods that flourished during the war years declined steeply, factories were closing and now lay idle, along with the work force, many of whom like myself, had taken to the road. Veteran soldiers were a common sight, some still in military kit, ancient and worn, the so-called Knights of the Road. At times we would walk a stretch together, revealing their lives as we travelled. I wondered how they had survived so much in the war, only now to be cast out and drifting, forsaken by the very society they had fought to protect. Who, apart from a simple fellow traveller like myself, would hear their stories?

Though tempted at times to return to the Cut, I pressed on, inhabiting the woods and lanes, sleeping wherever I could find shelter. Sometimes it would be a dry barn in return for a day or two of work cutting turnips or beets, sometimes I would try my luck in a town where I could beg the floor of an outhouse behind an inn if I shifted barrels, cleaned the pumps or swept the floors. Sometimes I would draw attention from the young women working there. Serving me an extra pint or two after hours, they would make it clear that more than company was on offer. I seized such comfort thankfully, life alone on the road took some weathering.

Apart from my sketchbooks, I had little reminder of the life I'd lived with Daniel, of the world he'd opened up for me. From time to time I found an old newspaper, but the contents often failed to engage me. Neither was I allowed access to the places I might turn to fill this void. As a boatman I was no stranger to living on the margins and as I'd found in London, when visiting a gallery or museum, deep suspicion followed me. Many libraries even boasted a sign prohibiting food, unaccompanied children and tramps. After two years, with work still scarce and a hostile reception commonplace, I began to see my life less as an inspiring adventure and more a worn-out folly. But sometimes there was goodness to be found, and later that autumn an elderly man with a mission restored my faith.

By the time I met Samuel Jones, I had unwittingly headed back towards the Cut and arrived in a small market town a couple of miles from the water. Searching for a quiet place to eat, I discovered a terraced house in a back street with a large chalkboard outside. *The Readers Rest: Books for Weary Travellers. All Welcome!*

Samuel greeted me warmly, offering me a hot drink and an invitation to make full use of anything that stirred my interest. The walls of his front room were stacked with every type of book from literature to science, from history to religion, politics to needlework. In the far corner, a man dressed much as myself was leafing quietly through the pages of an encyclopaedia.

'Have you come far?' my host asked, adding a slice of fruit cake to the welcome mug of tea. I fully expected his courtesy to switch at any moment, driving me off with the familiar threatening scowl. But as we sat together in the

217

warm, I took time to explain my journey here, the life I had grown up with, the work I had done at the school. He listened with care, nodding as if he understood it all.

'There are many like yourself,' he said. 'Men of learning, some self-taught whose faces no longer fit, whose place is no longer confined to hearth and home. Some have lost employment and fallen on hard times, others have found no respite since the war and cannot settle to the life they once knew.'

'And you offer this as a place of safety?'

'As the sign says, we are here for all who care to call in. I've collected books for years – not only personal copies but from every house clearance, every auction.'

'A true public library then. But why?'

'The suffering didn't end with the war. Many are suffering still, the next wave of youth gone or reduced to wandering by injury or economics.' He lifted his chin towards the corner of the room. 'Some have a good education behind them, all snatched by the madness of what happens when wrong decisions are made.'

I took a moment to give thanks for my own lot, the solidity of my growing years, the accident of birth that meant I had not been caught up in recent events.

'It's different for me,' I told him. 'I had a home, it was my choice to leave, to wander.'

'We make no distinction here,' he said. 'Whatever your reasons, you are welcome. Feel free to sit as long as you wish, my wife will serve lunch in the kitchen and there's a privy and an outhouse in the garden. If you wish to stay with us and rest a while, please do.'

I stayed a month with Samuel and his wife, sleeping in the outhouse, and carrying out repairs around the town wherever cheap labour was needed. On nearby farms I stripped and sorted the last of the autumn produce, and on days without work I settled in the haven of Samuel's front room, as immersed in culture and scholarship as I had been at St Mark's.

But often across empty fields I would feel the pull of the water and find my way to the canal, where I walked the towpaths I'd known long before. One morning, along a scenic stretch where the Grand Junction reached into the Midlands, I discovered an unmanned lock, the old lockhouse deserted and in need of attention. The doors were hanging loose, the windows cracked or broken, rafters gaping open to the elements. Though a busy stretch of water, it seemed decay had now reached this far, the old ways threatened and spent. The lock was deep, its walls moss ridden and crumbling in places, but the gates themselves had not succumbed, and on inspection were still in good repair.

I took my books there whenever I could and sat reading on an old bench by the door. If a boat passed through, I manned the gates, at ease with the boatman and his family, the stretch and power of old skills fuelling my wish to be back on familiar ground.

By mid-November I had stayed long enough with Samuel and could no longer prey on his kindness, but for the first time since leaving home and with winter close at heel, I could not decide where to travel next. It made little sense to go further afield, I was now familiar with the town, it offered more than many I had passed through, a generosity of spirit embodied in my benefactor. One evening, after the meal, I shared my concerns with Samuel.

'We've grown used to your company,' he said. 'Don't feel you have to leave on our account. But you'll be needing your independence, the freedom that's kept you this long on the road.'

As he spoke, I realised it was not freedom I craved, but structure, a routine that did not involve the constant shift of one foot in front of the other, the endless search for work.

'There's a lockhouse near here,' I said, 'a couple of miles west across the fields. Do you know why no one lives there – why the lock is unmanned? I've noticed it's a busy stretch of the water.'

Samuel was silent for a while. 'There's been a dispute over the land for many years – it belongs to the Manor at Stanford and is leased to the canal company. As you know, times are changing. It's a deep lock, dangerous and tough to operate, and when the last tenant left there was no interest in taking it over.'

'Do you know if they're still looking for someone?'

'It's possible. You'd need to enquire at the office in Braunston. It's no more than twenty miles from here – you'll be there and back in a day or so.'

I left at dawn the following morning, taking only a small pack and a lightened heart. All that remained was to convince the Board.

THIRTY THREE

It's late morning by the time Kate arrives and she finds me lost in thought in our usual spot on the bench. She sees that my sketchbook is closed, my time unproductive.

'Not to worry,' she says. 'I've brought something rather special this time.'

Kate reaches into the straw basket and with great care, brings out a photograph album. It's one I recognise, dark maroon, silk tassels that bind the pages. I stare at it, distant yet familiar, lying here in Kate's lap. I know what's coming now, daring me to take up the challenge. I touch the soft downy suede of the cover, draw a mark across the nap. I feel the weight of it in my hands, the weight of all it signifies – the passion and the loss. I close my eyes and breathe in the missing years, the memories excised, or hidden beneath the dusty flaps. The pinch in my stomach sharpens, a hammering starts in my chest. I'm impatient now, and just a little scared.

Kate watches closely as I open it up. My unsteady hands release the musty age of it, the fluted corner mounts that slide out of place. On each page the images lie, fresh and familiar, redolent with life. Beneath each one in my own white copperplate, a place and a date.

And then I see her. After fifty years she's there. The smile, the dark hair cropped, falling in waves around her face. I see her head tip, her hand move to push the strands away, in slow frames like an old cine film. Her eyes meet mine across the decades, half a century lost between us, seared into the pages, made real again: the house by the lock, the workshop, the gathering clan. I see the others outside by the wall, the dog at their feet. And she's there with them, in the long white dress, shielding her eyes from the sun.

I turn to Kate, willing her to understand, to know what the sight of this woman means. How knowing her was my homecoming, falling in love the simplest of things. But perhaps she does know, perhaps in these long patient hours with me, she has worked it all out.

We met by chance at the lock one day, the dog facing off an angry gaggle of geese. I'd been living in the lockhouse for a couple of years by then, setting it to rights and managing this stretch of the water. I'd seen her many times from a distance, in the village or further up the towpath, the dog at her heels, and wondered idly where she came from, too shy to speak. My world framed by the Cut, the School and then the road, I'd known a few women but none so striking. She wore the white dress that day, neat boots, her hair a flash of chestnut in the bright afternoon.

'I'm sorry,' she said, holding the dog round his neck to quieten him. But he wore no collar and slipped way, chasing the geese down towards the lock until they gave up and took flight. When she stood up, there were streaks of mud across the front of her dress.

'That won't clean up too well,' I said, mindful of my mother's battle with laundry.

She looked down at the damage, shook her head and smiled. 'It's no matter. I shouldn't wear a white dress to walk the dog.'

Her voice was quiet, well spoken. 'He loves the water, you see. Often jumps in and can't always get himself out. He's a bit wild, I'm afraid – a product of loose discipline.'

I knelt down and ruffled the dog's neck. He looked well enough, elegant and bright eyed, unlike the feral creatures that ranged around the wharfs or the sturdy ratters some families kept on board. I asked his age, how long she had owned him.

'We're not sure how old he is, he just turned up at the door one day before I came here. They assumed he was a stray, or abandoned, so they adopted him, called him Stan – short for Stanford – after the village. We live just outside it, in the redbrick cottages near the mill. Perhaps you know them? They've just been done up.'

I had watched with interest as the renovations took shape, chatted to the builders, given them a hand with the heavy work. 'I believe it's a workshop now,' I said. 'For artists?'

She laughed, tucked a piece of hair behind her ear. 'Not all of us are artists, I'm more of a hanger-on,' she said. 'I'm a writer of sorts – not in the true sense of the word, but I scribble.'

I found it hard to think of this young woman as an appendage, her presence here on my home patch the most welcome sight I'd had for some time. I dared to mention my own work, much of which I had completed since coming here. 'It's only small stuff, you know. Line drawings, watercolours.'

Her face lit up. 'You must come over to the workshop – meet the others. They'd be delighted.'

I wasn't so sure. Despite the praise and reassurance that had come from Daniel over the years, I knew he had a biased eye. The occupants of the redbrick cottages might well see things differently.

By now the dog had turned his attention to the nearest hedgerow, setting up a flock of noisy sparrows. We watched as he leapt at them, barking as they rose. The young woman called him, though he took no notice. 'He needs to let off steam, so I'll let you get on.'

She set off towards the cottages and I stood watching them awhile, about to resume my work when she turned, walked a few steps backwards and called,

'Issy! My name's Issy. Come and see us at the house – anytime!'.

The rest of that afternoon seemed to drift more slowly than usual, the sky took on a sharp, clear hue, the canal banks outlined in rich tones of green and brown. Long after she'd gone, I could see her still, and between passing boats I sketched a new vista, one that stretched the other way following the path she had taken. Later whilst laying out my supper, instead of the usual gnaw of hunger, I found I had no appetite. My mind swam, dwelling on the afternoon, on this chance encounter.

★

To my shame, I'm crying, tears falling onto the page unchecked. How can such sadness rise from so long ago? Surely it must all be out now, my soul laid bare. My hands shake, a pain rises in my throat and I can no longer see. I fumble for my handkerchief and push the album away.

Kate takes it from me, gently wipes the page and closes it. 'I'm so sorry,' she says. 'I thought it might help, but I see it's too much. This is a lot for you to deal with Leonard, we don't need to do any more today. You've made amazing progress – it's bound to be hard.'

We sit in silence awhile, then she says, 'Can I ask you something? The young woman here in the white dress – it's not your wife is it?'

I shake my head, cough a little, wipe my nose.

'But she has a special place in your life?'

I'm fighting for the words to explain, to tell her.

'You must be tired,' Kate says. 'Would you like me to stay, or would you rather be alone? You'll need time to process what's happening.'

I don't want her to go. Her presence is a strengthening force, filling the empty spaces. I shake my head, put my hand on the album. Now I'm calm again, I can see the innocence of it: not a loaded missile, nor a box of unknown fears.

'But you do remember, don't you,' Kate says. 'And that's a good thing.'

It is more than a good thing. I close my eyes and swallow hard, getting the words straight. When they come out, it's a low growl, a grating rattle in my throat, and though I doubt it makes sense, by the look on her face Kate knows exactly what I'm trying to say.

'Yes,' I tell her, my voice a slow rasping croak. 'It is the very best thing.'

THIRTY FOUR

After leaving Leonard safely back in his room, Kate raced downstairs to find Walter. When he wasn't in his office, nor anywhere around, she guessed he'd already left for home. Her news could wait until the morning, they were both rostered on for the early shift, but what had happened with Leo was too much to keep to herself and Walter would want to know. Kate even had a duty to report it, but contacting him after hours – how would that go down? She had no idea about his home life, whether he had a partner, a family.

Overcast skies had shifted with the wind and Kate walked the back way home along the towpath. In Leo's day, the waterways would have been carefully managed, but now in spite of regular efforts to clear them, rubbish still gathered on the banks. By the time she reached home, she had made a mental note to join the local volunteers.

Kate hung around the flat for an hour before deciding to phone Walter. She let it ring a short while and was about to hang up when she heard his voice, distant above loud music.

'Hello, Walter? It's Kate. Sorry to bother you but I just wanted a quick word, if that's ok?'

227

'It's no bother – hang on, I'll turn the music down.'

When the line went quiet, Kate began again. 'Is this ok – I'm not disturbing you?'

'Not at all. Nothing that can't wait. What's up, Kate?'

Faced with explaining, Kate now doubted her own version of events. Did Leonard actually speak, or had it simply been wishful thinking on her part?'

'There's been a development – with Leonard.'

'I see. What kind of development?'

'He started speaking… at least I'm fairly sure he did.'

'When, today?' Walter's voice was cautious.

'This morning during our session.'

'And it happened just out of the blue?'

Kate ran through details of the session, the album, the effect it had on Leonard. 'It was powerful stuff. I think it finally opened something up.'

At the other end Walter gave a low whistle. 'Kate, this is brilliant! Not just for Leo but for the project too. It's what we need to validate what we're trying to do. Evidence if you like.'

Kate hadn't thought beyond Leonard's progress, but now she saw how much was at stake, the trust Walter had placed in her. She just hoped it was not all a fluke, that the next time Leo would be silent again and they'd be no further forward.

'I hope you're right. It's early days – it could be back to square one tomorrow.'

'Don't be so hard on yourself, Kate. This is your success too. Have a little faith.'

After she hung up, Kate stood looking at the phone, turning over Walter's words. *Have a little faith,* he'd said. It was always an issue, her lack of self-belief, the sad realisation that art could never be the centre of her life. But what was it that made Leonard give up? Why did he put it all away?

Letting Walter know Leonard's progress had been the right thing to do, clearly he appreciated her efforts and what this would mean for Leo, but something was not right, something else she couldn't quite grasp. She poured a glass of wine and went back to her notes.

THIRTY FIVE

Another restless night, I wake many times and long for the morning. There's no mention of another session with Kate on the calendar, but I will need to find her, I need to know what happened with the photos of Issy. Did I try to speak, or was it all still in my mind? I go to the wardrobe and lift the blanket. The album is still there, with my sketchbook and the canvas roll. I take them down, put them on the bed and begin to leaf through the drawings.

I've not spoken a word since, not even to Walter. When he brings my breakfast, he puts the tray on the table and sits down with me.

'So, Leo,' he says. 'How's things today? Kate keeping you busy?' He nods at the pile of work on the bed.

Should I tell him what has happened? He too is a safe pair of hands. Maybe he knows already, maybe Kate has told him. I want to show him the album, explain the past these photos represent but will he, after all, have the patience to wait, to listen?

I clear my throat, try get my words in order and pass

230

him the album. He leans over to take it and when I start to speak, he looks up surprised by the sound.

'Ah. So it's true then – Kate wasn't making it up! This is real progress, Leo. I knew you'd get there, it just takes time.'

'And Kate.' I croak.

'And Kate,' he says with a smile. 'I reckon she's done some good, don't you?'

I revert to a nod, my throat tight and dry, then Walter reaches for the album and opens it up, scanning the pages.

'Handsome devil weren't you Leo?' he says with a wink. 'Bet you set a few hearts on fire?'

There was only the one that mattered. Walter turns to a photograph of Issy by the lockhouse. 'And who's this? I'm guessing she's someone special?'

I point to the date beneath and try to speak. But my voice catches and the words falter. 'She was, but it's all gone now. Another life.'

'Fifty years or yesterday, we still live with it, side by side,' Walter says. 'The sweet moments and the sad.'

He studies the pages further back, photos of all the outings we took that summer. I think of how we'd go to the city on my days off, raiding a little art shop in a backstreet, spending money we could ill afford on materials for my painting. I think of our train ride to the Norfolk coast, or the times we piled into the horse cart and took a picnic up to the Vale.

Walter slowly turns the pages and when we've been through them all, he leaves me with a promise to send for Kate and come back when his shift is over.

★

The usual clatter comes from the kitchen, as I wait in the dining room for Kate to find me. I hear voices from the television in the day room, the distant chatter of staff. I'm wondering what will happen now, when they discover I've found my voice.

When Kate arrives mid-morning there's a new energy about her. I wonder, vainly whether it's to do with me and what happened yesterday. She sits down beside me, asks me how I am, tells me how pleased she is with progress.

'The thing is,' she says, taking out her notebook, 'we do need to report back on this. Any significant change in a patient's condition needs to be registered, you see.'

I get my thoughts together. I've grown used to the way things are and I'm not sure I want it to change. 'Can it wait?' I ask.'

'I've spoken to Walter and he suggests a few days to let things settle down. Time for you to practise, to strengthen your voice. It's not going to happen overnight.'

'I wasn't sure it would happen at all.'

'Neither was I. But it has. You should be proud – you've worked hard and it's paid off.'

Kate writes rapidly for a minute or two. I understand she has to give a report, I just hope she doesn't let on to my wife. I'm not yet ready for that and Kate doesn't press me further.

'Last time was hard for you, but we had quite a result. I'm wondering where you'd like to go next with our sessions?'

I realise that all along the choice has been mine, the effort mine to make. 'The album,' I say. 'There's a lot there.'

Kate picks up the album and opens it at the last page. 'These photos – where were they taken?'

Again it hits me, reaching up from the pages: the dog by the water, the geese. Kate knows nothing of this. 'This one,' I look again at the photograph by the wall, a bright day, three figures and a dog. 'Outside the artist's workshop on the canal. I worked at the lockhouse a mile away, along the towpath.'

Kate pauses, then points to the image of Issy. 'And this is…?'

I clear my throat again, feel a smile creep across my face. What I have felt since that first meeting opens again like a sluice gate, flooding my heart. Issy leaning on the rough bricks, studying her feet neatly crossed at the ankles. How she would turn her head and smile, the lock of hair that fell across her face, how she'd hook it back behind her ear. The gesture mirrored in Kate the day she came for lunch.

'This is Issy,' I tell her, my voice cracking again. 'She was…a friend.'

Now it's Kate who doesn't trust herself to speak. Instead she lays a hand on my arm and lets her silence fill the space.

'Come on,' she says, helping me to my feet. 'I'll get something to drink and we'll go outside.'

On our seat by the Albertine, the morning sun catches my face, warming the tight muscles of my throat. Kate puts down two glasses and a jug of water and waits beside me for a sign that I'm ready to begin.

Does she realise how much I remember? Has she made

anything of it from my drawings, or the old stuff my wife has shown her? I had my doubts at first, what good it could do. But she's won me over. Like Walter, she's won me with kindness. I wonder how this can be, how come I've been so fortunate, why she keeps coming back calm and unperturbed, no matter what state I'm in. As I start to speak, in a voice still strange even to my own ears, she nods and smiles, urging me on as if she's understanding every word.

'Her name is Isabel – Issy. After we met, she often came to the lockhouse with the dog. She'd bring an offering from their kitchen, produce from the garden or simply to pass the time of day.'

'And you became friends?'

'Over time, yes.'

'But it was more than that?'

So much more. I shift in my seat, wondering how to explain quite what it had been. How I would find myself waiting and hopeful, checking the towpath all too often for a sight of her, her dress billowing, the dog chasing back and forth around her heels. And whenever she appeared, the air between us flowed warm and charged, a surge of joy brought a grin to my face and set my heart to beat a little faster.

I pause and take a drink, lost in that time we had. No doubt it's vague, a tangled ribbon of words but I press on, hoping it will all make sense. I explain there were others at the workshop too, Michael the printmaker and his wife Annie. Her family had made a mint in textiles and supporting the arts was seen as a way to give something back. Annie's sister Lilian had worked for a publishing house in London but returned home after some issue in the workplace. She became the driving force behind the workshop, setting up bursaries and scholarships for anyone who might need help with funding. Out of tact, they never broached the subject with me though they probably guessed how little money I had.

Passionate in their thinking, they believed the art world needed to change, that art should be accessible, not locked away for the privileged. More galleries were needed, places anyone could visit and feel welcome, and not only in the big cities. Though I shared their views, radical talk did not excite me in the same way. I didn't see how my work could change things and besides, I had crossed so many barriers already, simply finding a job had been hard enough.

I close my eyes, lift my face to the sun. Beside me on the bench, Kate waits while I gather myself, take time to rest my voice. We've been sitting for a while, Kate making notes, hopefully piecing things together as I speak.

'You know, this is quite a story you're telling, Leonard,' she says, handing me a glass of water.

I take a few sips and put the glass down. 'Does it make sense? In my head it does but I know it can all change somewhere along the line. That's why I stopped speaking. Couldn't bear the confusion, all the fuss.'

'It makes perfect sense Leonard.' Kate nudges me gently, 'Perhaps a little tidying up round the edges, but it's all good. Better than good – you're doing fine.'

'Is our time up, or shall I go on?'

'You're not too tired?'

I am exhausted but I shake my head and Kate opens her

notebook again. 'Ok, so what happened? Did you become part of the workshop?'

'I visited now and again. It was a new world for me, not one I expected to be welcoming.'

'And was it?'

'It was, surprisingly.'

'So you went to the workshop in your spare time? Is that how it worked?'

'More or less. They supported me, respected my heritage, the way it was reflected in my work.'

This had touched me deeply. Such people moved in circles a world away from mine and though they all spoke with the clip of high birth, their eyes did not slide across my clothes whenever I opened my mouth. But I never quite lost the fear that my origins would affect working with them, no matter how generous they might seem towards my art.

'Did you feel at home there?' Kate asks.

'I did. There was comfort in the whole place, a kinship. Like pulling on a pair of old boots. Confined spaces, neat clutter, the smell of paint, oil and cooking, the clack of Annie's loom at the rear brought memories of home on the *Albert Jack*. Or maybe it was simply the presence of Issy. Looking back, perhaps it was only that.'

Kate looks up, her pen poised then puts the notebook to one side and stretches her fingers. 'Perhaps we need a break, Leonard?'

I take another drink of water and try to carry on but by now any fluency I may have found is fast escaping. There is so much to tell, too many words to find and I lapse again into my own thoughts. Once early on, Michael told me that my art had a unique quality, that I shouldn't keep it to myself. Thinking of Michael's words all these years later, I wonder how different things would have been if I'd never found it and brought it out into the open. I would never have felt its loss so keenly, yet without my art, without that connection, would Issy and I have passed each other by, a mere nod on the towpath? And for all the pain that came after, the visceral cut and scrape of those weeks and months that followed what happened, I would not have changed a moment of it.

THIRTY SIX

At home that evening Kate searched around for her tape recorder. Whatever Leonard's next disclosure might be, Kate was determined to capture it. Though transcribing the tapes would take time, time she could ill afford, it was better that trying to listen, understand and write all at once. Now she had grasped the context, Kate was trying to stitch together a cohesive narrative from the fragmented pieces he offered.

Before work the following morning, Kate called to see Walter in his office. She handed him her latest set of notes and stood by the window watching a pair of wagtails strut across the driveway.

'This is quite a breakthrough Kate,' Walter said, looking through the papers. I hope you're pleased.'

'I realise it's a breakthrough,' she said, 'but I'm not sure it's a success.'

'How come?'

'It feels more like an ending.'

'And that bothers you?'

Kate sat down and put her elbows on the desk. 'For two

reasons,' she said. 'Firstly, if Leo's placement here was due to aphasia and a reluctance to speak as his wife implied, shouldn't he now have the option of going home?'

'He needed to rest from his broken ribs as well, he wouldn't have done that at home. Is that a problem?'

'I'm just not sure if going home is the right move for him. When he first came – or at least when I first met him, he was like a fish out of water. Or maybe a boat in dry dock,' she added with a wry smile. 'Yet in spite of all the odds, he's found himself a niche, a routine that suits him. His daily trips outside, Tom and the greenhouse, his fondness for you, establishing his art again and our sessions together. But with this project nearly done, how different will Leo's life be without that support? Shouldn't he be consulted, given a choice – the chance to manage his own future?'

'I see.' Walter leaned back in his chair. 'You have to understand, you're not responsible for what happens next, Kate. If you feel the project has come to a natural conclusion and been successful, you can draw a line under it, it's as simple as that. We've no official remit here remember.'

'I suppose so. Perhaps I've just become too fond of him and I realise that's not a good thing – professional distance and all that.'

'It's hard to keep a balance – objectivity versus care and empathy. It's not an easy mix. So what else, Kate? You said there were two reasons.'

Kate reached for her notes and flicked through them. 'Leo is entitled to confidentiality. We've assured him of that, but isn't there a power of attorney in place? Aren't we duty bound to disclose the clinical improvement, both here and to his wife? And if we do, where does that leave us – or the project? I really don't fancy my chances when Matron finds out.'

'*If* she finds out.' Walter sat down beside her. 'Let's not panic. We've managed so far and I believe the more evidence we gather, the more chance we have of providing a valid case. Look at what's happened – look at all you've achieved so far. Do you think Leo would be speaking again without it? No, no way. Trust me Kate, only good can come of this.'

Kate looked up at him and shrugged. 'I hope you're right.'

'By the way, did you ever discover why Leo's name was familiar?'

'Actually, I did,' she said. 'He cropped up in an essay I wrote years ago.'

'Small world, eh? So, do we keep going?'

Kate sighed. 'I don't want to dig too deep – and I certainly don't want to cause him any pain, but I know Leo trusts me and he has more to tell, especially now he's literally found his voice. I have a feeling something happened to him all those years ago and I'd like to find out what it was.'

Walter handed back her notes. 'Ok. Tread carefully and keep me in the loop.'

THIRTY SEVEN

Kate returns on Thursday as promised. We sit outside on the bench by the Albertine arch that's in full bloom, its heavy scent filling the space we share. I have the album on my lap, and though prepared, even eager for the story to be told, I still hesitate, knowing what is to come. Kate waits too, then she brings out a small black box. Not a camera, it looks like some sort of recording device.

'I've thought a lot about your story Leonard,' she says. 'I'd like to record your voice this time, if I may? That way I can transcribe your words and keep an accurate record of them. It might also help you to hear back what's being said, then you'll know how much progress you've made.'

I'm not sure about this. I'm still not keen to have my voice heard in every quarter. Not here, and certainly not in my wife's presence. I need to retain an element of control, there's precious little else.

'It will all be confidential,' Kate assures me. 'No one has access to this without your permission.'

I shake my head. 'My wife has access to everything of mine. It's the way it works now.'

'Not everything, Leonard. You still have rights as an individual. And your wife won't see or hear anything that passes between us. Not unless you want her to.'

Kate clips a microphone onto the side of the tape recorder, then rests it on the bench between us. 'You know this could also be useful evidence when you need it,' she says. 'With the return of your voice – of your speech – that might mean the power of attorney could be lifted.'

'Power of attorney?'

Kate smiles. 'The legal document your wife has in place.'

I think about this a moment, then slowly nod. It seems not only the past is sorting itself out. 'We'll have to see. There's a way to go yet.'

'Where would you like to start today? Is there more about your time at the workshop?'

I'm beginning to understand Kate's powers of persuasion, how she'll suggest, not insist, request and not demand. As I start to speak, I know it's not the workshop she wants to hear about, but Issy. I begin to talk of those early days together, I tell her how the first swifts arrived, and we'd watch them swoop and dive across the water, how we heard the skylarks rise. How in the weeks that followed our meeting, life took on new meaning, my thoughts filled with light and hope, joy and pride overriding any fear I may have held regarding my background. Kate would call it my 'self-worth' but at the time I knew it simply as being helplessly in love.

Issy often chose to be away from the workshop, coming down to the lockhouse and settling outside to write on an old table we found in the washhouse. She would work on her small typewriter, the tap of its keys beating a steady rhythm to those hours we spent together, the sound of it rooted deep in the memory of that time. I had read of love, of the soaring lift that paints the days and stirs the nights. And this was ours now, evenings that would drift beyond the parting we could neither of us bear. In my humble room, Issy lay with me in the warmth of that summer, until morning crept in and took her back to the workshop. We gave no thought to convention, to expectations set outside our little community. If the village thought us strange, greeting us with frowns and whispers, this was no more than I had known all my life, my skin thickened in more ways than one. Neither did my own social code forged in quite another world, follow convention. There had been those times on the road, when not every door was closed to me, the women who had taken my education far beyond anything the school had taught me. But this, hitherto unknown, this I cherished, a lodging house for the soul.

THIRTY EIGHT

Kate switches off the tape recorder and goes to fetch some tea. While she's away I wander off down the cracked path to the greenhouse. It's market day in town and the benches are empty of the seed trays and herb bundles Tom gathered at first light. Memories have stirred a new restlessness and I'm suddenly filled with a wish to go with him, a need to be away from here, back in a world of bustle and churn, where the days are not empty spaces waiting for Kate, or Walter or even my wife. Days where I follow my own footsteps, where I can decide what's to be done.

Kate comes back with tea and biscuits, most of which she eats herself. By now she knows I will only leave them for the birds.

'Ok Leo,' she says, wiping crumbs from her hands, 'Where to now? Do we carry on, or leave things for today?'

I'm tempted to talk about my thoughts of leaving, the need to escape, to move forward and not back, but though I trust her, there may be some rule about disclosure, she may be obliged to pass it on and I can't risk that. Besides, I'm not yet done with the past, there's more to tell and yet I'm not sure how much further I want to go.

'We'll carry on, if that's alright with you. You've sat through so much so far, my long hours of silence and now my faulty ramblings. I hope Walter appreciates what you've done for me.'

Kate dips her head and smiles, but it's a secret smile, warm beyond friendship. 'He's a good boss,' she says. 'He doesn't miss much.' Then she switches on the tape recorder and I carry on, recalling those distant summer days at Stanford.

Michael made good his promise of support, meeting with me each week to discuss my latest efforts, offering guidance, keeping my output steady. Annie's sister Lilian would visit from time to time and she and Issy would wander off together, deep in conversation, no doubt their London lives discussed at length.

As summer drifted by, a public show was planned for the end of August in the gallery of Annie and Lilian's family home. Michael's new set of prints, posters for the city tram and bus companies, and Annie's textile pieces would be shown alongside my own paintings, the entire exhibition devoted to work from the Atelier. I had heard such promises before and did not expect much to come of it but Michael's words of encouragement kept me going, Issy's presence acting as a muse, to inspire and to guide. By the time the exhibition was due, I had gathered enough pieces for a worthwhile contribution and this time the promise of a public showing held good. Second only to the joy of knowing Issy, was the knowledge that my work, stylishly framed, would now hang on the walls of a reputable gallery.

We drove to Stanford Manor in the horse cart one Sunday, four of us with the dog and all our work stacked in the back. When we had hung the exhibition, and drunk a toast to its success, Lilian swept us all into the dining room and sat us down at the long refectory table. She and Annie fetched an abundance of food from the depths of the house, waving away any offer of help, and ladled it onto the plates themselves. I saw no one in service, no help of any kind. On closer inspection, despite its size, the whole house seemed steeped in desolation, an air of faded grandeur, of obsolescence. A way of life outmoded, overtaken by progress just as mine had been on the Cut. I thought of the term *genteel poverty* and wondered how such an estate would survive in the coming age. If democracy was creeping in, perhaps supporting the workshop was one way to embrace it.

Later as we jogged home, singing loud to a full moon over the night sky and the old horse every inch a ringer for Riley, all the stages of my life seemed to fold one upon the other like cards shuffled in a pack, blending into one perfect moment of unity. I have since learned the rarity of such moments, how precious their gift, and how desperate the shift when fate snatches them away.

I'm lost in that other world again, wondering how much I've spoken and how much is just a random flow of thought. Kate seems pleased enough, the evidence will all be there somewhere, at least she no longer has to scribble while I struggle with my words.

'I'm sorry – I'm not sure what comes out and what stays inside. It's probably all a waste of time anyway.'

'Not at all. It's not surprising there's some confusion Leonard, you've been silent for many months. This is quite a change for you.'

'It was a great success you know. The exhibition.'

'So I gather.' Kate dives into her bag and pulls out the scrapbook. She's not brought it since those early silent sessions when all I had to offer was my drawing. Scraps of paper fall into her lap as she flicks through the pages, then she picks one out and passes it to me.

'I found this,' she says. 'It seems you had quite a following.'

I take the cutting, which like the others has yellowed with age. There's another grainy photograph like the one in the album, with us surrounded by a small crowd at the opening of the exhibition. The article mentions the acclaim we received, often from circles beyond our small provincial arena. It explains the flood of interest in the Atelier itself, how we lived and worked together, what inspired it.

'There were sales and commissions too. We spoke with buyers from Bristol and Birmingham, and as far afield as Dublin and Edinburgh. Visitors came, articles were written – you see we even merited a small column in the national press!'

Kate takes the cutting from me and slots it carefully back in the scrapbook. Then she asks, 'When your work started to sell, were you tempted to give up your job at the lockhouse?'

'Not straight away, though it did cross my mind. Some of my pieces fetched a good price and even after a contribution to the workshop's funds, I had more money than I could ever have imagined.'

'So you carried on working?'

'The Cut was in my bones, and now there was Issy and my art as well, I saw no reason to leave.'

'How much did Issy talk about her own work? Did you know what she was writing?'

'Only a little. Issy was quite... protective of it – refused to let me see the job half finished.' It's like a painting, she would say when I pressed her for a few pages. You wouldn't want me to see something half done, would you? And a book takes a long time, you must be patient. I had all the patience in the world, I would have waited a lifetime if need be. But then, a lifetime is what it took after all, both hers and mine.

Kate is silent for a while, running her finger up and down the edge of the scrapbook. Then she packs it away with the tape recorder and gets to her feet. 'We'll leave it there for today, Leonard. Thank you – you've done well.'

I heave myself up from the bench and stretch. 'I'm off for a walk then, if we're done. Stretch these ageing limbs.'

Kate slings the bag over her shoulder. 'Would you like some company? I don't have anywhere else to be just yet.'

But this time I tell her I'd rather be alone. There's enough to reflect on, and in my head I'll have company every step of the way.

THIRTY NINE

This afternoon Kate and I sit beneath the rose arch again. I'm thankful no one else risks the fresh air or we might have to draw lots for the bench. I know our time is almost up, our *sessions* coming to an end. Have they served their purpose, I wonder? Have I *moved on*? Kate seems to think so but she hasn't heard it all. There's more to the story, the tucked away final part that will turn me inside out with the telling.

'Where would you like to start, Leonard? Last time you talked about the exhibition, how you'd had some recognition, even a little money. Issy was writing, you were making a life together.' She speaks softly, there's a question in her voice and I know it's time to tell her what happened. I breathe deeply, gather my thoughts and begin.

It was a day like any other at that time, waking together in my narrow bed with the sun low at the window, a dawn full of hope and promise. I had a series of tasks ahead of me: lock paddles needing a second coat of paint, clearing the banks a mile up the water towards town. Issy gathered her belongings and left early, promising to return later with

Stan. As always I watched her walk away, along the towpath until she rounded the long bend and moved out of sight.

I remember each task I carried out that morning, the exact hour I finished the painting, the exact stretch of bank I cleared between eleven and one when I stopped for lunch. I knew Issy would be back mid-afternoon, her word count reached, her pages complete for the day, the rhythm to our days marked out by moments of separation and reunion. But that day, I had an extra task on my list, and planned to spend an hour or so with my neighbour across the field helping to fix loose slates on his washhouse roof. My neighbour's cottage is no more than three hundred yards from the lock, with a clear view of the water and any passing traffic as it approaches. I can run the distance in a couple of minutes and be back in time to work the gates.

A barge was due upstream and the lock was full. I'd hoped to be back at the lockhouse before Issy arrived, but fixing the roof took longer than expected, hampered by a high wind that had sprung up during the morning. From the washhouse roof I saw her approach the lock, her favourite dress blowing around her, the dog at her heels, barking at the wind. I called to her but the wind in the wrong direction snatched my voice and left her searching for me by the house. I knew she would fetch the chair from my living room and settle by the door with her writing, and that while she worked, the dog would set off, nose to the ground, on his routine explorations.

I did not look up again until the job was done, but as I stowed the hammer in my belt and prepared to come down, the familiar racket of Stan and the geese reached me on the roof. I remember thinking, one day the dog will not object to their presence. He will get used to them. But that's the last clear thought I have of that day, that moment, when my world still turned in its glorious cycle. The rest is a scattered mess of fragments swept up, lost in the wind and the turmoil, of an angry gaggle at the water's edge, the calamitous yelping of the dog. Of Issy there one moment, and gone the next. Of my desperate run across the field when I could no longer see her. All this that turned a moment to eternity.

How could I have missed her falling, not heard the splash? How did I not know what she would do to save the dog, his foolish bid to catch a goose, his leap into the lock? He paddled still in circles, eyes wide and terrified and Issy face down below the surface, the white dress around her floating, a life belt that did not save her.

I recall how light she was, lifting her lifeless from the water, her face pale, tinged with blue. I must have worked to empty what I could from her lungs, there was bruising on her back, the coroner said later, and a deep cut on her head where the lock wall had struck her as she fell. I must have hauled the dog out too, for he recovered and lay confused and whimpering by her side.

I kissed her, fetched a blanket still hopeful it was not too late, that she could not bear to leave me, that love would be enough. But as we sat together, the dog and I, we heard the wind sigh, the trees knock and clack behind the house, the gentle slap of the water, but not the sound I longed for, not her waking.

I must have kicked off my boots before I jumped, oddly I recall my feet cold and wet in the hours that followed, when Michael and Annie arrived from the workshop, alerted by my neighbour. The chaos of questions, of anger and tears, of blame and recriminations, quick to condemn as if I alone had caused this. But later, others took matters in hand, sombre and efficient, their words of condolence calming the waters between us.

I staggered through the days that followed, worked the lock gates, ate and slept little. Out of pity, the dog stayed with me, lying outside my door, or searching for Issy in the scent that lingered, up and down the towpath and in my rooms. Adrift and broken we bore our shared guilt, the cruel weight of loss. All this comes in piece by piece, patched and nailed and rearranged by time. Much of it is gone, the mind stunned and cold. Other grief has visited since then, scouring and deep, but that first cut, in the raw crudity of youth, left a sturdy heart cautious and afraid, its wounds unhealed.

Grey clouds have covered the sun and though it's still warm, I'm shivering, intensely cold. Kate turns off the tape recorder, puts her jacket around my shoulders and takes my hand. I'm not sure how much I've managed to say, whether she's understood any of it or whether she's just being kind, indulging an old fool in his wanderings. But then she says,

'I can't imagine how painful this must have been.'

I drop my head, put my hands in my pockets. Though I'm still shaking, something inside is calmer now and I need to go on. 'We had so little time together. It's foolish for those months that summer to have such power, but they did. And what followed, all the years since, nothing ever quite made up for losing her.'

'Not even your wife?'

I take a moment to answer. For all our differences, I've no wish to appear disloyal – even to Kate. 'We've not had the easiest of times,' I say.

Kate is too tactful to comment. Instead she says, 'Thank you for sharing so much with me. You look tired now, perhaps we should leave it there?'

She's right, I've done enough. There may be more to tell, I'm not sure, but my story is safe and Kate will be back soon.

FORTY

After her session with Leo, Kate was due back at work but her mind grew restive, her shift endless. His words, the tragedy of his story had left her deeply moved and now she simply wanted to go home. Walter caught up with her in the empty day room as she cleared tea cups and plates from the afternoon visits, bending awkwardly, clutching a pile of crockery.

'We have trays, you know,' he said, taking some of the load from her. 'No extra charge.'

Kate thanked him, dragged a hand through her hair and sank onto the arm of the nearest chair.

'Are you ok?'

A lump rose in her throat, she fought off tears that had threatened to spill all afternoon. 'I'm fine. Really.' Clearly she was not.

'Wait here a minute.' Walter took the crockery into the kitchen then sat down next to her. 'So, what's happened? Is it Leo?'

Kate nodded, letting her tears fall, then blew her nose on a tissue. 'His story. It's just so... sad.'

'You've found out something else?'

Kate began to explain but failed again. Walter got to his feet and glanced around the room, now empty of residents and visitors.

'I finish in half an hour, why don't you knock off too? Better still,' he said, pausing on his way out, 'maybe a quick chat over a glass might help?'

Kate shoved her hands into the pockets of her overall. 'It might,' she said. 'Thanks.'

'There's a place near the canal that's just reopened.'

'Sounds good. I've not been out much.' And I usually do my drinking at home, she thought, but Walter doesn't need to know that.

Only the hours with Leo had got her through these first months, without them she'd have been off long before now. Walter must have known this, and trusted her to see it through. Trust is a powerful thing, she thought, driving home after her shift. She would need to beware, not tempted to confuse gratitude for something else altogether.

At the kitchen table Kate plugged in the tape recorder, and clamped on a set of headphones. A moment passed, seconds of doubt before the sound kicked in and she heard Leo's voice, halting and cracked, stumbling through the painful scenes she'd heard that afternoon. His voice still came in rough waves, harsh and indistinct at times, and though background noise intruded, drowning his words in a wash of wind and birdsong, the headphones helped. After hearing it through, Kate began the transcript, each audible word noted with care, until the whole piece emerged. Only now, over the pain of Leo's story hung a wavering cloud of regret. With their sessions together drawing to a close, Kate knew it wasn't only his story that had captured her.

She packed away the tape recorder and her notes, then took a shower and tried to work out what to wear.

At the pub, they chose a table by the water where another stretch had been cleared. Kate wondered how Leo would respond to this – would he see it as something positive or too far removed from its origins? Walter fetched two beers and sat down beside her. Now they were here, Kate could think of nothing to say. Away from work, it seemed wrong to talk about it. Adding to the doubt, Walter had changed out of his uniform and now wore jeans and a pale blue shirt. He looked a lot less like her boss.

'When did you move here?' he asked, following her gaze to the opposite bank where the waterfront buildings had been turned into expensive apartments.

Kate had to think hard, since starting the project she'd lost track of time. 'About six months ago, just before I started the job.'

'And before that?'

Kate knew the subject would come up sooner or later. There was a long pause as she sipped her beer, wondering what to say. She'd not achieved much in her twenty-four years and for some reason, quite unconnected with work, Kate didn't want Walter to know her fault lines. 'I had a job in the city,' she said. 'Nothing special, just shop work.'

Thankfully, Walter didn't dig any deeper. 'So, tell me more about Leo.'

He listened as Kate ran through the details of Leo's

story, the lockhouse, the workshop, meeting Issy and what happened to her.

'It's a lot to deal with,' he said. 'For you and for him. How was he when he'd told you all this?'

Kate recalled Leo's face as he'd spoken. 'Distressed, not surprisingly. But there was relief too, as if he'd been holding his breath for a long time.'

Walter finished his beer and put his glass down on the table. 'Now he's speaking again, I think we'll have to wind up the project. As I've said before, you're not responsible for what happens next.'

'Thanks, Walter. I appreciate that but I don't feel we've got to the end yet.'

'It's your choice, Kate. But things might have to change anyway.' He paused, took a deep breath. 'There's something I should probably tell you, before you hear it on the grapevine. It will affect what we're doing.'

Kate held on to her glass for support.

'I've found another job,' he said. 'I'll be leaving in a few weeks.'

Kate looked at him, his dipped head in profile. Why now, when things were going so well? 'I see,' she said. 'Is it far, your new job?'

'Not too far – on the edge of the city. It's a new place just opened, rather different from here.'

'In what way?'

'Where do I start? For one thing, the work you're doing here with Leo is there for all the residents – anyone who needs it. There are exercise classes and music – there's even an art group!'

'So, it's a promotion, then?' Kate tried to keep her voice level.

'In a sense, yes. There's no more money but more responsibility, more autonomy. Coming here was never a permanent thing.'

Kate risked a step out of line. 'So why start the project if you weren't going to be around to see it through?'

Walter took a moment to reply. 'The whole idea came from the new place anyway. I know it's bad timing but in my defence, I applied for the job before I realised the success you'd have with Leo.'

This wasn't right. Kate could understand Walter needing to move on – he was young, with so much to offer. Yet she had risked weeks in a new job, on an unofficial project, put in hours of extra work, all so that he could waltz off into the sunset!

'What happens now, then?' she said, her voice rising. 'I can't just leave Leo without support – without winding things up properly.'

'I know, Kate. I'm sorry if you feel let down, that's the last thing I wanted. It's clear to me you have a gift for this kind of work – a rare insight that doesn't come with training. It's there, straight from the heart. Think of what you've done for Leo – where would he be if you hadn't worked with him, if we hadn't taken those risks?'

Kate sighed, the heaviness easing a little. 'I guess so. It's just that I've learnt so much working here, from being with Leo – it's become rather more than a job.'

'I felt like that too, not so long ago – I even said as much to Leo once after a bad night episode with his neighbour.

But things change, we have to grab new chances when we can. And I'll make sure there's still time to close things down – I haven't handed in my notice yet.'

There was some consolation in that. Kate listened as Walter went on about the new home, the facilities, the endless career prospects. 'And,' he added with a grin, 'there's always room for another new recruit.'

Ah, Kate thought. Who knows?

'Well, thanks for filling me in. At least now I know what's happening.'

'Don't worry,' Walter said, gathering up the glasses. 'We still have time to finish the work with Leo.'

Kate took this as her cue to leave but then he said, 'They do food here. If you're hungry?'

FORTY ONE

Kate and I have set up camp by the window in my room where it's quiet and we won't be overheard. I still don't speak much when we're downstairs, I don't want to broadcast that bit of news, at least not yet.

Since our last session, I'm sleeping better. Angela has been quiet too, I think they give her something fairly hefty at night. I can't say I miss those episodes. Walter hasn't been around much either, and though I manage perfectly well without help, it's his company I like – the news he brings, the attention he pays. I ask Kate if she's seen him, they've become quite pally, I think. I've noticed the way her head tips when she's with him, the way his face lights up when she's here. I tease her a little, like I did with Walter, but she pretends not to know what I'm talking about.

I notice she's quiet today. Something about her worries me, she's withdrawn a little, not like herself at all. I wonder if I should ask her, if I can help, but that's the wrong way round here. I've scraped out my soul and laid it bare for her to deal with, yet to ask her a simple question seems close to intrusion. I'm not sure how much more Kate will want to hear from me, or even how much I want to say. I have finally managed to speak of Issy, to tell her what happened, so is it best to stop now? Can I bring myself to talk about the aftermath? Kate plugs in the tape recorder, settles in her chair and picks up the notebook.

'The last session was hard for you, Leonard. You spoke of raw and painful things, but you spoke of beauty too, of the joy that knowing Issy had brought to your life, the place she's held in your heart for so long. We can let it rest there, if you like, or do you want to go on?'

It strikes me again that whenever I'm with Kate, I have a choice, a space in which I'm free to choose, to take my time. She waits for me to make up my mind, she listens.

'There's more to tell, if you've a mind to hear it. Who'd have thought it, eh?'

Kate leans over to switch on the tape recorder. 'It's an honour, Leo. I hope you know that by now.'

So once again I'm on my rambling way, hoping there is some connection between my thoughts and the words coming out of my mouth. Like so much else, it's hard to remember how I stumbled through those raw, bleak months after Issy's death, but the presence of Rhona who now came often at weekends, helped soothe the anguish. In these moments, her calm efficiency her quiet contained grief touched us all. Together we talked of Issy, the sister Rhona had begrudged and loved in equal measure and yet, in spite of this, I could not let her know the true nature of my intimacy with Issy, of the love that had grown between us. Neither, thankfully, did the others see fit to tell her. Perhaps I feared disapproval, perhaps it was simply too precious for words, but Rhona knew it only as a close friendship, a fondness we all shared for her sister and the light she had brought to our lives.

Then as autumn drew on and the shock waves settled, Rhona's visits dropped away, her new research post absorbing the edge of her sorrow. By Christmas, the occupants of Stanford House were carrying on much as before, immersed in their work with subdued determination. But I could not. Restless again, trailing my loss, I began to look for a new challenge, a new place, anything to remove me from the pain of Issy's absence. Returning to London had some appeal but there would be no livelihood there unless I moved back to the Cut, and I had no wish to intrude into the settled lives of my sisters. So I stayed another year at the lock, working at the mechanics of my life with little sense of purpose. I could no longer bear to paint, and when the exhibition closed, I stored the unsold work at the workshop together with all my other attempts. It became clear it was not only Issy that had perished in the lock that day.

From time to time I visited Samuel at the *Readers Rest*. I found his company pleasing, a gentle reassurance that helped still my distress. With his failing eyesight, he could no longer read much in the winter months and after work, I would cross the dark fields to sit and read with him, then bed down in the outhouse until day break, heading home when the first boats were due. But I knew this was a mere interlude, marking time until I'd formed some kind of plan. There had been too many years adrift.

Gazing out of the window in my room, I notice the rain has stopped. Is it my age, I wonder, or is the past so much more alive than all the years since? Am I falling into senility – is my wife right after all? Perhaps it's more like hypnosis, a trance-like state brought on by Kate's soothing presence, the tone of her voice. Kate turns off the tape recorder with a loud click that brings me back to the present. 'I think we should stop there and let's see where the next session takes us,' Kate says. 'Whether you'd like to go on, or call a halt. It's completely up to you. Just let me know.'

But after she's stowed her things away, the change in her is still there, a sadness I've not seen before. Has all this been too much for her? Again, I wonder whether Rhona has a point – Kate is very young to take on so much of an old man's pain. I've no idea how much practice she's had at this sort of thing, but I do know she's a joy to have around. When she picks up her bag, I take a chance.

'Is there something wrong, Kate? Something I can help you with this time?'

Kate pulls on her jacket and pauses a moment. Then she shakes her head, smiles and goes off to fetch some tea. Later when she's gone, I take down my sketch book and turn again to a clean page.

FORTY TWO

Suffering from a heavy cold, Rhona spent the day drifting around the house, dosed up with paracetamol, lemon and whisky. She'd been unable to visit Leonard for several days and had hoped for a further report on his condition, a word from Matron to reassure her things were progressing as they should. But there was nothing, and though impatient for news, she avoided the phone call that might put Matron on the defensive, speaking in those patronising tones that so infuriated her.

A couple of weeks had passed since leaving the photograph album for the young care nurse to deal with. Though reluctant to hand it over, Rhona now felt certain that photographs would be suitable material for Leonard's therapy. She remembered finding the album after Issy's death, those distant dark days as she cleared her room at the workshop. Then returning to Hampstead to do it all again, fielding Edith's grief and regret, keeping a lid on her own. Now she thought about it, perhaps unexpressed grief for Issy had compounded the agony, years later, of losing her son. That, and the guilt she'd never come to terms with.

Resenting Issy as a child, only to lose her when they finally found affection, resenting her unborn son only to lose him eighteen years later. Both so young, so unformed, so much promise needlessly taken. There was a pattern there. Grief, after all, was simply love with nowhere to go. And was Edward the reason she and Leonard had drifted? Or was it before that – was it, in fact to do with Issy? So much rushing to the surface. Far too much.

For a while after Issy's death, Rhona had kept in touch with Michael and Annie, visiting the workshop from time to time, consoled by the people and places Issy had known in those final months. But it was not until Leonard left the lockhouse and returned to London that they began to connect, driven by a shared love of the natural world that reached beyond their memories of Issy. He had now taken a teaching post at a secondary school in Paddington, nothing prestigious but all that his training and background would allow. There was comfort in his letters, amusing tales of his pupils, their exploits and the effort it took to engage them in meaningful learning. Leonard could never accept that young people did not always find learning as joyous as he did.

At times Leonard would come to visit her and they'd walk in the clear air of the parkland that surrounded her workplace. Her rooms at the top of a large Victorian house were a far cry from the fog and grime of his own existence, and he rarely invited her to his home. Perhaps he feared the shock of a London she had never known would prove offensive, but in time that changed. When he mortgaged a small terraced house near the school, the invitations began. Rhona travelled to see him often, offering advice on his small patch of garden, informing him of the soil type, the geology beneath, of what would grow best and where. Perhaps romance had never been part of her life plan. Unlike her sister, she had neither beauty nor flair, her strengths seen as barriers or threats by most men she encountered. But Leonard was different. At ease in his company, his warmth, their shared loss of Issy. Whatever it was, Rhona found herself drawn in ways that even logic could not dispel as trivia. How inevitable was it that the affinity they shared would shift again, that the night he cooked a meal and she offered to stay, they would be bound for good? Such details are gone, caught up in the rolling of time, but looking back, perhaps the shift from friendship to marriage came sooner than either of them were prepared for.

Had she suspected then that Leonard and Issy had been more than friends? And if so, was this just something else she'd buried? How incongruous her personal self was with her working self, the self that explored and probed and sought out the truth. How inept she was in matters of the heart.

Silly woman, Rhona thought, rummaging around for a handkerchief – a large blue one of Leonard's. Just a lot of old nonsense. But stuffing the handkerchief back in her pocket, she knew it was not the cold that made her eyes run.

FORTY THREE

Kate is here again. We're outside on the Albertine bench, watching the swifts dip in half circles beneath the eaves. She seems more like her old self today, and I carry on as usual, in the soft hiss of the tape recorder, telling her more about the time after Issy's fall, the time Rhona and I spent together, the growing bond between us. Kate asks about my teaching, the effort it took to get started.

'It was hard,' I tell her. 'I hadn't reckoned my early life would be such a hindrance.'

Kate looks up. 'Your wife mentioned it was difficult for you.'

'I needed a qualification and that meant passing exams. I went to night school, worked on the Cut during the day but it was costly, money I could ill afford.'

'But you did manage it, and found a job?'

'Eventually, yes.' I explained how time and again my applications were ignored, or if I secured an interview, my background intervened. The fact that I'd been unemployed and on the road, that I'd worked as a lock keeper and took up painting in my spare time. None of that went down

267

well. It seemed that since I'd not attended school until the age of twelve, it was not much of an example to be setting young people.

'But surely,' Kate said, 'your years of pupil teaching at the school must have carried some weight?'

'Not in the eyes of officialdom. It was a help for me though, I knew it was something I could do.'

'And what about your art – what happened to that?'

I look down at my hands, run them over my knees. 'Ah now, there was a problem.'

'You'd lost your muse?'

'Yes. But that was only part of it. After a while I did try to carry on, thrashing out my weariness on a different canvas. I moved towards other forms, those favoured by Klee or Kandinsky and for a while the change was good. It soothed my disillusion, gave me a new direction, but the style was not my own and didn't sit well with my view of the world.'

'And after that, did you stop painting altogether?'

I nod slowly, aware that this too has been a loss ungrieved. I think again of Daniel and his words after Issy died. He asked if Issy was the only reason I painted, told me I had a rare gift, one I should cherish, that even in bleak times, I could make it work for me. Change the style, he said, do anything, but don't give it up. That would be the greatest loss of all. But in the years that followed, the way my life took shape, I hid that away too. Until now.

Kate stands and reaches for her jacket. Now, there's the same unease I saw last time, a preoccupation. I don't want to question her again but then she says, 'I gave it up too, you know. I wanted to make a living from my art but it didn't work out.'

'You know you have talent, Kate. I've seen it. Why give up?'

'For one thing, it doesn't pay the bills. But coming here, working with you and…' she pauses, looks away into the distance, '…it's something special. Now it's all coming to an end.'

So is that the sadness? The irony that my new beginning, is also an ending? There may be more, but I look at her, my spark in this dismal place, the hours of care, of kindness she's given over these long months, and hope that she too has a champion in her corner.

FORTY FOUR

After leaving Leonard, Kate called in to see Walter, but then remembered he'd taken the afternoon off to ferry a patient to hospital. She collected the rest of her things and was about to leave by the main entrance when Matron stepped out of her office.

'Ah, Miss Davies. A word, if you please?'

The voice alone was enough to send her spinning back to school. Kate turned. 'Yes, Matron. Of course.'

Matron waved her into the office, closed the door and indicated a chair in front of the desk. Kate sat down and waited while Matron busied herself with a pile of papers, neither looking up nor speaking. Shifting in her seat, Kate suspected the reason for being here and when Walter walked in a few moments later, it became uncomfortably clear.

'Right then.' Matron tapped the papers together noisily and laid them on the desk. 'You two have some explaining to do.'

Walter and Kate exchanged a look. 'About what, exactly?' he asked.

'Don't be smart with me, Walter. I know what you've been up to and it's totally unacceptable!'

Kate thought of their out of work meeting. Had someone seen them together and reported it? But Walter calmly sidestepped. 'I'm sorry Matron, but you'll have to be a bit more explicit. I've given you my report on Miss Davies' induction period and her work easily meets all the necessary criteria. I'm convinced she's a valuable addition to the team.'

'I'm aware of that,' Matron snapped. 'This isn't why we're here.'

Still calm, Walter stood up. 'Then perhaps Miss Davies can be excused. Any other issues can be discussed between ourselves.'

Matron signalled him to sit down. 'For goodness sake Walter, you know what I'm talking about. This concerns you both.'

Walter continued to hedge, and though touched by his attempt to shield her, Kate just wanted this over.

'It's the project, isn't it? she said. 'The work I'm doing with Leonard Gardner.'

'It most certainly is.' Matron turned the full force of her disapproval on Walter. 'A project that I expressly refused to endorse. And now I find that not only have you gone against my wishes, but you're using an inexperienced new recruit with no relevant qualifications into the bargain!'

Walter looked over at Kate, his eyes full of concern. 'Kate, you don't need…'

'I think perhaps I do,' she said. 'I need to explain. A few weeks after I started to work here, Mr Robinson – Walter

– suggested a project that could help bring new meaning to the lives of many patients here, something more than simply sitting in a chair or eating.'

Matron huffed loudly. 'Miss Davies I really don't see how you're in a position to suggest that's all we do here. True, we may run this home along traditional lines, but I have many years of nursing experience and I can assure you we offer an exemplary experience for our patients.'

'With respect,' Walter broke in, 'Kate is right. I've become aware that practice at the Poplars is a little behind the times. Many other nursing homes are offering a rich and varied programme of events for their patients, similar to the work Kate has done – is still doing – with Leonard. If you took the time to visit him, to see what's been achieved, it's possible you'd see things differently.'

Matron studied her hands in silence, pondering her next move. When it came, it surprised them both. 'I am aware that things are changing, the world is a very different place now. Most of our patients were born before the first world war. Perhaps the policy has always been to protect them, to shelter them from further harm.'

'Of course, that's vital too,' Walter said, getting to his feet again and pacing up and down. 'But don't we have a duty to protect *and* enrich at the same time? Draw on their personal lives, seek out their past interests and skills?'

Matron watched him but made no comment. Something about her manner had shifted, the set of her shoulders a little less rigid.

'That's as maybe. But my concern right now is what happens next. We are all in serious trouble if regional office or Mr Gardner's wife find out. How will I justify what you've been doing without consent and using unqualified staff? As you're probably aware, they won't take too kindly to it.'

Walter stopped pacing. 'But do they really need to know? Kate is winding up the project anyway, no harm's been done and it's my guess this has given you something to think about.'

Matron stood and faced him. 'Don't push it Walter,' she said. 'By rights I should dismiss you both.'

'Matron, please!' Kate too was on her feet. 'I understand if you need me to leave, but I don't regret doing this, not for a moment. I know what we've achieved and the work Leo and I have done together is more valuable than my job. Just spend some time with him and you'll understand.'

Matron sat down again. 'I'll let you know what I decide to do by the end of the week. That's all.'

Kate followed Walter back to his office and slumped into a chair. 'It's not good, is it?' she said.

'Kate, I don't know what to say. I'm so sorry I got you into this – it's my mess.'

'I did have a choice – you didn't exactly twist my arm. Well, only a bit,' she added.

'I wonder how Matron found out?'

'More spies than we thought? Or just a sharp pair of eyes. Either way it makes no difference.'

'I won't leave you to face this on your own,' Walter said. 'I will sort it before I go. That's a promise. Meanwhile, the least I can do is shout you a meal.'

Kate had her doubts. 'Is that wise, after what's happened?'

Walter grinned. 'Maybe not, but what's the worst she can do – threaten to sack us?'

FORTY FIVE

Kate walked home along the canal. This had become her favoured route, there was a stillness here, a promise of renewal, of pulling good from the ruins. She wondered what good she could pull from the current mess. She'd come here to work, to change tack completely. New start, new place, new life. Yet how could she have known six months ago that this job, this project, would work its way into her heart? What spending these hours with Leonard would reveal? She found it was not simply her art she'd hidden away but a side she'd never thought to exist. A better side, one she could cherish after all. But with the project and her job threatened, coupled with Walter leaving anyway, where exactly did that leave her?

Walter was already waiting when Kate arrived at the restaurant – a new Italian place in the square, all sparse décor, candles and cheerful staff. He stood up to greet her, hesitated a moment, then kissed her briefly on the cheek.

'This is nice,' Kate said, casting her eyes around, taking in the tiled floor, the chatter and bustle.

Walter smiled his slow smile. 'It's a small town, but at least I can eat here without too many heads turning.'

It never occurred to Kate that a small provincial town might be a problem for him. Something else she was learning. 'Is that why you're going back to the city?'

'It's one of the reasons, yes. But it's mainly the job. As I said, there's a lot more scope – they've even started to work with art therapists. Now, that's something you might want to think about – you'd be perfect.'

'Have you let Matron know yet?'

'I went back later this afternoon and told her. Hard to make out whether she was relieved or indignant. She knew I was looking elsewhere – had even given me a good reference but probably didn't think it would be taken up.'

'How's Leo, by the way? I haven't seen him for a day or two.'

'Leo's doing fine – the recordings have helped a lot. I shall miss him.'

'You can always keep in touch. I know how much he appreciates what you've done for him.'

Kate was doubtful. 'In the end it's all come to nothing. I really thought we had a chance to make it official.'

'That may still happen – who knows. What does it matter anyway? It's been a success, isn't that the best we could hope for?'

Kate studied the menu. She didn't really want to talk about work, or what had happened in Matron's office or her future. She really just wanted to enjoy being out, away from the flat, with Walter. Sitting opposite, she could feel the heat from his knees as they brushed hers beneath the table. Something was going on, something she didn't want to run away from.

Last time over food at the at the pub, Walter had told her a little about his family, his mother's battle to keep three sons in check, the work she took on to support them all. But he'd made no mention of his father at all. Again Kate wondered how much to venture into the rather dull waters of her own past, how much of it would put him off. When the waiter came with their food, Kate risked another glass of wine and noted Walter's lime and soda. As he tipped his glass with hers, her curiosity didn't go unnoticed.

'I'm driving,' he said. 'And on the early shift tomorrow.'

Kate shook her head. 'Sorry. I just wondered, after last time – at the pub.'

Walter looked up at her, his dark eyes serious. 'My father drank enough for both of us,' he said, 'so I… I like to take it easy.'

'So did mine,' she said. 'Especially after the pit closed. But it didn't stop me, I'm afraid. Quite the opposite, in fact.'

If she'd shocked him, he gave nothing away. 'You do what you have to,' he said gently. 'Whatever it takes.'

The evening drifted by without further mention of work, and as the restaurant gradually emptied out, they stayed on in no hurry to leave until the waiter began laying up for the next day's lunch.

For a Friday the town was quiet. A few drinkers sat outside taking in the last of the summer warmth, music issued from a basement venue, a couple argued in a doorway. Kate and Walter wandered through the main street, down to the waterside and along the towpath.

'Do you ever see your family?' he asked.

'Not as often as I should. But my Gran and I write every week – I've told her all about Leo and the project and… you. That you're a good boss,' she added.

Walter said nothing more, but as they walked the length of the towpath as far as the lock, he took hold of her hand, resting it gently in his.

FORTY SIX

Rhona arrived at the Poplars well before visiting time, anxious to meet Matron or Walter to demand an explanation about the project. Matron's phone call had suggested some urgency but now neither she nor Walter were anywhere to be found.

Rhona made her way up to Leonard's room and managed to catch him before he left on his wanderings. In any case, she wanted to show him the folder and he was always less distracted in his room. Less amenable too, but she'd come to expect that now. She settled herself in the chair by the window and took out her knitting whilst Leonard perched on the bed trying to put on his socks.

'Why on earth are you putting your socks on now?' she said. 'It's three o'clock in the afternoon!'

Rhona guessed he'd already been outside, walking in the garden to clear his head since his wet slippers now lurked beneath the bed. Seeing him struggle to bend, she got up to help him, rolling the socks down to the toes with her thumbs inside, the way she used to when her sons were small. A forgotten act, touching in its simplicity. Leonard caught her eye, then took the socks from her and finished the job.

For a while they sat, Rhona's needles clicking, the familiar silence returning. 'I had wanted a word with Matron or that staff nurse chap on the way in,' she said, not looking up. 'I think there should be a case review meeting soon. I'm not convinced this *project* is doing you much good. I'm not even sure that young woman is qualified to do this kind of work. I've been doing some research and as I suspected, it's quite specialised. I might have to lodge a complaint.'

Leonard sighed and moved off the bed. She expected he would start pacing back and forth, his caged animal act, but instead he came and stood next to her by the window and rested his hand on the back of her chair. He coughed slightly and made an odd growling noise as if clearing his throat. It was the first sound she'd heard him make for months.

'It's actually working out well,' he said, his voice steady if a little rough. 'Better than expected.'

Rhona put down her knitting and stared at him, blinking rapidly. She searched for something suitable to say but this time it was her own words that failed.

Leonard cleared his throat again. 'I wanted to let you know, Rhona, but in my own time. I wanted to be sure things were working, that it wasn't just a fluke. I still get muddled at times. That may never change, but it is progress.'

If this was what Matron had wanted to explain, no wonder she said it was urgent. 'Well, you're a dark horse, Leonard. I assume Matron knows?'

'I've no idea – but Kate does, and so does Walter. It's all thanks to them anyway.'

Rhona put away her knitting and sat for a moment, fingers tapping the arms of her chair. 'Does this mean you'll want to come home?'

Now Leonard did begin to pace. 'I'm not sure what I want yet,' he said. 'But I do know that I need time to work it out. Stuck in here, having no part in how my life runs – that can't happen any longer.'

For weeks Rhona had been aware of a change in him, only now did she see the extent of it. Not only had he found his voice, but it came with a certainty, a conviction she hadn't heard for years. Part of her still wanted to find Matron, but another side held her back. Could she really complain now? Besides, she had the folder to deal with and a revelation of her own to deliver.

'The rain's stopped,' she said. 'Why don't we go outside? It's easier to think.'

FORTY SEVEN

It's market day and thankfully Tom isn't around. My wife has a habit of asking too many questions when the subject is close to her heart. And when it's not. We sit down at the table where I began to paint with Kate. Last week was it, or last month? I see how time moves in and out like air from a pair of bellows. *Fifty years or yesterday*, Walter said. *The sweet moments and the sad.*

When my wife bends down to the bag at her feet, I expect her knitting or a book to appear. But I watch astonished as she pulls out a manilla folder and lays it in her lap. Then I remember. A harmless thing, it should be a joy to see, part of the permission I now have to restore my memories of Issy, but this lies there like a warning, it's wrong for it to be here, as if two worlds have collided, the old and the new. Not a gentle unveiling, the touching reminiscence that happens with Kate, but a headlong crash.

I try to keep things calm, stop the shake in my hands, gather my thoughts. 'Where did you get this?' I ask.

My wife looks up and speaks gently, in a voice unlike her own.

'In the loft. I found it with your things in the old chest.'

I take it from her, open it up and read: *London 1929*. Inside on thin pages are the words Issy wrote in our summer together at the lockhouse and now it's here, in my wife's hands, fifty years later.

'Why didn't you tell me you had this?' she says, in her quiet unfamiliar voice. There's no rancour there, simply sorrow. 'I was Issy's next of kin, I dealt with her belongings, her estate. You had no right to keep it from me.'

I'm struggling now, what to tell her, what to hold back. It was the past, she doesn't need to know. But she persists.

'And I think there are some pages missing, Leonard. At the end. Why is that?'

I think back to the day, months after Issy's death, when I took out those pages and hid them away. Our private story, the words she had meant for my eyes only. Yet even then I could not hand over the folder. To give it up would have given away those hours and weeks and months we'd shared, priceless moments as she set her story down on the page. Then later, after Rhona and I were bound together, it was as if I'd betrayed her, betrayed them both – Issy for loving her sister and Rhona for not loving her enough. Hidden truths. I buried them all, as far and as deep as they would go.

'Do you think I'm stupid Leonard?' my wife says now. 'Did you think I didn't know? That I haven't suspected all along what passed between you and Issy? That you were lovers?'

I'm leaning on the table for support as she carries on, her voice still calm but with an edge now. 'Did you ever plan to say anything – was I just a substitute? I waited, you know, waited years for you to tell me the truth, but you never did. I should have guessed you never would. Was it to spare my feelings, or to hang on to Issy?'

And it's this that tips me over. 'Enough, Rhona! All these years, I've never raised my voice to you. I've put up with your bitterness, your disappointment. You knew exactly what I was like and it didn't seem to bother you back then!'

'And if you'd been honest with me, then maybe I wouldn't have had years of living a lie, of living with Issy's ghost between us.'

'There was no ghost, Rhona. You could have had more faith in me. Instead, you chose to turn it all sour. Even after we lost Edward, it was your misery that took over, as if William and I were not suffering too.'

She turns to face me. 'Don't bring Edward into this. Or William for that matter. You've no idea what it was like for me, what I had to give up.'

Oh, believe me Rhona, I do. I have lived with it for far too long.

FORTY EIGHT

Rhona left Leonard sitting at the table by the greenhouse, and drove home faster than she should, as if putting some miles between them could cancel out the scene with him. She could make no sense of what had happened. Leonard's voice, recovered with a vengeance then raising it to blame her for what, exactly? For their faltering marriage? For wanting a life beyond domesticity? For envying Issy? All of it, most likely. Messy conversations she could never quite get to grips with.

Rhona could only conclude that Leonard had no wish to come home, that having found a new voice, it would suit him to have a new life, a separate one. That was how they'd begun after all. Living apart might even suit them both as it had done years before. At the time, there were practicalities involved. Before her marriage, Rhona had secured work at a research station north of London, significant work on the principles of crop nutrition, the development of organic fertiliser, analysing the results of long-term field experiments. Here she was not side-lined, her work not confined to preparing slides, cleaning equipment and making tea. Her findings were valued, her opinion sought, her papers published. Life after Cambridge had opened up, awash with hope and possibility. Rhona would not give it up lightly but neither did Leonard wish to move from his home and an equally hard-won teaching post. Instead, they spent the weekends together, took holidays on the coast and lived alone the rest of the time. Save for convention, there had been no need for marriage at all.

It was not until later that events forced them to think again. A child had not been part of the plan, certainly not for Rhona. When her pregnancy was confirmed, she'd riled for weeks at her stupidity, getting 'caught' was for the uneducated, the stuff of cheap fiction not for those who understood the science. For a while, they continued to live apart, but as the months passed, plagued with sickness and fatigue, Rhona had no option but to leave her beloved workplace and move back to the city.

Leonard had worked hard on the house, restoring it to a clean and habitable state. He was no stranger to modest living but for Rhona, the two of them thrown together in a cramped terrace, mourning the loss of the work she loved, it was too much. She would fill her days reading and walking, sometimes as far as her old familiar ground of Hampstead, then return to sleep for hours until the sickness woke her again in the morning.

Even before Edward was born, it seemed they had retreated further into separate camps, their sparse affinity thinning out with each month that passed. Leonard tried to interest her in his teaching, even suggesting she might find some consolation there too, but he failed to realise that married women were not permitted to work in schools. Women with a husband were not permitted to work in many fields at all, certainly not women with a child as well.

Now though, just as she feared, she could see the truth of Leonard's words. Losing Issy, losing her work and then her son, Rhona had never quite come to terms with any of it. She had laid the blame firmly at his feet.

Rhona put the car away in the garage, locked the door and paused on the driveway, looking up at the house, the home they'd shared, in spite of everything, for all these years. Late afternoon sunlight crossed the eaves where swallows were gathering for their long journey south. A willow dipped and shivered, casting shadows on the front lawn, such a far cry from Leonard's early roots. She had hoped he would find his place here too but perhaps it had never worked for him, had never been the home he'd longed for. History intervening, too late to fix. And no matter what he confessed to, Issy would always be there between them. Beloved sister, bane of her life.

Whether or not Leonard chose to come home was his decision. Rhona understood that frail as he was, he might just need to take off. Through all her resentment and pain, all the angry and bitter years he'd stayed with her. Perhaps now it was time to let him go.

FORTY NINE

I wake in the small hours with a weight on my chest, a familiar weight, the weight of grief. Seeing Issy's folder again, dragging up so much really is a step too far. All this will have to stop, whatever is left of my past can lie buried for all I care. Tomorrow I will tell Kate we've done enough.

Walter comes in early as he often does, to check I'm still here, that I've not popped my clogs in the night. I tell him I'm fine, that he can leave me to it. I'll have to manage soon anyway, because I gather he's leaving at the end of the month. I can't quite get my head around that, though it's a good move for him. I think of Kate and wonder if this is what upset her the other day. I have a feeling she'll miss him too.

I begin the slow task of ablutions and dressing, leaning on the bed to manage my socks without falling. I'm almost done when there's a gentle knock at the door. A good sign this, not a brusque invasion.

'Mr Gardner?' A familiar voice calls from the corridor. 'Can I come in?'

It isn't Walter, it's Matron hovering outside. She hurries into the room and closes the door behind her. I should offer her a seat but this doesn't seem like a social visit. I sit down on the bed and wait.

'I know Staff Nurse Robinson has already been in this morning but I wanted to talk to you about something,' she says carefully. 'Something that has only recently come to my attention. I'm afraid there are several issues to be addressed as a result. I've given the matter a great deal of thought of course, and I'm concerned both for your welfare and for our ...er... reputation here at the Poplars.'

I have no idea what she's referring to and I must look blank because she carries on, hands clasped in front of her. 'I understand that Miss Davies has been visiting you on a regular basis, outside her prescribed duties as a member of staff. Is that correct?'

I nod slowly and wonder where this is leading. If Kate's in trouble we have a problem.

'And during these visits, you've been er... drawing and painting?'

I nod again, as Matron looks down, avoiding my eye.

'Well, I'm here to let you know that these sessions will have to stop. There has been... an issue shall we say, and it looks as if Miss Davies will be handing in her notice. Mr Robinson, as you probably already know, is leaving anyway.'

I'm not sure I've heard correctly. What kind of issue? How can Kate be leaving too – and why? She would have mentioned it but she's said nothing. I don't have to wait long – in the next breath, Matron explains.

'It would seem,' she says, 'that these so-called visits have not been authorised. Mr Robinson came to me some months ago with a proposal to which I did not give my consent. The matter needed to be discussed at regional office but it seems he went ahead anyway and now I have your wife asking some rather awkward questions.'

I'm really not sure what all the fuss is about. Authorised or not, Matron needs to know how much Kate has done for me.

'Under normal – or rather, different circumstances,' Matron prattles on, 'you would be called upon to give a statement. Or even,' now she shuffles her feet and coughs lightly, 'even make a complaint. I realise that in your case this would not be possible but I wanted you to know –'

I get off the bed and clear my clogged throat. 'Thank you for coming to see me Matron, but you've no need to be concerned – either for my welfare, or the reputation of the Home. I've no intention of making a complaint.'

'Mr Gardner?' Matron stares at me, her mouth open. She's a little less forbidding now. 'I don't understand. When did…?' She looks me over from head to toe as if I've just dropped through the ceiling.

I cough, clear my throat again. 'About a week ago.'

'And you didn't think it necessary to let me know? Does anyone know?'

'Kate knows, of course. And Walter. I have them to thank for this – especially Kate.'

'And your wife, Mr Gardner? Is she aware of what's happened?'

'Yes. I explained it to her yesterday.'

'I see.' Matron clasps her hands again and frowns. 'I will of course have to discuss this with her since she…'

'Holds all the cards?'

Matron drops her hands, searching for the pockets of her uniform. 'I was going to say, is legally responsible for you. I have no choice, I'm afraid.'

And there it is. In spite of all the progress we've made, Kate and I, all the corners she's helped to prise open, my life is still not my own.

Matron turns to go then pauses at the door. 'Mr Gardner, you may be aware that it is possible to reverse the power of attorney. That if you are mentally and physically fit again, our doctor can issue a certificate to that effect?' Her voice has lost its harsh edge and she looks almost kindly.

I tell her I'll need time to think this through.

'You may want to talk to your son, perhaps, before making any further decisions.'

As she leaves, I see the faint trace of a smile.

FIFTY

When Matron has gone, I go in search of Walter to tell him about her visit, but he's not in the day room, or the kitchen. It's now too late for the morning rounds and his absence concerns me. Outside, I find Tom on the tractor-mower sweeping round the lawn in a noisy shower of green. He stops when he sees me and climbs down.

'Everything alright, Leonard? Can I help with something?'

There's a flash of panic, until I remember I can speak again and now it makes no difference who knows. 'I'm looking for Walter. Have you seen him?'

Ignoring my question, Tom stares at me, just as the others have done. 'Leonard, your voice? When did this happen?'

I supply him with brief details while he scratches his head, squinting into the sun. 'And you're looking for Walter? Can't say I've seen him this morning. I'll keep an eye out though. You take care, now.'

He starts up the mower again and I return to the day room, a little lightheaded. I've not had my breakfast, not even a cup of tea, and there's no sign of anyone around apart from the sleepers and shufflers. If I go back to the kitchen, they might find me something to eat, or better still, Walter might have turned up. It's not far, twenty yards or so, I've done it dozens of times but half way there, the room begins to spin and the floor leaps up to greet me, a dramatic thud that no doubt rouses even the armchair brigade.

Seeing stars is an apt expression. There's a flurry of activity, someone turns me on my side, there's a sharp pain in my left temple not unlike the one I woke up with in hospital after falling off the ladder.

A voice close to my ear calls urgently. 'Leonard, can you hear me?'

It's Walter's voice. He's here now, at just the right time. I nod slowly, put my hand to my head, afraid it's starting all over again.

'Don't try to move,' he says. 'We'll need to fetch the doctor to check you out. Does it hurt anywhere?'

There's a gathering of feet around me on the floor – slippers mainly and Matron's smart lace-ups. I tell them I'm fine, relieved when I'm understood. I couldn't bear to go through all that again.

'Can you sit up?' Matron asks, holding out a glass of water. 'You need to drink this.'

With Walter's help I sit up slowly and take the glass. He holds my hand steady while I drink and Matron ushers the others back to their chairs. 'If you can stay here, Walter, I'll go and ring the doctor. It's my guess Mr Gardner will be fine but we'd better be sure.'

'So, Leo,' Walter says when she's gone. 'You need to take better care of yourself – no more laps of the garden for a while.'

The pain in my temple subsides and the room settles down. 'Missed my breakfast, that's all. On my way to find you.'

'Ah, I've been busy this morning. Lots to do. But you have to eat, Leo.'

Walter helps me to an armchair, away from the others. Stay here, Leo. I'll fetch your breakfast.'

'Now eat,' he says, returning with my tray, and don't go skipping meals again.'

The toast is cold but welcome. Walter fetches me a fresh mug of tea, pulls up a footstool and sits down.

'So what were you coming to see me about in such a hurry?'

I take a swig of tea and tell him about Matron's visit, the project and the power of attorney. I also tell him about Kate, and Matron's words of praise.

Walter grins and looks away. 'She's a bit special, isn't she? But don't tell anyone I said so.'

He waits with me until the doctor arrives followed closely by Matron. The doctor leans in and speaks loudly. 'Not been overdoing it, have we Mr Gardner?' He turns to Matron. 'Perhaps we should get him back to his room first, then I'll take a look.'

They take me up in the lift. My legs are still a little disconnected and it's a relief to lie down. The doctor does all the usual prodding and poking, shines a light into my eyes, checks my head and shows me in a mirror where a small shiny bump has appeared.

'This is nothing to worry about – everything else seems to be in order. No need for a hospital trip I think, but keep a close eye on him for the next few days.'

He's about to leave when Matron stops him.

'Doctor, we have a bit of good news regarding Mr Gardner's general progress.' She turns to me. 'Isn't that right, Leonard?'

Leonard? I'm not sure why she's dropped the formality but as they stand expectantly waiting for my response the full force of my situation here strikes me and I'm suddenly aware of what I've become – of what these long weeks and months have turned me into. Despite finding my voice, I am old and dependent, slumped on a bed surrounded by concerned faces, yet none of them really knows what I want – not even Walter.

I cough a couple of times, swing my feet to the floor and stand upright by the bed. There's an eruption of voices – 'Mr Gardner…Leo, you must keep calm… you've had a fall… take it easy…'

But it's all too much. I don't want their concern or advice any longer. I don't need it and it's my right to refuse, even if there is some legal piece of paper that says I can't. I hold up my hand and lean on my chair by the window. If I'm ever going to have a life again, I need to take matters into my own hands and if the doctor needs to know about my progress, I'll be the one to tell him. I draw breath and face him.

'Last week I started to speak again. What's more, I'm told most of it makes sense. So I need to think about what happens next, if you don't mind. If you need to do anything, it's probably time to call my wife.'

In spite of this surge of energy, my knees are still weak. As soon as they've left, I sit down again and stare out of the window. Having been here so long, even small acts are exhausting.

FIFTY ONE

It's been a week since my fall. A long week confined to barracks and without Kate too, since our sessions have drawn to a close.

Walter has left now. He called in to see me a few days ago, gave me his phone number, told me to keep in touch. It's hard to imagine life here without him and I'm not the only one to think like that.

My wife must have spoken to William because a day or two later he comes to see me.

'You know Mother's against your moving from here,' he says. 'She still thinks you're not ready to be at home.'

We're outside on the rose bench, watching a finch pull at a length of clover on the path. 'I'm afraid your mother has no idea what's right for me. I'm only just beginning to realise myself.'

William turns and rests his arm along the back of the seat. 'Couldn't you talk to her now? I know she's not always easy but now you're... better, she'll have to understand.'

'There's a meeting with the solicitor tomorrow – Matron arranged it through the doctor.'

'To revoke the power of attorney?'

'Exactly.'

'And has Mother agreed?'

'Your mother has agreed to be there. It's my guess she'll have to accept the doctor's judgement.'

William looks doubtful. 'I can come too, if it would help?'

'Thank you but there's no need. It's a trek for you and I have to do this on my own. I've been dragging my heels for too long – even before I ended up here. In spite of everything, I've learned a lot, these past months. It's not too late to change, to set things right.'

William frowns, looking disturbingly like his mother.

'I'm not sure I know what you mean.'

'I mean it's time to put myself back together – my whole self. And that includes my art.'

'You mean the work you've done here, with Kate?'

'More than that. All the work I did before, in my early years, I shut it off. What I didn't realise until now, was how much of myself I'd shut off with it, denying who I was – who I am. That needs to change. *I* need to change it.'

'Did Mother take exception to your art?'

Poor William. I realise he's been a victim in all this too. 'Not exactly. But there were reasons I gave it up. I'll explain one day, but right now, you can give me a hand to prove I'm fit to make my own decisions.'

The following day Matron summons me to her office. The walls are dark panelled wood, with a scattering of dull portraits, none of which I recognise. I've only been in here once before, the day my wife brought me to visit the place. To see if it's suitable, she'd said, though I found out later from William that my room was already booked.

This time, in addition to the wood panelling and lifeless portraits, I'm confronted by a row of faces. My wife is there and the doctor, and seated to one side away from the others, is another man holding a clipboard and pen. Matron guides me to a chair and I sit, half facing them, disturbed by the formality of it all. No one speaks, but there's a rustle and a cough as if waiting for the curtain to go up.

'Thank you for coming Mr Gardner,' Matron begins. 'Or may I call you Leonard?'

Without waiting for my reply, she speaks in that loud voice, addressing the room at large. 'As you know we are gathered to review Leonard's situation here at the Poplars and to consider whether, in the light of his recent progress, he might be more appropriately placed elsewhere in the future.'

My wife shifts in her chair, her face inscrutable. I look away, fearful for my resolve as Matron introduces the man with the clipboard, the solicitor I assume has been appointed to hear the case.

'Leonard has been with us some six months, during which time his progress, though not always steady, has been considerable. Many of the problems faced by his wife when he first came, have now largely been overcome, thanks to the excellent care he has received here.'

The seated bodies in the room nod wisely and make notes, whispering among themselves. I might just as well not be here at all. If I thought this was to be a fair assessment of my progress and that I would have a platform to plead my case from my own standpoint, I was much mistaken.

'The doctor will account for Leonard's medical improvement, he has regained his speech and moreover, he has had many opportunities to enjoy the garden and grounds. I believe he even helps our groundsman out from time to time!'

Matron beams at the room, waiting I think, for a round of applause. How well she's done – nothing at all to do with me or with Kate. It's this that stirs me from my seat and I stand, straighter than I have for years. The group watches closely as I begin the testimony I prepared with William on the rose bench.

I speak of Walter, of his care and friendship. I speak of Kate and the power of the work we have done together, of how this, and this alone has been the key to my progress, to finding my voice again. And not only my voice but a large part of me that has been absent for many years. I try not to look at Matron, I avoid my wife's eye. I expect at any moment she will pipe up and tell me to stop wasting everybody's time. But it doesn't come. The room is silent and I tell them that after discussions with my son – and with Matron too – I feel the power of attorney should be revoked, that I would like my rights fully restored, to be free to decide my own future, whatever and wherever that might be. Then I leave the room, go to the kitchen for a drink of water and head outside. Whatever is decided, I can do no more.

FIFTY TWO

After the case review meeting, Rhona has no choice but to revoke the power of attorney. As I suspected, she's concerned about it. Now that I'm free to make my own decisions again, she worries what they might be. Yet I've seen the change in her, a loosening of the ties that have bound us for all this time. Ties born out of grief and of loss.

'If you're not staying here,' she says, needles clicking as we sit in the armchairs by Matron's office, 'presumably you'll be coming home?'

This is one option. I dare say we could rub along together for a few more years even though the place was never quite home enough for me. We could set new ground rules, I could start to paint again, open up the past she and I have avoided for so long. But in truth, I haven't yet decided what my plans are and when I have, my wife may not be the first person I share them with.

'I'm not sure, Rhona. I've had plenty of time to think since I've been in here.'

My wife studies her knitting, counting the stitches. 'You may be an old fool Leonard but... I have missed you.'

She lifts her head a moment, and says softly, 'I did love you once you know but I was never much good at the emotional stuff, was I? Not like Issy – she had a gift for it.'

I stare at her, this rush of affection, wondering where my wife has gone. 'I never meant to be dishonest, Rhona. Omission is not dishonesty.'

'No, it's not. I suppose we're both guilty of that.'

'Did you never think to ask me about Issy – about what we had?'

'It was simpler not to. You and I were together, Issy was dead. What good would it have done to bring it all up again?'

Rhona begins to wind the wool and pack her knitting away. 'Why don't we get some air, Leonard. You can show me round this garden you've become so fond of.'

This time, we walk the length of the wall together and all the paths I've trodden these past months. We go again to the greenhouse and the herb garden but not the Albertine bench.

Rhona stoops to pick up a handful of earth, rubs it between her fingers and lets it fall. 'This is good,' she says and I know she's not just referring to the soil. As she's leaving, she clutches her bag and leans in to kiss me on the cheek. 'Those missing pages, Leonard? I don't need to see them – it's your story, not mine.'

I catch a whiff of our bathroom, the soap, the face powder she's used for years, and I fight a sudden urge to go with her. Yet I know it is not the answer. The answer comes one morning a day or two later when I open my window and chat to Tom in the greenhouse. I see him there, in his element, potting up, tying and tending. I see how each of us has that space, a niche that claims the soul, where the face fits and the heart belongs. Sometimes on this long journey we may find it briefly, as I did with Issy at the lockhouse. Sometimes we can only catch a glimpse as it slides past, just out of reach. But as I watch Tom in his space, every movement confident, tender, familiar, I know then exactly where I want to be.

FIFTY THREE

After her shift, Kate went to find Leonard in the garden. He was due to leave in a few days and though their sessions together were officially over, she wanted to bring him a copy of her final report.

'It's still against the rules, so keep it quiet,' she said, handing it over.

Leonard tapped his nose. 'I'm good at that.'

Kate had worked long and hard on it, not only to do justice to the project and the time they'd spent together but to do herself credit, to be more than just a vessel for Leo's progress. With luck, the report might also convince regional office this was something worthwhile. Since the case hearing and the public acknowledgement of Leo's progress, Matron made no further move to discipline her, and Kate had begun to have her own ideas about what to do next. If the project was accepted, she might suggest coordinating the work here at the Poplars, even if they had to recruit a qualified therapist while she trained. Walter's suggestion had again struck a chord, he had a knack of understanding what she needed.

'Have you decided what you'll do now, Leonard? Will you go home?'

'I might, for a while – for the winter anyway. These old bones don't take kindly to the cold. But I have a plan.'

'Can I ask what it is?'

Leonard reached into his jacket pocket and handed her a photograph. Not a cracked and ancient relic this time, but a bold new one in full colour. Kate studied it a moment then looked up and smiled.

'Your boat?'

'My very own – the *Albert Jack*. It's been idle for twenty years, since Alice's children left the Cut.'

'So you're going back on the water?'

'Not yet. There's work to do, it needs a lot of attention. But in the spring, when it's ready, I'll be off. My floating studio.'

It sounded perfect.

'There's always room for two, you know, if ever you feel like joining me.'

The offer touched Kate deeply. 'Thank you,' she said. 'I might just do that. But I have plans too.'

'Will you stay here, carry on the good work?'

'If I can. There's a lot to do, I think many of the patients would benefit. Your neighbour Angela for one – she could do with some company.'

Leo smiled. 'You know, I think you may be right.'

They wandered back along the path and for the last time in this place, sat together on the Albertine bench. The nights were drawing in, there was a touch of autumn in the air: wet leaves and smoke from Tom's bonfire. A couple of pigeons fluffed and scrapped on the lawn, a lone thrush called the day to a close.

'I always knew you'd come through, Leonard. That you'd find yourself again.'

'I have you to thank for that, Kate,' he said. 'And Walter.' There was a long pause before he added, 'Have you heard from him, by the way?'

'As it happens, I have. We've seen each other a couple of times. He's fine – loves the new job.'

Leonard nodded slowly, watching her face, waiting for the subtle shift she could no longer hide.

'I'm pleased about that. He'll do well there.'

'I don't think Matron's going to chuck me out yet,' Kate said. 'Would you like me to stay a while, if you're not too tired?'

'Yes,' he said, 'I'd like that very much.'

Kate stays with me until darkness falls, long past my regulation bedtime. She leaves me in the hallway and I creep up the backstairs to my room. Since I'll soon be out of here, I have the feeling they no longer watch my every move.

I take off my jacket and hang it on the back of the door. Then from the wardrobe I fetch the manilla folder and the canvas roll and take them both to the armchair by the window. Leaving the folder on the table I pick up the roll and untie the thin straps, but this time my fingers don't hover over the pencils and brushes. I hold it upright and carefully search for the concealed zip. It's a little stiff, it takes a while to coax it open, but then I reach in and draw out a sheaf of folded paper, half a dozen or so typed pages. The last words Issy wrote, the closing chapter of her life. I lay the pages out, my hand smoothing them flat, bringing them into the light. And as I read through our blissful months together, I hear her words aloud, rising from the hidden years. In those long hours with Kate, I've opened them all up, swept the dust aside and laid them finally to rest.

FIFTY FOUR

Postscript

1988

Kate helped herself to a glass of champagne and a catalogue from the tray by the entrance. They were gathered in the gallery at the Manor for a private view of work by members of the Stanford Workshop, featuring the artist Leonard Gardner. By the door Kate studied the display of photographs, some dating back as far as 1929, the Stanford Four by the wall outside the workshop, the exhibition of 1930, even the fatal lockhouse where Leonard had made his home for five years. There were later additions too, Leonard at his easel on the *Albert Jack,* or picnicking with Rhona on the towpath. Another showed a smiling Leonard on the steps of City Hall holding an award for his contribution to the arts.

In the main gallery, Kate paused a long time at each piece, lost in the beauty of it, fielding memories of her early days at the Poplars and the work she and Leonard had done together. She was about to leave when she caught sight of

William, also holding a drink, quietly surveying the room from a corner by the open French window.

'Excuse me,' she said. 'It's William, isn't it?'

William took a moment to register, then smiled. 'Kate! It's good to see you.'

'I thought I'd find you here,' she said. 'This is such a lovely event – long overdue.'

'It's been a lot of work for the organisers, gathering all his work and getting it off the ground – but it's worth it.'

Kate surveyed the room cautiously. 'Is your mother here?'

'No, sadly. She had a stroke a while ago and died soon after.'

'I'm so sorry,' Kate said. 'Though it's hard to imagine. Your mother was always so... robust.'

William sipped his champagne. 'I thought so too. After Dad left the Poplars, things changed. True, Dad spent a lot of his time on the boat, but Mum went too sometimes – he even taught her how to handle it. Not surprising really – she always did like to take the helm.'

Kate thought a moment. 'I'm not so sure,' she said. 'Leo's strength was just less overt. He was an inspiration to me.'

The room began to fill, the clatter of voices coming between them. They stepped outside onto a wide terrace overlooking the lawn. 'It's good to be here,' William said. 'We've not been up this way for a while. I gather when the family sold, they left the place in trust – to become a permanent centre for the arts.'

'It's doing very well, by all accounts. They run residential courses now too.'

'What about the old workshop by the canal?' William asked. 'It's been derelict for years.'

'Apparently the Waterways Board have taken it over and plan to turn it into a canal museum.'

'Ah, Dad would have liked that – he was proud of his heritage.'

'It's so good to see all his work together at last. He's very popular now, even the recent ones he did on his boat.'

'I always knew he'd be acknowledged eventually,' William said. 'It's just sad it came too late for him to see.'

'I don't think that would bother him at all – far from it. I was so fond of him. He was one of a kind, your father.'

William nodded. 'He was indeed. I'll always be grateful for the help you gave him. You and Walter.'

'Actually, Walter's here somewhere. He's on pushchair duty – there wasn't room to bring it inside. Come and say hi – and meet the family.'

Kate led William round the corner of the house to where Walter waited with the pushchair and a small child hopping beside him on the path. The child looked up, ran towards them, and Kate scooped him into her arms.

'This is our little one,' she said, brushing the hair from his eyes. 'His name is Leo.'

ACKNOWLEDGEMENTS

Many sources have provided invaluable background information for The Boatman's Journey, among them The London Canal Museum at Kings Cross, the Canal Museum at Stoke Bruerne, and the publications Women and Children of the Cut by Wendy Freer and The Canal Boatmen's Mission by Wendy Freer and Gill Foster.

I would like to thank Lorna Fox for her advice on speech therapy and Melissa Hynes for her encouragement and support with the early draft. Many thanks also go to my brother Rob and sister-in-law Jacqui for the chance to travel on their narrow boat.

My grateful thanks again go to Cressida Downing for her welcome editorial advice and guidance, and to the team at Troubador for their expertise and patience.

Finally, I am indebted to the late Fred Jay Girling, whose paintings were the inspiration for the work of Leonard Gardner.

This book is printed on paper from sustainable sources managed under the Forest Stewardship Council (FSC) scheme.

It has been printed in the UK to reduce transportation miles and their impact upon the environment.

For every new title that Matador publishes, we plant a tree to offset CO_2, partnering with the More Trees scheme.

For more about how Matador offsets its environmental impact, see www.troubador.co.uk/about/